The Good Doctora
Copyright ©2025 by Todd Merer
All world rights reserved

This is a work of fiction. Names, places, and incidents are the products of the author's imagination or are used fictitiously. Any resemblance to actual events or locales or persons, living or dead, is entirely coincidental.

No part of this book may be reproduced, stored in a retrieval system, or transmitted in any form or by any means electronic, mechanical, photocopying, recording or otherwise, without the prior consent of the publisher.

Readers are encouraged to go to www.MissionPointPress.com to contact the author or to find information on how to buy this book in bulk at a discounted rate.

MISSION POINT PRESS

Published by Mission Point Press
2554 Chandler Rd.
Traverse City, MI 49696
(231) 421-9513
www.MissionPointPress.com

Design by Sarah Meiers

Softcover ISBN: 978-1-965278-02-4
Hardcover ISBN: 978-1-965278-03-1
Library of Congress Control Number: 2024917837

Printed in the United States of America

AN ELECTRA, ESQ. LEGAL THRILLER

THE GOOD DOCTORA

TODD MERER

MISSION POINT PRESS

For Soraya

"Give a girl the right shoes and she can conquer the world."

–Marilyn Monroe

CHAPTER 1

Call me Electra.
Not many people do. Legally, I'm Electra, Esq., reachable at ElectraLaw.com. Formally, I'm Ms. Electra, and socially, just plain El.

Actually, the only person who calls me Electra is Gino Moskowitz, who'd invited me to his Thanksgiving dinner. Much as I adore Gino, the prospect of spending the holidays in gray New York was depressing, and I'd declined. Instead, I was now two miles up in the Colombian Andes at *La Penitenciaria de Combita,* where a gate guard was breathing down my cleavage while I signed in.

Just because I'm a hot-looking lady lawyer, every mutt seemed to get the idea that looking was free. It wasn't. Men loved to think they had all the cards, but they didn't: their inflated egos always played right into my hands. Don't get me wrong, I don't seek male attention, but when it comes—which is often—I put it to good use. Like right now.

The guard's lingering gaze gave me time to scan the visitor register and note that the inmate I was there to see had already been visited by half a dozen drug lawyers. The usual gasbags: New York guys wearing necklaced Stars of David, and Miami Cubans dangling gold crosses, all pitching their God-given powers. I signed with my usual scrawl—illegible to others and impossible for competitors to decipher—because I prefer to keep my business private.

"*Bienvenida, Doctora,*" the guard said.
Colombianos' honorific for lawyers is "*Doctor.*" I don't like the appellation because it lumps me among a group I abhor.

"*Mil gracias*," I said, entering.

Combita's grounds replicated the tended lawns and floral paths of American federal jails because it was financed by the U.S.A. as part of the multi-billion anti-drug program known as "Plan Colombia." What a joke. The War on Drugs was a long-term losing affair like Vietnam and Iraq. But, hey, wars gin up the economy and create jobs and wealth for a fortunate few, myself included. Judge me not lest you be judged, my millennial counterparts, struggling for a slice of the tech or banking or what-have-you pie, for the justice system industry is a very lucrative enterprise. Besides, it's more fun.

At least it is for me.

Not so for the unfortunates in Combita, imprisoned behind concentric rings of barbed fences in moldy concrete cells. Roused before dawn, subjected to butt-naked, cold bucket showers, then confined all day in courtyards huddled against the frequent rain and constant chill. At twilight, they would be locked down again, fed a gruel of spoiled meat and moldy potatoes, allowed five minutes for prayer as per the prison *padre's* redemption program, after which the naked light bulb went out.

The man I was there to see wasn't among the sufferers. As boss of the notorious Santa Fe cartel, he was a Midas, and in Combita, money bought everything. Even his own private suite and, I hoped, my services.

I paused at his door for a pre-arrival checklist. The checklist had nothing to do with lawyering for narcos—I've dealt with more cocaine-powdered gangsters than I can count. I just like my appearance to reflect my attitude: calm, cool, and unruffled.

Despite the four-hour drive from Bogota, my St. Laurent jumpsuit was unrumpled. Check. My signature blue silk Hermès scarf was a touch off-kilter, so I adjusted it. Check. I took my Chanel compact mirror from my crocodile shoulder bag for the finishing touches. Indulging in fine things is a trait I inherited from my poor Mama, who believed in living every day to its fullest because you never know if it's going to be your last—ironically, she ended up choosing her own judgment day.

But I digress.

My point is that I am not a vain material girl who flaunts; I dress my style purely as a self-indulgence, and don't give a hoot how the world views me—though from the looks I get, the world seems to like what it sees. So I glossed my lips—putting the polish on my armor before battle, so to speak—and blew a kiss at my mirror image—*mwah!*

Looking good, kid.

CHAPTER 2

Martin Montez was an attractive man.
Sturdy, in his prime-silver years, a shock of wavy salt-and-pepper hair, a pencil mustache above a white smile. A charmer. Gracious.
I disliked him at first sight, although I wasn't sure why. I mean, what was there not to like?
It wasn't what he did for a living. For goodness' sake, I'm a white-powder lawyer. It was something else hovering just beyond my ken. Sort of a subliminal light suggesting caution in the presence of a particularly abominable snow-dealer.
"Welcome to my humble abode," Montez greeted me, gesturing around his quarters. "*No es exactamente* a Beverly Hills Hotel bungalow," he said. "*Pero qué diablos*, one must make the best of circumstances, you agree?"
"*Claramente*," I said, thinking he sure had.
He wore a fine cashmere polo over tweed trousers tucked into polished low boots. His cave had a mini-fridge and an electric cooking iron, a curtained-off shower and shitter, and a cellphone plugged into an outlet.
"Forgive me for being forward, but you're even more attractive than I was told."
He was hitting on me, but it wouldn't get him anywhere. No doubt he'd swept many women off their feet, but for me his appeal was best swept under a rug. Men are not my thing. Neither are women. Life is filled with monsters, and some had managed to chew me up when I was younger and more vulnerable—a mistake I would never make again, having

fashioned myself into a lone ranger. But at the moment, I had a flirtatious client to convince.

"To be honest," he continued, "when you came to my attention, my first thought was that a man like me being defended by a lady lawyer seemed, shall we say, unconventional? But then I thought, yes, why not? The women jurors will admire you, and now that we've met, I believe the men will as well."

"One never knows what jurors think," I said. "Until afterward."

He chuckled. "Well put. Our mutual friend says you're a better *doctor* than any man he knows. Like flies from afar, *doctores* buzz around me, promising this and that. I'm told you don't make promises you can't keep. That is why you're the only one with whom I chose to consult."

"I'm honored," I lied, thinking of his overcrowded legal visit register.

"I assume you're familiar with my case?" he asked.

I was. The indictment that led to Montez's impending extradition to the States was bare bones: the applicable laws that Santa Fe cartel had broken and brief references to the overt acts violating them: trafficking tens of thousands of kilos of cocaine, millions of doses of fentanyl, and laundering billions of dollars.

Exaggerated? Of course. Government press releases generally are. Still, no doubt his was a big case warranting a big fee, and I like making a lot of money because I like living well on my own.

"They say the name Santa Fe is a thief's religious homage to an act of faith," he said. "*Ridículo*. It's a trading company whose offices happen to be in Santa Fe de Bogota."

"Also the name of the Bogota football team," I said.

"*Muy perceptiva*. I am a big fan." He threw his head back and laughed. His neck was as smooth as a baby's which I figured was fifty grand worth of lift; well worth it, plus he could sightsee Rio with his plastic surgeon's other patients.

"Your analysis, *Doctora*?" he asked.

I paused as if for thought, but it was only for effect. His case was a lost cause. Martin Montez, a.k.a. *El Jugador*, "The Player," was the indictment's top-captioned defendant among twenty-odd others, but only he and his junior partners were listed by names: Leon Lemus, a.k.a. "Lucho," and Jorge Jaramillo, a.k.a. "Don J." Some of the other defendants' names were black-line redacted, which I took to mean that they were in custody and cooperating. Others were simply ID'd as FNU LNU—first name unknown, last name unknown—indicating they were fugitives. Among these was Montez's alleged Mexican kill team, a group whose shared alias was "*Los Xs*."

"The indictment mentions phone conversations between defendants and CSs, short for confidential sources," I said. "I think the sources were in your, ah, trading company."

Anger flushed his face. He stood and crossed to the window and stood with his back to me. Beyond the jail perimeter I saw the armored SUV he'd provided for my trip. Thoughtful of him, because Bogota was four hours away on a highway alternately controlled by army units, guerrillas, and paramilitary outfits by day, and by independent *banditos* by night.

"Why would anyone betray me?" he asked without turning. "For what reason?"

I knew he knew why but answered anyway. "For a get-out-of-jail-free card."

"Your *recomendación*?" he asked.

I glanced at my watch. It was late afternoon. I'd left Bogota early, but we'd gotten stuck at an army *barricada*—some kind of dustup, not unusual—and although I'd just arrived, it was nearly time to leave. Time to take my best shot at being retained, then go while the going was safe.

"Cooperation is your only option," I said.

He turned to me. "You're afraid to fight?"

"No point in fighting a losing battle," I said. "Join Team America and I'll get you a short sentence you can do standing on your head—as opposed to pacing a cell for decades."

He showed me his smile. No surprise that his teeth were the best money might buy with the requisite minor imperfections—a shade deliberately less than bright white, a slightly misaligned lower incisor, a teeny chip on an upper's corner—all meant to suggest his choppers were not false.

"*Me gusta* the manner in which you speak. The *aliraciónes*."

"Unintended," I said. "My words express my thoughts."

"I, too, speak bluntly," he said. "Cooperation? The other lawyers advise that—to my friends, I mean. I think all they care about is money. Do you, *Doctora*?"

"Of course I do, *señor*," I said. "And success as well."

"Ah. Honesty. And you stand by your guarantee?"

"There are no guarantees," I said.

"Hypothetically?" he asked. "Supposing I could cooperate? I am informed that Lucho and Don J began cooperating as soon as they were arrested. Against me, of course," he added. "I am the sacrificial lamb."

For a very bad actor, his acting wasn't half bad. I added an extra point for his tacked on, rueful smile, and reminded myself to watch my step with this character.

"Months after them, I was also arrested," he went on. "The fugitive life was enjoyable, and I thought I was the lucky one, but it turned out to be my bad luck. By now I am sure your government has accepted their cooperation."

"Very possibly," I said.

"If the prosecutors already know everything about Santa Fe from them, they will not need my cooperation. I doubt there's anything you can do for me. Oh, you'll come up with something, *los doctores* always do, but who knows if it will work ... until, as you put it ... afterward."

I believe I can find ways to improve a bad situation better than any drug lawyer out there, but saying so would sound as weak as wishing upon a star. Best to come on strong.

"If you think that, then there's no point in continuing our conversation," I said.

"*Tranquila, Doctora*," he said. "I meant no disrespect. I am distracted because there are complications. In my absence there are many who wish to assume my position. They are determined not to allow anyone to block their ambitions."

I nodded. Same old same old. The way it always was.

He held my gaze. "You're not concerned?"

"Only about driving to Bogota at night."

"You truly believe you can help me?"

"I know I can help you," I said.

His face grew stern. "Do not make promises you cannot keep."

I'd already said no guarantees, but I'd just implied a promise: "I know I can help you." Not a wise statement to make to a lion in his den, but technically true, to a degree. To paraphrase an old song: anything another lawyer can do, I can do better. I believed this. Truly.

"Your fee would be?" he asked.

"One million five," I said.

"One. It's not negotiable."

I'd deliberately overreached, thinking we'd meet in the middle. Still, hard to walk away from a million-dollar score. But to save face I'd have to one-up him on the deal.

"Agreed on one condition," I said. "Paid in full, up front."

He nodded noncommittally, then glanced at his watch. Stood. "Thank you for coming."

He didn't offer his hand, so I just nodded and left, disappointed because I'd thought the Mighty Electra was about to hit one out of the park, but instead had struck out.

As I left, a woman was entering. A visored hat covered her face, but the wind outlined her slender, curvaceous body. *Señor* Montez's conjugal visitor, no doubt. In Combita, money even bought love.

CHAPTER 3

For a few minutes I brooded about my wasting a long day's journey so Montez could kill time picking my brain while waiting to be pleasured.

Oh, well. Win some, lose some, and there's an upside to everything—one being that the holiday season in New York is cold and bleak, but here it's all sunshine and green valleys between snow-capped peaks. Also, I'm not an action junkie but I do enjoy adventuring, even in the remote heart of Colombia, where the terrain isn't the only thing that's edgy....

Ufff!

Bit of a jar there, a rough patch of road above a poorly repaired pothole—*Oh*—there's a wilted memorial shrine on the road shoulder, so I guess the pothole was a crater. Stuff happens hereabouts. Not to worry—the SUV was armored and the two thugs up front were armed and suitably dangerous looking.

Anyway, forget looking back, look ahead. This evening I'd enjoy a fine dinner, tomorrow morning fly to home sweet home, maybe do a little shopping, then get back on the merry-go-round and wait for another chance to grab a gold ring.

I kicked back and enjoyed the ride. Or tried to.

I noticed the driver and his sidekick sharing an awareness: glances in the dash and side mirrors, looking up at the hillsides ahead, unspoken acknowledgments. Something was up and I looked around but all I saw was a car half a mile behind.

Ahead was a roadside *arepa* stand: a crumbling brick hut fronted by an outdoor grill operated by two indigenous women. The driver pulled over.

"If you wish to relieve yourself, *Doctora*," he said. First time he'd spoken. His accent was Mexican.

Good idea. We were still two hours from Bogota. The pissoir was a hole behind a bush next to the hut. I lowered my jumpsuit, squatted, and—

KA-BOOM!

Shotgun?

From the hut?

Should I go in?

Stay here or run?

I froze.

A man brandishing a pistol rushed from the hut. He saw me and hesitated, as if surprised to discover a woman.

CRACK!

A hole appeared between his brows. For a moment he stood still, his expression frozen puzzlement. Then, like a building being demolished, he slowly crumpled to a cross-legged squat as if meditating. A thin line of blood trickled from his new eye and ran down his face, but he seemed not to mind.

"*Cabrón*," my driver said, putting his boot to the man's chest and tilting him over.

"You finished, *Doctora*?" the driver asked me.

"What? Oh." My bodysuit was around my ankles, but I was saved from sight by the bush. I yanked it up and zipped.

"*Bueno*," he said. "*Vamos.*"

I followed him into the hut. His sidekick was reloading a shotgun. Another man lay on the floor. His middle was torn apart revealing gray intestines filled with undigested food.

I turned and vomited, then staggered out of the hut.

Next to the SUV, another car was parked. Clearly the vehicle that had been following us. The indigenous women were gone. My driver brought an arepa outside and offered it to me.

Sick to my stomach, I declined. He tossed the arepa to his sidekick and went back in to take another for himself. I staggered into the back of the SUV and curled up, trying to parse what had happened.

Had the attackers been banditos? Unlikely, as it was still day. They wouldn't dare, would they?

Were they Montez's would-be cartel heirs, intent on taking

out his lawyer? Had the gunman hesitated because he expected the lawyer to be a man? Not that I was Montez's lawyer, but they didn't know that.

Whatever had made him flinch, it had been the weirdest moment of my already bizarre life. Yet, although I was shaken, I was also strangely stirred. I had a hell of a story to tell, but the only one I'd tell it to was Gino Moskowitz, and he'd laugh it off as just another day at the office.

CHAPTER 4

Casa Medina is a discreet hotel in Bogota's upscale district, Zona G.

Most American lawyers hawking extradition work tend to stay in flashy hotels, the better to see and be seen by potential clients. I prefer flying beneath the radar because all kinds of law enforcement also frequent the flashy hotels to observe the players. Sometimes I think I take my paranoia too seriously, but my work entails walking the razor's edge between the law and the free-fire zone of the War on Drugs, and I don't want anyone noticing if I misstep.

Casa Medina's dining area is an inner courtyard with tropical flowers and stone fountainheads whose gentle gurgling underscored muted violins. Freshly bathed and made-up, sleek in clingy black Versace offset by pearl strands, my roadside pitstop now relegated out of mind, I was led to my pre-reserved table.

Three men were seated there: the two facing me wore suits, the third was seated with his back to me. The ominous emptiness of the fourth setting drew out an old memory from my childhood family dinners. I shook myself out of it before its significance could settle in; now was not the time for reminiscing.

"I think there's a *confusión*," I said to the maître d'. "I'm dining *sola*."

The man with his back to me turned. He was thirty-something and might have been handsome but for a too-small chin, a shortcoming compensated by his cheerful demeanor. He squeezed my arm and grinned.

"Here she is," he said happily.

"And here you are," I said, wondering what Pacho Grajales, whom Montez had referred to as our mutual friend, was doing here.

I'd first met Pacho when he was a new immigrant facing deportation for a dubious violation of IRS policy I'd managed to dismiss. He was penniless then, and I hadn't charged him, a favor he'd since paid back many times over when he became a well-known businessman in New York's Colombian diaspora with a finger in various enterprises, one being a chain of fast-food joints called El Pollo Loco. His was "the Original," and seemed a legitimate business, although he'd referred many drug-dealing miscreants my way. I didn't know his relation to them and didn't ask, preferring to view Pacho as simply a hale fellow, well-met. After all, everyone who was someone ate at El Pollo Loco.

Hmm. Since Montez was a no-go, was Pacho here to refer another client?

He gestured me to a chair at the fourth setting, then introduced the two men. The plump one was Adolfo Arias, the grim-visaged dude was Victor Vizcaino. When they stood to shake hands, Arias's palm was moist, and he smelled of drugstore cologne. Vizcaino's fingers were thin, his grip dry. I noticed they both wore square-toed shoes, the style favored by Colombian lawyers. Hmm. A man who refers drug cases and a pair of Colombian drug lawyers at a pre-planned meet meant a business agenda, so I kicked into working mode: pretend everything is being recorded.

Evade and dissemble: no moments of conscious avoidance or knowledge of criminality or silences that might be interpreted as acquiescence.

No discussions about who was paying my fee or how it was to be paid.

The maître d' popped a champagne cork and poured. Pacho raised his flute. "A toast, *señores*," he said. "To the health of our friend."

The fizz tickled my nose. And my fancy. I was back on the criminal-defense merry-go-round. Whoever their friend was, he could afford two lawyers.

"*Salúd*!" Arias drained his flute and burped.

"To our collaboration," Vizcaino said.

Collaboration? A word uncomfortably related to conspiring. "To our legal efforts," I said.

"To *Señor* Martin's quick return," Pacho added.

Martin? As in Martin Montez?

Eureka! My playing hard to get had succeeded after all.

"Arias and Vizcaino are facilitating your fee," Pacho told me.

Facilitating my fee? Not appropriate words with potential law-enforcement surveillance in play. See, receiving fees that I knew or should have known were proceeds of crimes conceivably could put me into an overarching conspiracy. Not to mention, since it would most likely be paid in cash, it might create problems with IRS-required cash transaction reports mandating the ID of the payor, which is why I restrict fee-talk to myself and the client.

"Mr. Montez is fortunate to be assisted by such friends," I said, countering Pacho's ill-advised comment. "After all, being confined in Combita, he personally can't arrange means to legitimately pay me."

Arias and Vizcaino, recognizing my self-protective evasion, exchanged knowing smiles.

"Long trip back, eh?" Vizcaino asked me.

He knows what happened, I realized. Don't know how he could, but he did. Probably from my Mexican escorts.

"Actually, I slept most of the way," I said.

Pacho, working on a refill, was oblivious to the exchange. "I'm returning to New York tomorrow," he said. "The following day I will personally see to it that according to your understanding with Martin, your fee—"

"Let's order, I'm starving," I interrupted.

"Our client says you believe there are informants," Vizcaino said. "He wants you to learn who they are."

A fastball I needed to foul off. "During the course of the case, I shall force the government to disclose informants." I didn't add that such disclosure would only be made if Montez went to trial, but since I was sure he'd be cooperating—all cartel *jefes* do, or try to—the info would remain secret.

"¡*Mesero*!" Pacho called to the waiter. "Another bottle, *por favor.*"

CHAPTER 5

Two bottles of bubbly had grown to four by the time the meet ended, and the next morning I awoke mildly hungover.

During the flight, I nestled in my usual first-class bulkhead seat, 1-A, lowered the window shade, closed my eyes, and re-ran the situation.

Pacho. Definitely in with the in-crowd.

Arias and Vizcaino. Lawyers who doubled as *consiglieres* who well might be among the FNUs and LNUs in Montez's indictment. Guilt by association was contagious, and I'd have to distance myself from them—and from Montez's Mexicans, who likely were the "X" killers mentioned in his indictment.

I knew that Montez would be a difficult client, but since he was paying for first-class service, I'd do him well—although it would be strictly business class.

In fact, I felt a tingle of anticipation. Despite what I said before, I do have a minor addiction—to action—and the feeling that complications might set in didn't deter me. Funny how things happen. Years ago, a coincidental meeting had turned me from a cocaine junkie into a white-powder lawyer, and now I was addicted to the thrilling taste of courtroom victory—a flavor made all the more delicious when narrowly dodging the agony of defeat. A side benefit being that, since I didn't work well with others, I alone controlled my agenda.

Did I have moral reservations about my work?

Nope. The way I see it, representing drugsters is no different than defending corrupt politicians or corporations whose products kill people. Also—and yeah, I know it sounds corny—I truly believe everyone is entitled to a lawyer. This is one of many maxims drilled into me by Gino Moskowitz, my patron saint who changed my life.

At touchdown, seat 1-A allowed me to be the first passenger off.

I had a Global Entry card and ten minutes later was in the chopper I'd hired. Another fifteen minutes later, I was back in the Big Apple. Compared to Bogota, New York was a breath of filthy air.

My office was a suite in a midtown art deco building that's been near-empty since the pandemic. The premises were slightly spooky now, more so because I don't employ a secretary—I don't want anyone knowing my business. The office smelled stale, so I opened a window, then reviewed my mail and messages.

I was jazzed. The Thanksgiving Thursday aloneness was over; thank God it was Friday, and a damn good one, because I was getting a visit from a Mr. Green.

I took my gun—a Sig with a silvered custom-job—from my safe. I didn't envision any problems, but there are a lot of money-hungry bloodhounds out there, and Pacho's naïveté didn't exactly put me at ease. The idea of having to shoot someone wasn't something I relished, but if things ever came to that, I wanted to do it with style.

And not necessarily with the Sig. An inappropriately grateful client had once said I had the brass balls of a man, and since I was a woman, he'd gifted me a set of brass knuckles to protect myself. I shoved the knucks and the Sig in my top desk drawer.

My phone rang.

"*Hola*," Pacho said. "Confirming tomorrow's meeting."

"Right," I said. "I don't know much about the fast-food business, but I'll try to help you."

"What? Oh. Ha-ha. You know the Elmhurst Manor?"

"Yes." It was a popular joint among the Colombian expat community.

"Tomorrow evening, say eight o'clock? After we, you know, talk, you're invited to my daughter's *quinceañera* there."

Uh-oh. A million greenbacks are hefty. Lugging them from

a fifteenth birthday party was definitely not cool. Maybe leave via a rear exit? Whatever, I'd find a way. As Gino Moskowitz often said: "When a client puts money on the table? Take it off."

"See you then," I told Pacho.

"*Otra cosa*," he said. "A car has been following me. I turn, it turns. I'm worried it's the police."

"*Ridículo*," I said. "Why would the police follow a law-abiding businessman? Friday is payroll day, right?"

"Not really, I ..."

"Maybe people think so and want to rob you," I said. "My advice is to be careful."

"I got the license plate. You have ways of finding out whose car it is?"

I hesitated. Pacho's followers might well be cops. I could easily learn who owned the plate. But if it was a law-enforcement vehicle, a search would come up empty—a giveaway that, if I passed it on to Pacho, was flirting with obstruction of justice. So, if the search came up empty, I'd tell Pacho I couldn't get the information. On the other hand, if Pacho was being tagged by a rip-off crew, getting him their ID was law-abidingly A-okay.

"I'll see what I can find out," I said.

I called a P.I. I use and asked him to run the plate. Ten minutes later he called back. The plate was publicly registered to one Brian DiMaglio, who lived in College Point, a nice neighborhood not favored by bad guys. I decided both the cop and robber scenarios were mistaken.

Saturday night the Elmhurst Manor was feverish.

Avoiding the packed restaurant and bar, I ducked into the private ballroom where the *quinceañera* party was in full swing. Girls in cute yellow *Pollo Loco* aprons and caps were carving roasted birds. People were dancing *bachata* and drinking *aguardiente*. Pacho was at the head table with his wife, Marisol, and just-turned-fifteen daughter, Cleo, plus another woman he introduced as his younger sister Laura.

My gaze lingered on Laura. I felt *simpático* toward her. She was young enough to be my daughter, and yet I saw something about her that resonated; a fleeting sense that she was troubled in a way I had been at her age, before Gino Moskowitz had changed the course of my life.

Pacho nodded toward a side door. I went through it and found myself in a room filled with freezers and stacked with cartons. I figured my million was in one of them. When Pacho joined me a moment later, he locked the door.

"Did you find out what I asked?" he said.

Although it seemed a harmless favor, I don't like leaving paper trails. Or talking aloud in what might be electronically monitored air. Accordingly, I'd memorized the info the P.I. had given me, and whispered it in Pacho's ear.

"*Mil gracias.*" He jotted it down, folded it away, then produced an envelope, which he handed to me.

I had no idea what was in it—maybe a communication from Montez or one of his lawyers—but I slipped it in my jacket pocket and mouthed, *the fee*?

"That's what—"

Something smashed against the door. It burst open and three men wearing blue windbreakers stenciled with large yellow lettering—DEA—entered. Their guns were drawn.

One confronted us, another snooped the room, the third, a lean guy I made as the team leader, said, "Mr. Grajales, you're under arrest. You have the right to remain silent."

"I'm Mr. Grajales's lawyer," I cut in. "I do not want you to question him."

"I know who you are," the leader said disdainfully.

Pacho was spread-eagled against a wall and patted down. His pockets were emptied, and their contents put atop a freezer. The note he'd jotted was found and passed to the team leader. His face reddened as he read it.

"Sonofabitch," he said. "Pat counselor Dirtbag down too."

Dirtbag? No matter how confrontational or litigious a criminal matter is, my rule is to always keep things civil—never get personal. In turn, I am accorded the same feedback. Usually. More troublesome was that he already knew I was a lawyer.

"You've no cause to search me." I wasn't so sure about that, given the circumstances, but it sounded officious. I fished my phone out, and when I started recording, the team leader wavered.

"Forget her," a hoarse-voiced agent said from the shattered doorway. Sixtyish, very large, a big-boss aura.

Alongside him was a younger agent, dark-suited and suave, very un-DEA. "Do not create controversies," he said to the team leader.

The team leader nodded sullenly. "Guys, just bag up Pacho's ID and cash and whatever and read him his rights on the way to the paddy wagon."

While Pacho was led out, I saw that Pacho's wife and daughter were already gone, but his sister Laura was still there. "You're his lawyer," she said harshly. "Why did you allow him to be arrested for no reason?"

"I don't know the reason," I said. "When I do, I'll help him in any way I can."

Her expression softened. "I wish I could explain ... things."

"Feel free to," I said. "You can trust me."

"I want to, but ... I'm sorry, I didn't mean to be rude. My brother considers you a good friend, and I know you'll be there for him."

"You can count on me," I said.

"Thank you," she said, and left.

I noticed the agents had left one of Pacho's personal effects behind: a white plastic card left unnoticed atop a white chest freezer. It was the size of a credit card, but blank. It was meaningless to me, but if it had been among Pacho's things, it meant something to him. I picked it up and pocketed it along with the envelope he'd given me.

The DEA team leader was still in the ballroom. "Maybe your status as a lawyer changes Monday in court," he said to me. "Consider that over the weekend. Okay, beat it."

"What's your problem, agent?" I asked.

He held up the note on which Pacho had jotted the license plate information I'd given him. "My name is Brian DiMaglio and I live with my wife and kids in a home you broadcasted to your scumbag client. On the record, we're opening an investigation. Off the record, anything happens to my family, you can expect a personal visit from me."

I kept my eyes on his and my feelings to myself, thinking *broadcasted?*

Figured. They'd been on Pacho's phone, which explained how they knew I was a lawyer. A nasty unforeseen situation indeed, but DiMaglio had created it by using his personal car to do surveillance work. His bad, not mine. I'd bring it up if push came to shove, but if nothing regarding my role or presence transpired, let it go. No point in waving a red flag at a raging bull.

Had DEA arrived a few seconds later, they would have caught me in constructive possession of the million I was certain was in one of the stacked cartons, which very well might escalate things beyond a mere pat-down. Still, they'd discover the money soon enough, so I wanted to get out while the getting was good. I left the ballroom, passing too-crisped chickens turning on spits. They didn't smell good. Nothing did. My intuition had been spot-on.

Complications had set in.

CHAPTER 6

I was confident they had nothing on me.

I was the three monkeys. Hadn't seen, nor heard, nor spoken evil. I knew nothing from nothing. Not that my ignorance was blissful.

Pacho was my only contact. Nothing I could do but wait until Montez found out what had happened and reached out to me. For sure he'd bitch and moan over the lost money. Accuse me of having been paid before Pacho went down, say the loss was mine. I'd demand my fee, but he'd counter with a demand for proof of a seizure, which I didn't have because I'd left before the money was found.

Pacho's wife, Marisol, called. I told her to go to Brooklyn's Eastern District Federal court for a bail hearing Monday morning, and to bring as many relatives and people Pacho did business with as she could, then amended, "I mean, people from his fast-food business."

"*Por* bail, ¿*sí*?" she asked. "From *legítimo* Pollo Loco?"

"Of course, legitimate," I said. Obviously, Pacho's wife knew the drill. Had Pacho previously put up bail with money of questionable origin for clients he'd referred to me? Could I, the lawyer who had argued for those bails, become a suspect in those scams?

I suddenly remembered the envelope he'd given me. Now I opened it and saw banded Franklins I guesstimated as fifty thou.

A puzzlement. Why hand-deliver fifty K separately instead of including it in the million-dollar bundle? I thought on that but came up empty.

On Sunday I searched for Pacho.

He hadn't been booked in any of the New York fed jails. Figured. Probably he was still being processed in one or another intake, and even if I knew which, no way they'd allow me a visit. Fine with me, because at the moment there was nothing I cared to discuss in an insecure environment with my too-verbal client.

Sunday evening, Pacho's wife, Marisol, called again. All was ready as I'd instructed. She'd bring Pacho's U.S. passport and tax returns, and his Pollo Loco franchisees would come to cosign a bail bond.

"His *mamá* called from Bogota," Marisol said. "She has the bad heart and cannot fly."

"Any other calls from Colombia?" I asked.

"No one. *¿Por qué* you ask that?"

"No reason. Eleven, sharp."

The Worth Street entrance to the Southern District courthouse faces Chinatown's Columbus Park and looks like it's populated straight outta Canton: Chinese kids shooting baskets, Chinese adults doing Tai Chi, Chinese elders gathered around *Go* matches ... and an accidental tourist, Pacho's wife, Marisol.

I sat next to her. She said her people were running late but I'd factored that in. Pacho's arraignment was scheduled for twelve. Before then, I needed to prep the people I intended to propose as bail signatories, then sit in while Pacho was interviewed by Pretrial Services to make sure the questions were limited to the usual name, rank, serial number stuff, and that he didn't volunteer anything beyond. I needed an hour to do all this. Because things inevitably tend to run on a slow clock, I had allotted myself an extra hour.

By eleven thirty, the family and would-be signatories were there. I asked Marisol if Laura was coming. To my surprise, she shrugged. I was curious about Laura because she'd seemed interested in talking to me. But other matters were more pressing: the bail signatories were balking, having learned that if Pacho jumped bail, they'd be personally responsible for the bond.

Fortunately, Marisol calmed their worries: surely, they

knew their good friend Pacho would stay and defend himself against the baseless charges. This took some convincing, and it was twelve thirty by the time it was accomplished. I told them to be in the courtroom at one and hustled to the Pretrial Service interview.

Too late; it had already been done. The PTS officer gave me the report, and I skimmed the boilerplate to the last words: "Defendant has substantial ties to the community and is not considered a flight risk. Recommend bail secured by a two-hundred-fifty-thousand-dollar bond, with home confinement and electronic monitoring."

Excellent! Precisely what I'd intended to pitch.

I went up to the assigned courtroom, which turned out to be the domain of one Judge Edward Graff, who by my previous experience I knew to be a grim curmudgeon. The morning session was for new arraignments and the usual suspect mix of lawyers and lawmen were there. I checked the calendar and saw Pacho's case was near the bottom. His prosecutor was assistant U.S. Attorney Daniel Mizrahi, who I didn't know. I went to the government table and asked for him.

A brown-suited guy on the wrong side of forty looked up from a document he'd been reading. "I'm Mizrahi," he said. "Can I help you?"

I introduced myself as Pacho's lawyer and asked for a copy of the indictment.

His eyes narrowed. "We'll discuss that soon, counselor."

"My client can't enter a plea until he knows what for," I said.

He smiled thinly. "We'll address that soon as well."

"Thank you for your time and consideration," I said.

He looked back down at his paper, exposing the bald spot on his crown. By age and attire, Mizrahi wasn't one of the usual-suspect twentyish bright boys and gals who graduate from top-ten universities, do a five- or six-year hitch fattening their resume lawyering for the G, then move on to making major money in a top-ten law firm. I made him as one of the few career prosecutors in the Southern District, who tend to be hard-nosed, by-the-book, resentful jerks.

I took a seat in the first-row lawyers-only bench. Gave a

sharp glance to the unsubtle flirtations of the male defense lawyers and received cold shoulders from their few female counterparts—an unlikely sorority of in-it-for-the-money-honey types, and demure public defender do-gooders. Being a crossbreed between both extremes, I was deemed an outsider. I couldn't care less.

The arraignments were briefly repetitious. By rote, Judge Graff asked each of the arraigned defendants if they had read the indictment, and did he or she want it read now, and blah-blah-blah—to which the lawyers replied that they had reviewed the indictment with their client, waived a reading, and entered a plea of not guilty, etcetera, etcetera, etcetera.

Ho-hum.

The last group of defendants was led in by court security marshals. Pacho wasn't among them, so I went into the holding pen behind the courtroom. The cellblock was empty, and he was alone in a cell. We spoke quietly, his voice quavering through the bars.

"Tell *el señor* not to worry," he said.

"When the judge asks if you understand, just say yes."

"Every dollar will be accounted for," he said.

"We'll discuss your fee later," I said.

"Grajales," a corrections guard called.

To my mild surprise, the arraignment was held in Judge Graff's chambers.

When AUSA Mizrahi entered, I realized why we were in chambers. In-camera proceedings are kept private when the subject matter is something the court or the G doesn't want to make public. Like discussing the contents of an ongoing wiretap.

Pacho was led in, cuffed and guarded by a burly marshal. Graff nodded, his deputy clerk, Brunhilda, called the case, and the steno's fingers began moving.

"The government requested an in-camera appearance so as not to jeopardize an ongoing investigation," Graff said. He looked at me. "You wish to be heard on that, counselor?"

"No, your Honor," I said. "But I reserve the right to do so later—"

"So noted," he said. "The government also requested that you be disqualified as counsel for Mr. Grajales. They state that you are the subject of an investigation related to the charges against Mr. Grajales and therefore are conflicted from representation. What do you have to say about that?"

"I can't say anything because I don't know what Mr. Grajales is charged with."

Graff frowned. "You haven't read the indictment?"

"Your honor, if I might?" Mizrahi said. "Although Counselor is currently a subject of an investigation, it well might be that she will become a target. Therefore, I saw no reason to give her the present, unredacted indictment, which is still sealed."

"Wherever you're going with this, stop," Graff said. "I will not allow you to screw up a case that will sit on my docket for several years. Give counsel the unredacted indictment, Mr. Mizrahi. Perhaps after reading it, she may voluntarily withdraw."

"Judge," I said. "No matter what's in the indictment, I can assure you I will not withdraw. Unless, of course, I am a named defendant, which I assume I am not, or I would be seated next to Mr. Grajales."

Graff snorted in agreement. "Yes, you would."

"At most, I may be a target in an as-yet unstated allegation. In any event, whatever my situation may or may not be, my present concern is to defend Mr. Grajales."

Graff looked at Pacho. "You understand what we are discussing, sir?"

Pacho nodded vigorously. "Yes. I am very fluent."

"You want this lawyer to represent you, sir?"

"*Si,* your Honorable. She is my lawyer."

Graff nodded thoughtfully. "Not going to open a can of worms and let them fester. Going to deal with this quickly. In one week, I want submissions from both sides as to the government's motion to disqualify counsel."

"The government requests their submission be *ex parte,*" Mizrahi said.

Ex, as in excluded, *parte,* as in me not being party to the submission. "Not seeing it deprives me of an opportunity to respond," I said.

"Cross that bridge if and when we come to it," Graff said. "One week to submit. No need to arraign Mr. Grajales until then. I take it both sides have no objection to waiving speedy arraignment time for a week?"

"No objection," Mizrahi said.

"I object," I said. "The delay deprives Mr. Grajales of an opportunity to seek bail."

Graff nodded. "I've read the pretrial report. It recommends that bail be set—a bond for two hundred fifty thousand to be signed by responsible parties—with the conditions of release being home confinement and electronic monitoring. What's the government's position on that?"

"I haven't interviewed the signatories," Mizrahi said.

"They're present in the courtroom," I said. "They're all citizens, as is Mr. Grajales. His wife is here and will surrender his passport. The signatories are all persons with substantial businesses, as is Mr. Grajales."

"Your Honor," Mizrahi said. "Mr. Grajales has been arrested; we can't just release him without his first being arraigned."

"And you can't keep him unless he's speedily arraigned, Mr. Mizrahi," Graff said. "Until then, the government shall release him. You figure the dynamics. Arrest him next week, whatever."

"Your Honor—"

"You don't like my ruling, take it up to the Circuit," Graff said. "Now go vet the signatories. Half an hour to let me know if you've any objections. If you've none, don't waste time arguing against bail, because I'm going to go along with the PTS recommendation."

Mizrahi was taken aback. "Your Honor, if there's no arrest, how can bail be set?"

"Ms. Electra's client is detained is how," Graff said. "You don't like my ruling, appeal it."

Clever old Graff knew the seams in the system—an appeal would take at least a week— and filing it would anger a senior judge, not a wise move for a career prosecutor.

Reluctantly, Mizrahi interviewed the signatories. Realizing they were bona fide, he sped through the inquiries cursorily.

"I'll send the indictment," he said to me, and left.

I knew it would take some time until Pacho was fitted with an ankle bracelet monitor, and I told the family to wait outside the courthouse until he appeared. Having no intention of waiting myself, I remained until they were gone.

When I left, the corridor was empty, except for a lawyer talking on a cell. I knew he was a lawyer because only lawyers are allowed to bring phones into the courthouse, and I knew he was a Colombian lawyer because he wore square-toed shoes.

CHAPTER 7

That afternoon, AUSA Mizrahi sent me a terse email.
It was a demand that I submit to being fingerprinted, warning that my refusal would trigger a subpoena.
My reply was terser: Affirmative. Send indictment.
I knew they hoped to match my prints to Pacho's note containing Agent DiMaglio's information. I could fight the subpoena, at best quash it, at worst trigger the defense lawyer's standby tactic: delay, delay, delay. But since my prints were not on the note taken from Pacho, I'd comply. The lack of positive results would bolster my thus far unnecessary Plan B: I would argue that Pacho could have obtained the info from another source; that there was not a scintilla of evidence suggesting it had come from me, and even if it had there was no way of proving I'd had the requisite intent to either obstruct or further a conspiracy.
So much for the good news. The sadder story was that I'd violated a cardinal defense lawyer rule—cash before work—and I'd already committed as Pacho's lawyer. By now, Montez must have heard about Pacho's arrest. I figured he'd be reaching out to me via an intermediary, possibly the Colombian lawyer I'd seen in the courthouse. The seized million would be our shared agenda, not to mention Pacho's fee, which I expected Montez would cover.
Problem: I wasn't about to discuss fees with anyone but Montez. And the only way to see him was if one of his Colombian lawyers escorted me into Combita. But I had no way of reaching Adolfo Arias or Victor Vizcaino.
Solution: An hour later, a courier delivered an envelope

containing a ticket for that night's red-eye to Bogota. I called Avianca and secured first-class seat 1-A, my airborne cubbyhole. Nestled there, I'd gird myself for confronting Montez.

When I emerged from Bogota Customs and Immigration, Montez's portly Colombian lawyer, Adolfo Arias, was waiting for me.

I followed him outside the terminal where the dour Victor Vizcaino waited behind the wheel of a Beamer 700L. It was morning rush hour, but he leaned on his horn and bullied our way through and around traffic. I thought we were headed for the northbound highway toward Combita, but we drove south into the slums and shantytowns of south Bogota.

"They moved him," Vizcaino said.

"El Modesto," Arias said. "Feh."

Modesto translated as "modest," but the jail was an immodest temple to the worst of human depravity. Ancient, rotting, filthy, dank, dim. A maximum-security dungeon. Four thousand inmates competing for fifteen hundred beds. Visitors were not allowed to bring in phones. Three check points, each requiring pat-downs and inked thumb prints whose cleansing amenity was a greasy rag. I made a mental note to super-exfoliate my hands later.

We went down a twisty staircase to the lower depths, passing caged inmates lying on straw. A constant buzz of insane murmurings reverberated through the metal corridors, accompanied by an occasional echoed scream.

Yet Martin Montez was perfectly composed, although they'd taken his fine clothing and replaced it with a stained jumpsuit. His hair was matted, and he needed a shave, but still was possessed of his phony self-deprecating manner.

"Welcome to the pit where the dregs of humanity are stored," he said. "Fellow on my left is a serial rapist of young boys. Gentleman on my right butchered and ate his grandmother. There's a fingerprint-ink stain on your Tommy Hilfinger."

My jacket actually was a classic Dior, but no need saying so. "Why are you in this horror house?" I asked.

"I'm being punished," he said as if amused. "Orders from

your country, I should think. The agent in charge of my case dislikes me. Unpleasant fellow."

Huh? Montez knew who his case agent was?

"How do you know DiMaglio?" I asked.

"Who? I'm talking about the large man who's fond of cigars."

Ah, yes. The hulking hoarse-voiced agent who'd told DiMaglio to back off me. An old-timer who'd seen it all and was smart enough not to start an unnecessary beef with a lawyer.

"He believes I threatened a prosecutor and must be isolated here without communication," Montez said.

Ah-hah. So Mizrahi's bad attitude with me was because I was about to rep a guy he thought had dared threaten a prosecutor.

"You're wondering if it's true," he said.

"Wondering if you'll tell me," I said.

"It's not," he said. "But let them enjoy their spite. A few days in purgatory is good for the soul. How much longer, Victor?"

"You'll be in the new jail tomorrow," Vizcaino said.

"You see, good things happen to those who wait," Montez said. "Particularly if one is aided by loyal friends like my two lawyers. They have some questions."

"Pacho," Vizcaino said. "Why was his case heard in private?"

I saw no need to reveal that I was a subject of an investigation. That glitch was temporary. No harm, no foul. But it might scare Montez off.

"The judge had a long morning," I said. "I suppose he wanted to rest his aching back in the comfort of his chamber's armchair."

"Pacho," Arias asked next. "Why is he now at home?"

"He had a good lawyer who got him bailed out."

"Thank you for that," Montez said. "Pacho is a dear friend."

"Is he going to sit on people?" Vizcaino asked.

Sit, as in cooperate. Always a possibility, but no way of knowing yet, and positively no way I'd discuss it if and when Pacho did.

"He mentioned that he wanted to make things right," I said. "I took that to include his fee."

"Fee?" Montez said. "You were paid."

"Fifty thousand, which will pay for Pacho's case," I said. "Nothing for your case."

"Pacho didn't explain?" he asked.

I recalled Pacho about to say something just before the bust. "No," I said. "Why don't you?"

"An American lawyer told me if the police seize money, they must give a receipt for it," Vizcaino said.

"You have another American lawyer?" I asked.

"You don't have a receipt," Vizcaino said.

I didn't have a receipt because I'd left before the money was confiscated. I wondered if the DEA team had kept a chunk or two, then decided a true believer like DiMaglio wasn't the thieving kind.

"I'm sure I will in time," I said. "The lost million is your problem."

"Not a problem because there was no million, *Doctora*," Montez said. "The fifty was the first installment of my fee."

"I don't do pay-as-you-go deals," I said. "My million as agreed or I'm out of here."

Montez laughed. "I advise you not to try. A beautiful *gringa* alone in El Modesto? You wouldn't get far."

"I believed you honorable," I said. "I was wrong."

Montez's expression hardened. "Be very careful what you imply."

"I didn't imply anything," I said. "I stated a fact."

Abruptly Montez grinned. "All right, we negotiate. One hundred thousand a month. In less than a year you'll be paid in full and then we can concentrate on achieving what is required for your bonus."

Bonus? Guy thought I was a horse straining for a dangling carrot. "Five hundred thousand now and one hundred a month for the next five months," I said. "Final offer. Deal or no deal?"

"With one provision," Montez said. "Take good care of Pacho."

Meaning, make sure Pacho wasn't cooperating. I'd never

agree to that but let him think what he liked. "I take good care of all my clients," I said.

"Precisely why I retained you," Montez said. "Come closer."

I moved a foot away. He beckoned me closer, and I lent him my ear. His breath was cold against my skin as he whispered.

"I do not want these two *huevones* knowing our business," he said, referring to his Colombian *doctores*. "In addition to the five hundred now and one hundred monthly, if you perform satisfactorily, you'll get another million as a bonus."

Nicer carrot, I thought, but maybe a bite too far, believability-wise.

I'd left my phone in Vizcaino's car, per the rules of El Modesto.

While visiting, I'd gotten an email from Mizrahi. Attached to it was Pacho's indictment—actually a superseder—including an additional defendant now revealed from the redacted first indictment. At the bottom of a long list of captioned defendants, Pacho Grajales had been named, charged with money laundering as per an overt act of transferring drug money.

I sighed. Transferring? Mizrahi was a bulldog. If he overheard a Santa Fe conversation about Pacho paying my fifty, he might go after it—drug proceeds, yadda yadda yadda—just to dirty me up for hustling a client who'd threatened a prosecutor....

Wait a sec!

Montez and Pacho were in the same indictment. Therefore, my representing Pacho conflicted me from representing Montez. Both might waive objections to such a conflict, but Judge Graff wouldn't want to complicate things. He'd conflict me out.

I'd blown off a Mr. Big for a minor player.

Or had I? Montez wouldn't be extradited for months. Pacho was charged with one dirty-money count—the fifty grand—which was a minor transgression in the grand scheme involving billions. Pacho was looking at months, maybe even house arrest. I could cut a quick deal and he'd be out of the case before Montez was extradited to the States. Ergo, no conflict.

I closed the attachment. The cover letter had been copied to Judge Graff. It made reference to the attached indictment AUSA Mizrahi was prosecuting, and now I understood his demeanor.

Mizrahi was the prosecutor Montez had allegedly threatened.

The case had gotten personal. I sensed a gathering storm.

Time to go home and batten down the hatches.

CHAPTER 8

Home again.

It was the only home I'd ever known. A huge place in a venerable Upper West Side apartment house where my family had lived for decades. But the family tree had been reduced to a sapling—me.

I have no memory of my father, who disappeared before I was born. Another woman, some said, discreetly. His work, others said, mysteriously. After my father left, Mama spent her days cooped up in her bedroom, trying on her superb collection of classic clothing, expecting my father to arrive for dinner as he once had. Thus, the perpetually empty setting on our dining table—and the answer to why the empty chair in the Casa Medina restaurant had given me pause. Otherwise, Mama never acknowledged my father's disappearance and never spoke about him, nor displayed any photographs.

My father was a ghost in an empty chair, but I remember Mama clearly....

She was an old-fashioned southern girl who taught me to refrain from obscenities and to always keep my privacies, just as she always kept hers—until the day she went out a high window. She fell, some said. Suicide, others whispered. I had no idea because there was no one to ask, no evidence to comb over, only an open window and an empty chair.

These unanswered questions were my inheritance, along with Mama's classic wardrobe—when it comes to fashion, what goes around comes around, and I made good use of it. And, of course, the grand apartment with a rent-controlled $1832 monthly rent in perpetuity—an inexpensive oasis among multi-million dollar renovated apartments, thanks to the liberal New York pols who cared about poor people. In a way, I was among them, because I dissipated my considerable earnings entertaining myself. Think Christmas in Aspen, a weekend at a chef cook-off in Paris, soaking sun in St. Barth; first-class travel and accommodations all the way.

But not this trip.

I'd left hurriedly and brought no luggage. The clothing I'd worn for two days was rumpled and spotted with fingerprint ink. The stuff was ingrained beneath my nails, and it took a brisk scrub to remove it. I consigned the suit to a hamper, then showered, shampooed, and conditioned my hair, wrapped a turban around it, and was about to shave my legs when my phone rang. I groped for the phone and put it to my ear.

"Who's this?" I grouched.

"Me, Pacho. Visit me now."

"I'm beat. Maybe tomorrow...."

"Now, please," he said. "About, you know, the thing?"

I assumed the "thing" was the half-mil Montez had promised. He sure had acted fast. Apparently, the requisite cash had already been in the States.

"Be there in an hour," I said.

Another rule in my playbook is that the bigger the number, the larger the precautions. I doubted Pacho stashed Montez's fee money at home, and since he was confined there wearing a monitor, it would be delivered by some worker. I trusted Pacho but didn't know about the workers. I wrapped one of my trademark blue silk Hermès scarves around my neck, stuffed my Sig in my waistband and covered it with an oversized hoodie, then grabbed my raincoat and headed for my building's garage.

Below its public-level parking was a lower level for long-term vehicles. Mostly Benzes and Rollses belonging to my neighbors. One car was covered by a tarp. I pulled it off, revealing the vintage Caddy I call "the Shark." Since my mother never drove, I assumed it had been my father's: a '75 El Dorado convertible in like-new condition. Probably had been his pride and joy, unlike the wife and daughter he'd cruelly abandoned. Which is why I'd abandoned his surname.

It was raining as I drove through Westchester County.
Pacho lived in a McMansion set on an oversized lot, accessible via a gravel driveway secluded by greenery.

By the time I pulled into his driveway, the rain had stopped, and I left my raincoat in the Shark. Droplets beaded the other cars parked there, including a midsize SUV and a black Porsche Carrera. I rang the entrance bell.

Pacho answered the door. He was jittery, but that made sense, considering how our last fee transaction had ended.

"I sent my wife to visit her mother," he said. "I thought no need for her to be here."

I arched a questioning brow. The Porsche was flashy for Pacho's low-key image.

"The Porsche is my sister Laura's," he explained.

"Laura's here?"

"No, she's with my wife. The other car belongs to the ... you know ... them."

Mr. Green, the fee deliverer was here? An uneasy feeling panged in my gut.

Pacho led me to a large living room, double-ceilinged with a rimmed balcony. Security cameras were fixed up there, but their wiring hung, as if disconnected.

Two men were in the living room. They resembled the pair who'd driven me to and from Combita. Maybe they were. One was seated on an armchair with his legs crossed; the other sat on a nearby couch. A coffee table was between them. Atop it, white powder glittered—cocaine, I figured.

"Have another hit," one of the men said to Pacho. His accent was Mexican, like the guys from the SUV. Both were likely among the list of unnamed co-defendants in Montez's case: *Los Xs*, his team of hitmen. Not good.

"Really, I've had enough," Pacho said. "*Gracias.*"

"You seem *nervioso*," the other man said.

"No," Pacho said. "*Todo está bien.*"

"Maybe you were expecting the Pollo Loco friends you

usually work with," one said. "We're your new friends. I'm Ximeno, he's Xavier. You've heard of us?"

Pacho shrugged uneasily. "Indirectly."

"We're informed the lawyer carries a weapon," Xavier said. "I don't blame her. But now that we're friends, we all need to show good faith."

He took out a 9mm automatic and placed it on the coffee table. He wore transparent surgical gloves. Both of them did. These boys were shy about leaving fingerprints. My unease evolved into panic.

"Show your good faith, *Doctora*," Xavier said. "Your weapon, *por favor*?"

I wasn't about to give up my Sig, but then Ximeno uncrossed his legs, and I saw he held a gun leveled at me.

I heard Pacho's swift intake of breath and felt my own pulse jump. I took out my silver Sig and placed it on the table. Xavier picked it up and whistled appreciatively.

"*Muy bonita*, eh?" he asked Ximeno.

Ximeno chuckled. "*Plata y plomo*."

A take on the Colombian expression—*plato o plomo*, silver or lead—meaning live or die. But more ominously, with an "and" instead of an "or." The graph tracking my already precarious lifespan took a sudden zag downward.

"Pacho, is there something you want to tell us?" Xavier asked.

Pacho's Adam's apple bobbed as if he was trying to keep something swallowed. "*Mi casa es su casa*," he finally managed. "May I offer you drinks?"

"*No, gracias*," Xavier said. "If you've nothing to say, there is something we'd like you to do. Pick up the *Doctora's* gun and shoot her."

Pacho smiled feebly. "Funny," he said.

"It's not a joke, *amigo*," Xavier said.

My graph crashed like it was 1929. The silence was deafening—

A phone rang.

Pacho's gaze went to a landline installed as part of his probation monitoring system.

"*No respondas*," Xavier said.

The phone went on ringing. Then it stopped and a recording came on advising Pacho that he'd failed to make his scheduled call-in to Pretrial Services and he must do so now.

"*¿Cuál es el mensaje?*" Xavier asked.

"*Nada*," Pacho said. "A sales call."

"*En realidad*, the shooting was meant as a joke," Xavier said to me. "We just want to be sure your good faith is genuine. One can't be too careful nowadays, eh? It's possible you're not a lawyer but an American agent. Show us you are not an agent."

Ximeno produced another phial of white powder.

Criminy, the litmus test. Law enforcement agents were strictly forbidden to consume controlled substances when working undercover. If the target insisted, the undercover had to exit the situation. Trouble was, I wasn't a cop, and there was no exit.

Xavier opened the phial and tapped a mound of powder on the table. "Enjoy, *Doctora*."

Lord help me. I'd be breaking my self-imposed, strictly forbidden oath. Years earlier, I'd had a serious cocaine problem that nearly destroyed me until Gino Moskowitz straightened me out. Took every ounce of willpower to overcome my addiction, and I'd sworn never to do the stuff again. But life-or-death situations—for sure this was one—allow exceptions to the rule.

He handed me a rolled-up Franklin.

"Prove you're no agent," he said.

My hand trembled as I bent to the powder. Inadvertently, I exhaled, and a cloud of powder blew from atop the mound like snow dusting from a high peak.

"Do it now," Xavier said.

I put one end of the bill to my nose and the other end to the powder, anticipating the familiar feeling I'd once loved but now hated.

I took a snort of the cocaine.

Felt its harshness, then....

My world went black.

CHAPTER 9

I'd been a lonesome kid who'd had to find out the answers to life's mysteries on my own. I steeped myself in thoughts only the lonely can come up with. Like, after Mama died, I told myself the only difference between sleep and death was whether you woke up and transitioned from darkness to light, from mindlessness to mindfulness.

As I did now.

My sensory perceptions slowly kicked in. I saw a high ceiling rimmed by a shadowed balcony. I smelled the tang of a bitter odor. I felt a heavy object in my hand. I heard a slow, measured dripping....

I realized I was in Pacho's living room.

I recognized the stink as gunpowder.

I felt the Sig, weighty in my grip.

As if on auto pilot, I reverted to my firearm training. The Sig's safety was off, so I clicked it back on. Its silvered muzzle was smudged as if it had been fired. Was that the acrid smell of gunpowder on my right hand? Yes ... and on my face.

I had been the shooter.

Who, and what, had I shot?

The dripping emanated from the electronic ankle bracelet clamped to Pacho's ankle. His leg drooped from the couch where he lay sprawled. His eyes were open but unblinking. Below them, blood from his nose and mouth had flowed beneath his shirt and emerged as if a wellspring from beneath his trouser leg.

Pacho was dead. Maybe I was too. Maybe my life had

been a dream and I was now in the afterlife with Mama. And the men murdered on the road from Combita.

A wave of dizziness washed over me.

I felt disoriented. I closed my eyes.

I drew a deep breath.

Tried to stabilize.

To understand.

To remember.

But whatever I'd inhaled had lowered a curtain, behind which was a dead zone. I remembered nothing that had happened.

Try harder. Focus, El.

Alright. I remembered snorting cocaine from atop the coffee table.

But now the tabletop was empty. Yet my prints were all over it.

I undid my scarf and wiped the table. It was damp.

The scarf came away smeared with … blood?

Horrified, I threw it aside. I looked around.

Saw nothing but Pacho's body.

And a red light that winked.

On-off … On-off … On-off….

It dawned on me that the light was on the face of a landline phone. An alarm in case of emergencies? This was one. I wobbled to my feet, but before I could press the button, a voicemail message came on. I realized the phone's ringer had been silenced—the winking light had heralded an incoming call.

It was from a Pretrial Service officer wanting to know why Pacho hadn't checked in and warning that unless he did so by three o'clock, the PTS authorities would come to rearrest him for violating a condition of release.

I looked at my watch. It was four o'clock.

I heard a distant siren, growing louder.

I was bewildered but for one thought:

I shouldn't be here! Get out! Run!

The Shark was parked facing the house. I got behind the wheel and backed up, steering with my left hand while looking behind my right shoulder. Then I U-turned and hit the gas.

Gravel rattled the Shark's underbelly as I screeched from the driveway and whipsawed onto the street.

Gripping the wheel in both hands, I concentrated on the Shark's hood ornament. A winged nymph in flight—me—who swiftly consumed the dotted white line of a two-lane blacktop.

A vehicle rose out of the darkness in front of me.

I swerved right. It sped past. I glimpsed its US MARSHAL insignia, its angry driver gesturing at me. In my rearview mirror, I watched it enter Pacho's driveway.

The highway entrance was ahead.

The nymph guided me onto it.

I'd been so consumed by events I barely remembered getting home.

As I closed the door behind me, my exhausted mind raced: what to do next?

I undressed, tossed my clothes aside, and went into the bathroom to scrub my hands and face. Even after cleaning they still smelled of gunpowder residue—or perhaps I just imagined they did. I smeared them with Vaseline. The minerals and oils would neutralize the carbon-based gunpowder residue. I learned that from a forensic chemist testifying in a case—

No! Don't go off on tangents.

Stay in the here and now.

What happened?

It had started with the cocaine rendering me unconscious. Strange, that. I'd done more than my fair share of the drug, and although it occasionally knocked me on my ass, it had never knocked me out. Yet this time it had, and the next thing I remembered was awakening. Judging by the voicemail, I'd been out for at least an hour.

Had ... I killed Pacho?

No. I *couldn't* have.

I believe in the sanctity of human life. I believe killing is only justifiable in self-defense. But I had nothing to fear from Pacho—unless something unexpected had changed the equation.

Was it possible that I had killed in order to survive?

But who'd believe what I couldn't remember?

Was there any proof that I'd been there?

Fingerprints. Had I left any?

Unknown.

My image? No, the cameras had been disconnected, I remembered that now.

But were there cameras outside?

Unknown.

I had opportunity but had no motive. Or had one arisen?

Unknown.

The unknowns were piling up. All raising questions that elicited the same answer: I was the killer.

Impossible! Rethink!

I composed myself and replayed everything. I was foggy about what had happened before inhaling the cocaine, and after I awoke, my memory was a total dead zone. And only I was capable of retrieving it.

I stared at my mirror image.

There was a bruise on the left side of my forehead. Sore there. I had no idea how I'd gotten it. Otherwise, I seemed no different outwardly.

Inwardly?

I visualized the folds of my brain, willing them to spark neurons and reconnect links that would restore anamnesis. Two images struck me vividly:

Pacho's vacant eyes, so puzzled. *Why me?*

The steady dripping of his blood.

To put it all from mind, I meditated on nothingness, hoping to create a void, an emptiness perhaps remembrance might fill. But instead, I fell asleep.

When I awoke, midday sun peeked between the curtains. I did not realize it was a sound that had roused me until it came again: a loud knocking on my door—then a man's voice.

"Police! Open up!"

CHAPTER 10

The hoodie I'd worn was still on the floor.
I slipped it on and went to the door.
Its peephole offered a fishbowl view of two men. One had the seen-it-all expression of a homicide dick and wore an NYPD buzzer looped above a rumpled suit. The other was DEA Agent Brian DiMaglio. Their presence jolted me wide awake.
I chained the door and opened it six inches.
"You have a warrant?" My voice was hoarse, my throat raw from the powder. It had been so powerful I'd thought it wasn't cocaine, yet its numbing, acidic taste was like the old white devil I'd long ago escaped.
"Open or I'll bust in," DiMaglio snarled.
"Take it easy, Brian," the dick said.
Gritting his teeth, DiMaglio paused.
No warrant, I thought. Surely, they were here because of Pacho, but they didn't have anything on me—at least not enough to search, or arrest.
"You got a license to carry," DiMaglio said.
"I do," I said.
"Mind showing me your weapon?"
"I do," I said.
"Your client, Pacho Grajales," the NYPD dick said. "Your last contact with him was when?"
"I want you to leave."
"We have his phone," DiMaglio snarled. "His last call was to you."
I shrugged. "Attorney-client privilege, I believe."
"How about crime-fraud exception?" he asked.

"I don't know of any fraud or crime."

"Who clocked your forehead?"

"Get the heck out," I said.

"Ashes on your hoodie," DiMaglio said. "Up all night, chain-smoking until you fell asleep with your clothes on?"

I began to close the door but DiMaglio stuck his foot in the jamb. "Be back, Dirtbag."

I locked the door. My heart was pounding.

I suddenly remembered more.

It wasn't ashes DiMaglio had seen on my hoodie, but powder from when I'd sneezed before inhaling....

Good Lord!

The hoodie was the same one I'd worn to Pacho's place. Thank God I'd wiped the white powder from the coffee table. If DiMaglio had seen it there, he'd have linked it to my hoodie.

That was all I recalled for now, but I prayed it was just a precursor of more to come. Yet I couldn't wait until the memories emerged bit by bit. I had to be proactive. To remember and discover.

I brushed what was left of the powder from the hoodie into a plastic baggie. Then I scissored the hoodie into tiny pieces I flushed away.

My cellular buzzed.

The onscreen call number had Colombian prefixes. Montez? I didn't answer. I didn't want to speak in my muddled state. Couldn't. I needed to find things to hold on to, to understand by gaining familiarity.

The Shark was familiar.

My raincoat lay on the Shark's front seat.

The sight of it triggered another recollection. When I'd arrived at Pacho's house, the rain had stopped and I left the coat there before entering. Lucky me. If I had left the raincoat in Pacho's house, it would be traced to me.

I went to fold it and recoiled. My silver Sig lay on the seat.

I'd totally blocked it from my mind.

I hadn't even remembered taking it with me in my haste to leave Pacho's, much less putting it on the seat. Good thing I had. It, too, was traceable to me.

I drove onto the 59th Street Bridge.

I got onto the right-side single lane that exited into Long Island City. To my left was a fence beyond which three lanes of traffic whizzed toward central Queens. On my right was a bikeway bordering the bridge's edge. I stopped the Shark and got out. Wrapping the raincoat around the Sig, I carried it to the bikeway railing and opened the raincoat, letting the Sig drop. I watched it fall; a glint of silver flashed in the sun before a white splash erupted in the green water far below.

A horn blared—a car was stopped behind the Shark. I got back in and resumed driving. I glanced in the rearview mirror and saw the driver flipping me the bird. Another rude New Yorker thinking he's entitled because he drove a Porsche—

Porsche....

When I'd arrived at Pacho's house, a black Porsche had been parked there. Pacho had said it was Laura's. It had been gone when I fled.

Had Laura been in the house when ... it happened?

Was she a witness to the killing? Oh, the irony. A girl I saw myself in had seen the killer inside me.

Where was she now? Was she also a target?

Long Island City was long blocks of low buildings. Small industries. Tech start-ups. Busy, busy, L.I.C. But today was Sunday and the Shark cruised empty streets.

Still, I knew my destination would be open for business.

The guy who operated the forensic lab was a workaholic hermit who wore a perpetually worried look. Always so many things to do and so little time to do them.

"You should've called before you came," he said. "I'd've told you not to bother. I'm swamped here."

I showed him the baggie of powder. "Five hundred if I know what this is in twenty-four hours."

"You got no idea how much work I got."

"Make it seven-fifty," I said.

"I dunno if I can," he said. "Not much of a sample."

"Make it a thousand," I said.

"See what I can do," he said.

I drove back to the city.

When I was a kid, there was a man who visited the apartment from time to time.

He'd drop by and chat with Mom about the weather or some such small talk. He was a kind man, a physician, who became sort of my once-in-a-while father. He'd take me to a movie, sometimes to a show. He never said so, but I got the impression he'd known my mother for a long time.

I hadn't seen him in years but still got Hannukah cards from him. Must be an old guy now, but I needed to talk to someone. I trusted Gino, but he was too close. I needed someone distant from my doings to lend a nonjudgmental ear. I hoped the doctor would be happy to see me.

He was.

"Incredible," he said. "You're the spitting image of your mother. How are you, El?"

I related a redacted version of my problem. Said I'd been feeling well but all of a sudden blacked out and awoke sometime later without any idea of what had transpired between.

"Bruise on your forehead," he said. "Maybe something to do with it?"

"Don't think so," I said. "Don't know. Maybe."

"Or *someone*, considering your business," he said. "You had a case on the news. A couple seconds of you at the scene of a drug bust, but enough for you to come off as a tough operator. But I saw the nice kid I knew."

The doctor's name was Popstein, but I'd always called him Pops. "Maybe I'm not so nice, Pops."

"This bout of amnesia? Maybe you ate or drank or otherwise imbibed something disagreeable that rattled your system."

"I can't remember, remember?"

He examined my eyes and ears and looked down my throat. He drew blood. He prodded and squeezed and twisted. He listened to my heart. All seemed in working order. He wrote a script for me to get a brain scan.

"I'll let you know when I get the results," he said. "How do you feel now?"

"You kidding?" I asked. "I lost part of my mind."

"I have a colleague who might help you."

Pop's colleague was a psychiatrist.

I lay on his couch and related the same brief version I'd told Pops. He nodded sagely. "You're repressing an unpleasant event," he said.

"Effing brilliant," I said. "Sorry. Yeah, guess I am."

"Has this reaction ever happened to you before?" he asked.

"Never," I said. "Not once. Why would it?"

"Doctor Popstein's very fond of you," he said. "He confided that your childhood was … somewhat lacking. That in many ways, you were an orphan."

"What does that have to do with anything?" I asked.

"The mind's a reservoir," he said. "It can only hold so much memory. When it's functioning properly, it discards unimportant memories naturally. Stays level. But when things are repressed, such as by the sadness of orphanhood, they remain and build up until the reservoir spills over. To protect itself from the flood, the mind shuts down. Following me?"

It was true. I'd spent half my life caring for my childlike mom, long years in which I'd been deprived of the love and care I'd needed. Emotionally, I'd felt like an orphan. "You're saying I repressed things?"

He shrugged. "What do you think?" he asked.

"I don't know what to think," I said. "The floodwaters. They recede?"

"You'll have to find that out yourself," he said. "In the meantime, I'm prescribing Valium."

"Geez, doc, I don't need that."

"Let's say your anxiety does."

My fifty minutes were up.

I went for a brain scan.

The MRI machine looked like a torpedo. Being inside it was a claustrophobic ordeal of electronic noise, the perfect musical score for the horror show I was starring in.

CHAPTER 11

I went to my office.
My inbox was jammed with emails and notices from PACER—Public Access to Court Electronic Records—called "bounces" in the biz. At the moment, I had six or seven other active cases, but my only concern was whether there was a bounce indicating a case versus me.

There wasn't one.

Not yet anyway.

When my phone rang, I jumped. It was Pops. He'd gotten my MRI results. "Come over now and we'll discuss them."

Now? It was nearly six. Why couldn't we talk on the phone? Was it a discussion that merited a face-to-face? A fatal illness? Jaysus Christmas. If I had to go, I wanted to linger long enough to know whether I'd killed; if my soul was heaven or hell-bound. I went to Pops to find out.

"The good news is that the brain scan revealed no abnormalities or anomalies," he said.

"What's the bad news?" I asked.

"The blood report indicates the presence of cocaine." His tone was chastising but his expression sympathetic. He knew my history.

"I didn't slip," I said. Technically true and necessarily evasive because I wasn't about to share what happened after I'd been forced to indulge.

"There was also a toxin present," he said. "A plant-based substance related to a drug administered during procedures requiring anesthesia. You didn't undergo a surgical procedure recently, right? Perhaps at a dentist?"

"No, and no," I said.

"The toxin wasn't produced pharmaceutically," he said. "It was homemade. Not surprising. In some countries, it's the kind of stuff used by criminals, the same way knock-out drugs are used by American thieves. It induces a state of semi-coherence during which a person is devoid of free will and does whatever others direct. Some people suffer an after-effect: amnesia."

"What's the stuff called?" I asked.

"Scopolamine," he said.

And in Colombia, *burundanga*. I knew about it from my travels there. Walk down a dark street and a passing thief pauses to blows some in your face. You breathe it in, and welcome to the dead zone. It explained my blacking-out, but the presence of cocaine was a mystery.

"How long does the amnesia last?" I asked.

"Maybe a day. A week. A month. Perhaps years."

"Years?" I said, stricken.

He shrugged. "Whatever happened when you blacked out—if anything at all—perhaps it's trivial, meaningless."

"I need to know," I said. "Isn't there some kind of treatment? An antidote to the scopolamine?"

"There is, but it may be ineffective."

"I'm willing to try anything," I said.

"It may also be counterproductive," he said. "It may delete the forgotten memories permanently."

"I'll take my chances," I said.

"It's called an orphan drug," he said.

"Orphan? You told the shrink I was one, kind of."

"Coincidental usage," he said. "An orphan drug is a pharmaceutical developed to treat rare conditions which, lacking sufficient profit motive, would not be possible to develop without a government assistance program. There is one—*bacopa monnieiri*—designed to treat certain forms of amnesia."

"Like mine, you think?"

He shrugged. "Because its production is limited, it's too expensive for ninety percent of the population."

"I'm a top one-percenter," I said.

"The clinical trials are too small to be definitive. There may be unforeseen aftereffects."

"I want some," I said.

"Consider this carefully," he said. "What if it works and the memory is of something so awful it'll haunt you forever?"

"I like a good ghost story."

"Joking is escapism. Think seriously. Why not just let it go and continue life to wherever you're going?"

"I don't know where I'm going," I said.

"Then you'll be sure to get there."

"Ha-ha. Get me the darn antidote."

He sighed. "I already got some."

It was a pill. Ordinary looking, dull white, small. Resembled an aspirin but was slightly oval. No number or maker's logo. Just a pill.

Pops gave me two. "Take one now. Give it time."

I put it on my tongue and dry-swallowed it.

"When does it kick in?" I asked.

"You'll find out ... if it works."

CHAPTER 12

As soon as I got back to the office from visiting Pops, I logged onto PACER.

I did a name search for cases I was party to. Nothing. I searched AUSA Mizrahi's case and saw there was a third superseding Santa Fe indictment: four of the FNUs and LNUs—First and Last Names Unknown—had been identified. *Los Xs* were the four Monsalve brothers: Xavier, Ximeno, Xander, and Xenon.

Those names unearthed another buried memory. A voice, speaking Mexican Spanish, hardly a whisper, as if from deep within my memory bank: "*Doctora,* kill the thief."

Was this the orphan drug working? Or was my memory returning naturally? Didn't matter. There was no escaping the inescapable: I'd been drugged and hypnotized into becoming an instrument of death and left to be arrested.

Okay, assume the *Xs* believed that Pacho, Montez's banker in the States, had diverted cartel money into his own pocket. Why would they kill—or make me kill—the person who could lead them to the missing cash?

Unless they thought someone else could.

Pacho's trusted lawyer and friend. Me.

Did Montez believe I knew where his money was? If so, I assume the *Xs* gave me a hypnotic to loosen my tongue and lead them to the cash.

Before then, the feds had called and they'd fled. Yet if Pacho's death made me indispensable, why hadn't they taken me with them? Was there yet another person who knew about the money?

In my mind I heard the *X* again: "Where is *su hermana,* Pacho?"

Laura. Did they want her because they thought *she* knew what they wanted? It dawned on me that I wanted to find Laura too, desperately, hoping she could tell me what I had done.

My fragmented memory-bytes were coming together: Montez had wanted me to witness the killing, believing my knowledge made me his co-conspirator who would have no choice but to enable his murderous game of eliminating witnesses against him.

And I had.

Gino Moskowitz had taught me to never fight the current, but rather to go with the flow. But now the flow was quickly sweeping me toward a Niagara. I needed to fight my way ashore before I went over the edge.

Right ... but how?

I could let Montez think that Pacho had confided his thievery with me, but I didn't know where he'd hidden the purloined money. No, scratch the thought. If I didn't know, I was expendable.

Then again....

What if I told Montez I didn't personally know, but one of Pacho's Pollo Loco pals did? The guy was hiding, but I was close to finding him, and then I'd hand him to *Los Xs*.

That would work. At least for a few weeks. By then Montez would be extradited, and Santa Fe would be up for grabs, plunged into a state of confusion. Once here, Montez would be helpless, and I'd keep him isolated. Colombian lawyers could only visit inmates in federal jails if accompanied by an American lawyer, so I'd not help Arias or Vizcaino visit Montez, making myself his sole link to the outside world. Soon enough, he'd need my help, and I'd no longer be expendable.

My phone pinged. It was a text from an unknown number, again with a Colombian prefix. This time I answered. "Who's calling?"

"*El señor* must see you immediately."

It was the Colombian shuttle all over again.

I arrived in Bogota on the red-eye at dawn and Arias

whisked me through customs and immigration into the back of a sedan piloted by a pair of silent types. Arias was a man-spreader and I sat scrunched against the door. His cologne—Canoe?—was overpowering.

As we whizzed along the *autopista* he got a collect call from a correctional facility. He put it on speakerphone.

"*Si, señor,*" Arias answered. "I am *con ella.*"

"Hello, *Doctora,*" Montez said. "News?"

"My client suffered an unfortunate problem," I said. "Before it, he told me things of interest."

"I've heard things of interest as well," he said. "Show her."

Arias switched the phone to a video. I saw a long-shot of a large, featureless building at the base of a bleak mountainside. Then I heard the echoey tone of a large space as another image appeared: a dim chamber with a vaulted ceiling and a concrete floor pitted with large holes. Two people stood by the rim of a hole. One was a teenaged boy. The other was a man who held a gun at the boy's temple. There was a flash and blood and brain matter spewed from the boy's head as he toppled into the pit. The man with the gun leaned over it and shouted something below, his face wild-eyed with exhilaration.

It was Montez's lawyer, Victor Vizcaino.

From inside the pit, a woman cried.

"Save your tears, Señora Jaramillo," Vizcaino told her. "You'll need them for your other children if your husband testifies."

The screen went dark. I closed my eyes against the horror of another victim joining the eternals who had escaped from the nightmare that was Santa Fe ... and my again bearing witness to a killing that might make me a co-conspirator in Montez's murderous game of eliminating witnesses testifying against him.

Baffling.

If Montez was going to cooperate as I assumed, there would be no trial, no witnesses ... unless his cooperation was a ploy to prolong his case while he silenced his accusers ahead of trial.

Maybe he'd succeed with one—Don J?—but the other, Lucho, would still sink him.

Whichever, I had no intention of going down with his ship.

I considered my options: go to the Feds? But I was already in their gunsights, and perhaps they'd choose to believe I was not an innocent but a guilty turncoat. My public persona would instantly morph from a respected attorney to an untrustworthy mouthpiece, the word would spread, and I'd end up a target for vengeful X-men. Forget about the Feds.

Hmm....

I could resign from the case once back in the States. Uh-uh. I'd be out of Montez's sight but not out of his mind. I knew too much, and the only way the vindictive son of a gun would let me go would be in a coffin.

So I had to go with the flow for now after all, and hope there was time enough to escape the waterfall ahead—time in which I'd find absolution and escape the monsters I was consorting with before they destroyed me.

CHAPTER 13

"We're here," Arias said.

It was the next morning, and we were in south Bogota, turning into a driveway with an arched entrance that said *Penitencia Central Picota.* I'd been there before. It was the last rest stop on the road to extradition.

We passed a huge concrete hall of cellblock tiers where the echoes of metallic clangs mingled with the murmurings of American lawyers chatting up clients. Drug lawyers being my least favorite scoundrels of all, I thought of the old Groucho line about refusing to join a club that would accept him as a member.

But I had joined and was now paying my dues.

We entered a corridor where being fingerprinted was waived by a fistful of money—not *pesos*, greenbacks—and were escorted to a private interior apartment that looked like it had escaped from a Four Seasons. I entered while Arias remained outside.

Montez was swathed in a satin robe, relaxing with one leg over the arm of a deep leather chair, a velvet slipper dangling from a silken toe. He motioned for me to be seated with a wave of his ivory cigarette holder.

"We expected the police to arrest you for Pacho's murder," he said. "I've heard you resisted, but when your life was threatened, you murdered without pause."

Astounding how casually he said this. I didn't reply.

"You're not angry?" he asked. "I'm impressed. You're a pragmatic woman. You were left in proximity with, I believe the phrase is, the *corpus delecti*, yet you're not angry because you understand there are times when unpleasantries are necessary."

I interlaced my fingers to keep from clawing his eyes.

"You're strong and resourceful and I'm pleased that you survived. Now that you're aware of my plan, you have no choice but to be sure my trial is delayed."

I made a point of looking around the room. "Nice sound system, I bet," I said.

"*Muy agradable*," he said and picked up a remote. *Música romántica* came on.

"Make it louder," I said. When he did, beneath the music, I said, "Let's make things clear."

"By all means," he said.

"I was driven to some village in the mountains, dropped there, and told to wait," I said. "I waited. Only to then be driven back to Bogota. That's all that happened. Correct?"

"If you prefer, that is my understanding."

"Why was Pacho killed?" I asked.

"Hypothetically?" he said. "Supposing Pacho was stealing from his employer. Not just a few dollars, that's to be expected. But what if he'd concocted an elaborate plot to steal hundreds of millions? And then, to conceal his theft, he sunk a cargo ship supposedly ferrying his employer's money to Colombia so as to justify its loss. To his misfortune, the deceit was discovered. Pacho hid the money before his demise—perhaps he discussed it with you."

"He mentioned it," I lied. "He said one of his Pollo Loco workers knew where it was. The man is in hiding, but I believe I can find him."

"You have no other choice."

From a pocket he took a small photograph. It was a freeze-frame video shot of me aiming my silver Sig at Pacho's head.

He crumpled the photograph, dropped it in a cut-glass ashtray, and put a gold Dunhill lighter to it. I watched it wither and curl to ashes.

"The original shall be our own little secret," he said. "Prolong the trial and it too will vanish."

"Judge Graff moves cases fast," I said. "The only way to

prolong your case is if the government accepts your cooperation," I said. "But that threat—"

"Is nonsense," he said. "I am sure they will accept my cooperation."

"You said you had nothing to cooperate about," I pointed out.

"It seems I might after all," he said. "I have faith in your ability to gain time. As I told you, I was surprised you were not arrested. My workers said you'd taken enough burundanga to put an elephant to sleep. But then I realized you and I are the same."

Just two killers talking, I thought, bitterly.

"When it comes to the pursuit of money, nothing stands in our way," he said with a smirk I wanted to erase from his facelift. "By sheer force of will you awoke and escaped so as to receive your fees. Actually, I had no intention of paying them. But now you may rest assured that you will be paid, as circumstances have changed. We are clear, yes?"

"Perfectly, *señor*," I said.

CHAPTER 14

Hardly an hour after I returned to New York—which made me wonder if DiMaglio had known I was away, and where—he emailed a reminder that I was expected to appear at DEA for fingerprinting as agreed.

I thought the printing would be at DEA HQ, a discreetly unmarked building in far west midtown. But when I arrived there, I was redirected a few blocks uptown, to the Starrett-Lehigh building, a sprawling edifice of no discernable architecture, home to hundreds of anonymous start-up firms with zingy names—PING! POW-WOWY, NEXTO—and the ominously formal United States Drug Administration Northeast Regional Investigative Office.

The inner sanctum.

I figured printing me there was DiMaglio's way of rubbing my face in the shame of being the subject of an investigation.

Not pleasant but not problematic. My prints were never on Pacho's note ID'ing DiMaglio, and when he ran them, there'd be no match. My only concern was not soiling my clothes like when I had been fingerprinted in Colombia. Today, I had on one of Ma's tweed classics, a Saville Row trousered suit, because I didn't want to deal with cop-like comments about my legs.

"Okay," I said. "Let's get it done."

"You get around," he said. "Here, there, everywhere. Must be confusing sometimes. You do know we're not in Colombia?"

So I wasn't paranoid. He had been tabbing me. As for my meeting Montez, it was of no concern. It was my job, and he'd get my notice of appearance as Montez's lawyer soon enough.

"We gonna do this or not?" I asked.

"Soon as you roll up your sleeves," he'd replied. "Like I said, this ain't Colombia. We ditched ink pads years ago." He thumbed an electronic gizmo topped by a glass plate.

"Why not say so before?" I'd asked, rolling my sleeves up. "You get your kicks from bare arms?"

"From observing," he said. "The way you move? You're not a lefty."

"Wow," I said. "A deduction."

"Medical examiner says your former client Pacho's position and the angle of the entry wound indicate the shooter was right-handed."

"Gee, that puts me among ninety percent of potential suspects," I'd said.

"We're narrowing that down."

I couldn't blame him for being pissed at me, and I kept my mouth shut and held my hands out.

He rolled my fingers atop the glass, then took a full palm scan. He pressed some buttons, and a few seconds later, paper emerged from the print machine. I upgraded my awe for the G's supercomputers. Positively hypersonic.

He looked at the result, then lifted his chin toward the door.

"See you again," he said. "Real soon."

I was troubled when I left the DEA.

Not by DiMaglio saying the investigation was narrowing down, or adding that he'd be seeing me real soon, both of which I wrote off as bluster. Something else had disturbed me, although I couldn't put my finger on what.

I soon found out.

Much as I enjoy wheeling the Shark around, during weekday working hours I endure the subways, garaging the Shark rather than tempting road rage—including mine—in the stop-and-go traffic.

But now I headed to my garage because I had made an appointment to see a guy who lived way uptown, far above the gridlock.

When I arrived at the garage, the Shark was about to be lifted on the back of a tow truck. I stepped between it and the tow and asked the guy manning the winch what the hell he was doing.

"Following orders," he said.

"You Adolf Eichmann?"

"Who's he?" he said. "Here." He fished a folded document from his coverall and handed it to me. It was a search warrant authorizing the seizure and search of the Caddy, "to wit, specifically its tires."

I was fuming—why was this warrant issued?—yet there was no point in debating the point with a tow truck operator. Instead, I remained where I was, blocking the tow.

"Don't bust my balls," he said. "It is what it is."

"Then do what it is," I said. "The warrant's not for my car. So leave it and take the darn tires. What's your name, anyway?"

"I don't have to tell you."

"Fine," I said. "This will do."

There was a receipt stapled to the back of the warrant. I ripped it free and looked at the server's name. "Here's the deal, Munson," I said. "I don't move out of the way unless the car stays. You got a problem with that, call DiMaglio."

Munson had no problem with that. I figured he was paid by the hour, so why not prolong the job? As he began removing the tires, a grim thought entered my mind:

Tread marks.

The Shark was a heavyweight that left deep footprints. Had it done so in Pacho's driveway? Had they been plaster-casted and were now in an evidence room awaiting a match with the dinosaur who'd made them? The scenario at Pacho's house was still fuzzy in places, but I recalled my arrival before the dead zone, and my frenzied departure after it, looking backward over my shoulder as I reversed, steering with my left hand, then taking off in a spray of gravel.

Munson rolled a tire onto the tow truck bed. Sure enough, the treads were speckled with embedded gravel. I felt a stab of alarm, but then my legal mind kicked in: gravel had no DNA; it was just plain gravel. Like my not being left-handed, it signified nothing. But other things did....

Steering with my left hand.

My not being left-handed.

Left … left … *left*!

Then it came to me.

In Montez's photograph, I was pointing the Sig at Pacho with my left hand. Yet I must've fired a thousand rounds with my Sig at the shooting range, each and every one with my right hand!

Was the photo flipped, a reversed copy?

No. In the photograph, the oddly unknown bruise had been a fresh mark, clearly visible—on the left side of my forehead.

Was it a photoshop fake? My head pasted on another's body? No again. The shooter wore a blue silk scarf around her neck knotted in my distinctive way, one I'd never seen others master.

The puzzle was filling in.

If I'd shot Pacho, surely it would have been with my right hand. So, Montez's picture may have been doctored to show me shooting my client. But ultimately, I had no way of knowing whether it was I or someone else who had pulled the trigger.

"I wish you'd have let me tow it," Munson said. "I'm allergic to rubber."

He threw a tire in the flat bed and blew his nose, then took out a nasal inhaler and squirted his nostrils. I gaped at him as still another memory fragment drifted into my brain.

"Why are you looking at me like that?" Munson asked.

I wasn't looking at Munson but at his inhaler. It had provoked still another flashback: Montez had been wrong. It wasn't the pursuit of money that had roused me from my burundanga stupor. It was an object being held to my nose by someone—the *Xs*?—and I'd inhaled a bad, old acquaintance that never failed to energize me.

Cocaine.

The someone had blown it up my nose, awakening me from the drugged slumber. Who? Why?

I had ideas about who, but not why.

CHAPTER 15

I left the Shark on its blocks and ordered new tires, stat.
Then I took an Uber uptown to Riverdale for an in-person chat with what in the biz is called a paper man: a behind-the-scenes lawyer who does research and composes submissions and appeals for lawyers on the frontline—mouthpieces like me.

The guy I was visiting was the best paper man in town. He was also the guiding force that had led me to defense-lawyering.

Went down like so: after Mama passed, I discovered I was broke. Apparently, my father had some sort of pension, but it ended when she did. No longer burdened by caring for Mama, I'd ventured into the singles life. Hip-hopped into unsexy sex and abundant drugs. My personal school of hard knocks. To finance my debaucheries, I drove a cab.

Night-riding the big city turned out to be interesting. Passengers spoke to one another as if I wasn't there, providing insights into the human condition. Single riders spoke freely to me, imparting their deepest privacies. Taxi driving taught me what makes people tick. Some of it I found abhorrent. Other things—and people—I found attractive. Occasionally, I participated in one-nighters, not of the taxi stand variety. Just brief stops in the night—get undressed, get on, get off, get dressed, goodbye. More often than not these were fueled by drugs. It started with booze and weed—you know, the "normal" drugs. But eventually I got mired in cocaine. Sloppily. What I thought was a quickie turned into an assault. Left me hurting below and confused in my head, but for one thing: *no more men*. Topping this, a vigilant unmarked cop spotted me snorting and I did a night in jail, dreading my cab license—my livelihood—would be stripped. It was the lowest point of my life.

On an evening shortly before my trial, I got a call from a hotel cab stand. The passenger was a sharply dressed older man in a wheelchair. He asked what a girl like me was doing driving a cab. I'd thought he was headed for a sugar daddy proposition and brushed him off. But he'd persisted.

He said it seemed to him I was capable of better things.

"Name one," I said.

"Be a lawyer," he said. I laughed that off. Four years of college and three years in law school? Forget that. There was another way, he said. Clerking for a lawyer and enrolling in an online school made one eligible to take the bar exam. I asked how he knew that. He said he was a criminal defense lawyer. Said if I drove at his beck and call as he worked, he'd teach me the ropes.

At first, I rolled my eyes. *Me,* a lawyer? Ridiculous.

On second thought, I wondered why he was being so generous to someone he'd just met. Maybe he was lonely. Or just wanted a good-looking factotum.

But my third take was *darn,* why even consider it? Even a user-quantity cocaine conviction would bar me from lawyering. He sensed my reluctance, and I explained the problem.

"Don't worry, I'll take care of it," he said.

I was skeptical, but he did just that. At first, I had the impression he'd found a flaw in my arrest, but later I realized that the legal system, like all things transactional, often was subject to the favoritisms of old-boy networks, of which he was a member, and therefore an ace at bending its rules. That appealed to me, and I accepted his offer.

I found his way of lawyering to be fascinating: don't try beating doors down, forget picking locks—just oil the hinges. He loved divulging his ways and means and I loved learning them. Apart from the mysterious manner in which he'd vanished my case, he was an honest by-the-book lawyer and taught me to follow his lead.

I enrolled in an online law school, and for two years I chauffeured him in the Shark, observing his interactions with clients. Between his meetings, he talked me through my homework, reducing days of reading ancient cases into hours of listening to simple facts.

I passed the bar on my first try.

He gave me a desk in his office. Tested me with a case, a speeding charge that seemed unwinnable, but I won it. He upgraded me to a DWI—Driving While Intoxicated—*problemo*. I came through again. And so it went, the cases getting bigger and me getting better, with him gradually retreating to paperwork, while I took over the practice.

The man completely turned my life around.

His name is Gino Moskowitz.

CHAPTER 16

Gino's penthouse was on a quiet block overlooking Riverside Drive, the Hudson River, and Jersey beyond.

He greeted me with a fist bump, and I followed his wheelchair to his book-lined office. From the fifty thou Pacho had given me, I'd put ten in an envelope and placed it on his desk. Without opening it he put it in a drawer.

"Talk to me, Electra," he said.

I did. About everything.

Gino smiled. "We've seen it all when it comes to importing coke from Colombia—inside frozen broccoli, hardened and gilded like saintly statues, liquified. But the G doesn't pay much attention to how coke money is sent to Colombia."

"Your point being?" I asked.

"Contrary to popular belief, smuggling cocaine into the States is not the cartel's major problem. Transporting their money out is the real difficulty. There are brokers who specialize in doing so for a generous percentage of the number. This cost is avoided if fees are paid with drug money already in the States."

I recrossed my legs impatiently. I needed Gino's input on my situation, not a commentary on the biz.

"Golly, never occurred to me," I said. "I'd never participate in that. Knowingly."

"Don't nonchalant this, Electra. Montez already has two things on you—Pacho's murder, and your knowledge of the murder of a witness's kid. Don't give him a third. Last thing you need is a money-laundering beef. Be very careful how his fees are paid. You don't want a 1956 problem."

Section 1956 was the money-laundering statute. "I'll be careful," I said. "So. What do I do next?"

"Listen and learn, then think and act," he said.

Vintage Gino, simplifying everything.

"Another thing," I said. "In the recent past, somewhere between the States and Colombia, a southbound cargo ship sunk. I want to know the details."

"Southbound, eh? Ship was running drug money home?"

I shrugged. "Run the crews, see if any have criminal histories, outstanding warrants, known confederates. Look for relatives of Pacho, maybe first names starting with *X*."

"Stroll along the river for an hour while I do my thing," he said.

When I returned, Gino had earned his ten large.

"The ship was a rust bucket known at the time of its demise as *La Reina Celestial*," he said.

I smiled. Montez had a sense of irony. The Heavenly Queen ferried his manna from heaven.

"It went down a couple of miles outside of Colombian waters," he said. "So the investigation belonged to ISC, the International Shipping Commission."

"Whose portal you entered," I said.

"No big deal," he said. "The investigation turned out to be a back-alley blowjob not worth looking at twice."

"You're particularly obscene today," I said.

"Fucking listen to what I say, not how I say it. The ship? ISC determined the cause of sinking as unknown. Another way of saying *La Reina Celestial* was too deep down and unimportant to inspect closely. Maybe a fuel line that should have been replaced. Or an overworked boiler. Or overloaded cargo."

"What was its cargo?" I asked.

"Scrap metal," he said. "Actually, junked cars compressed into spheres. I liberated an image from their file. Here, have a look."

He touched his keyboard and a five-by-five sphere of compacted metal pimpled with glass and fabric appeared.

"Looks like junk—and it is—but there's worth to it," he said. "Bits and pieces of rare earth, valuable alloys, and so on. Cost too much to sift through the stuff in the States, but labor's cheap in Colombia. Scrap's a big moneymaker there."

"You said the ship's sitting on the bottom," I said. "With the load of scrap, I assume."

"Yeah," he said. "Each sphere must weigh a ton—more."

"If they didn't go down, how'd they get a photo?"

He enlarged the photograph. The sphere was sitting on sand, waves lapping at it.

"It beached," he said. "Takes some kind of current to move that."

I had a thought. "Either that or it's hollow," I said.

"Good point. I'll figure out how to get another look at it."

"Anything noteworthy about the crew that led you to the Celestial Queen?"

"Yep. One guy who went down with the ship. A fugitive. A Mexican national name of Xenon Monsalve."

One of the *Xs*. Figured.

My phone buzzed. The call was from the same Colombian-prefixed number as before. "Them," I said.

"Put it on speaker," Gino said.

"*El señor* has a cooperation," Arias said. "I just texted you the coordinates of a mangrove swamp on the Honduran coast where, in twenty-four hours, *lanchas* will offload two tons of cocaine. *Ciao, Doctora.*"

AUSA Mizrahi had made it clear he wouldn't allow Montez to cooperate. Still, DEA couldn't ignore a tip on a two-ton load, and it might induce Mizrahi to rethink now that Don J had been deleted from his witness list. It sickened me that I'd been duped into enabling it.

"Gino, I'm thinking to get off this case," I said.

"Maybe too late for that," he said.

"Montez can't hold Pacho and the murder over my head because he'd be incriminating himself. I don't like abandoning the girl, but every woman for herself."

"You got that right," he said. "But you're still on the case, and if you don't pass your client's info about a major load, Mizrahi might loop an obstruction charge around your neck."

I used my device to get into PACER and checked Montez's case docket. I saw Mizrahi had moved to withdraw from the case. Not surprising. He'd recused himself to shield the G from accusations of his being motivated by a personal vendetta—the alleged threat.

I'd gotten two other PACER bounces. One was a notice of appearance on the case from an AUSA named Jenna Wilkinson. I didn't know her but hoped that, unlike Mizrahi, she'd be receptive to giving Montez a chance to cooperate. I wanted the case to be signed, sealed, and stamped PAID.

The second was a G motion to revoke Pacho's bail—obviously filed prior to his murder—because one of the signatories to his bond had been deemed ineligible.

I called Wilkinson and started to introduce myself, but she interrupted.

"I assume you're calling in regard to Martin Montez," she said briskly. "I'm afraid I can't discuss the case with you yet, other than to inform you Mr. Montez is now in the final process of being extradited. When he's here, we can discuss things in depth."

"He wants to cooperate," I said.

"We'll discuss that as well."

"He's given me information regarding a large shipment arriving in Honduras," I said. "Specific time and place and a small window of opportunity: tomorrow."

"I see," she said. "Send me the information. But whether or not it proves valid, no promises we'll accept his cooperation. We clear on that?"

"As a bell," I said. "I'll text the details now."

I composed a text with the Honduran information. Hesitated a moment—do I really need to stay in?—then pressed SEND. The outgoing whoosh sounded like a door swinging, but whether it was opening or closing I had no idea.

CHAPTER 17

I don't read much fiction.

A few years back I started a novel called *The Extraditionist* written by a drug lawyer. Wasn't bad, the guy knew what he was talking about, but I didn't finish it. I'd already been there, done that, and grew bored because it was a retelling of stuff I'd been through. Besides, the lead character liked his ladies too much for my liking.

Non-fiction is more my thing. My reads are mainly biz stuff like the *Colombia Report* and subscriptions like the Treasury Department's SDNT—Specially Designated Narcotics Trafficker—which provides new listings of persons and entities forbidden to engage in any financial transactions in the States, directly or indirectly. Always good to know. Especially now.

I read through the listings, which are in alphabetical order by country. From Afghanistan to Zanzibar, there were thousands of names and entities. Lot of bad guys and terrorists out there, and no doubt a sprinkling of innocents, not that the Treasury Department cares if mistakes are made.

I scrolled to the recent additions. They were a mix of men and companies with Chinese and Slavic and Arabic names, but the last names, added just two days ago, were as Spanish as it gets: MARTIN MONTEZ, MARISOL GRAJALES, LAURA GRAJALES, and EL POLLO LOCO, INC.

Pacho's wife, Marisol, must have been the signatory deemed ineligible. Not surprising. But Pacho's case was history. What did disturb me was that, on its face, the SDNT listing suggested Laura was involved with El Pollo Loco's finances and, by extension, with Santa Fe. Yet it could also be that she was unknowingly used by Pacho to front his dealings. I hoped it was the latter. Be a pity if a girl like her was crooked up in the mix.

Got me to thinking if it hadn't been for Gino, that very well might have been my own path. I hoped Laura would also be blessed by a Good Samaritan, but hopefully it wouldn't be me. I wanted out.

The Shark cruised beneath Roosevelt Avenue's elevated tracks.

Ahead, Pacho's original El Pollo Loco location was dark and shuttered. Whether because of its inclusion on the SDNT list or Pacho's demise, I did not know. I'd tried telling myself I'd gone there hoping to have a heart-to-heart talk with Laura about my leaving the case, but I knew my real motivation was that I was still haunted by the uncertainty of what had occurred that night at Pacho's house. I was sure Laura had been there.

Whether as a participant or a witness, I had to know.

As I passed the restaurant, I saw a light on deep within. At the corner I looked up the side street and saw the place's back kitchen door was ajar. I parked and went in there.

An old woman was mopping the floor. I asked her if *doña* Laura was inside.

She pointed up the street. *"Ella está en el funeral."*

I knew the funeral home. It was where Jackson Heights butted against Elmhurst, in the heart of Little Colombia.

Outside it, yellow El Pollo Loco vans were parked. People were lined up outside, waiting to pay their condolences. I got in line. It moved slowly, which was okay with me because I dreaded what might happen when I encountered Laura. I hoped I was wrong and that she had not been a witness—that she'd just be distraught and in need of hand-holding. But I feared she'd confront me for killing Pacho, confirming my darkest worry.

Only one way to find out.

The funeral home was a converted storefront. Inside it, rows of collapsible chairs were filled, many with guys wearing yellow shirts backed with El Pollo Loco logos.

When the woman in front of me reached Laura, she lifted her face. In profile, Laura's cheekbones were high, her nose aquiline above a too-wide mouth. Her features were the epitome of white Spanish aristocracy, yet her skin had a light cream tinge suggesting a darker ancestor.

The woman moved on. My turn now.

"*Mis condolencias*," I said.

Laura looked at me. Her face was expressionless, and I wondered what she was thinking. In the candlelight, her dark eyes were flooded with emotion. Was it recognition and smoldering hatred for the woman who killed her brother? Perhaps, but I sensed it was something else—a strange blend of compassion, tempered by doubt.

"*Gracias*," she said.

"May we talk later?"

I thought she allowed a small nod before looking away, but I couldn't be sure.

I left the funeral home and got in the Shark, parking it behind the yellow vans.

I looked at my watch. The line outside the funeral home had shortened. I started the Shark up and ran through its pre-tech radio dials but reconsidered and shut the engine off. In Little Colombia, people took notice of idlers. I looked at my watch again. There was no longer a line outside the funeral home. I thought about Laura, wearing mourning black in a dim room reeking of incense and sadness. My phone pinged.

I had an email from Gino. His wizardry had spectral-analyzed sand taken from beneath the sphere and found it identical to that on the beaches of Guajira, the long peninsula that runs along Colombia's Caribbean coast. More proof that the sphere had come from the doomed *La Reina Celestial*, as the waters off the Guajira were the final leg of drug routes to and from North American and Colombian landfalls. A photograph was attached. It was a closer view of the sphere from another angle. Cracked open. Hollow. If there had been money inside, it was washed away or looted by beachcombers. Neither, I thought. Pacho hadn't put money in it.

A few more yellow-jacketed guys left the funeral home and got into vans. It began to rain, but without running the Shark's

V-8, I couldn't put the wipers on. The funeral home garage door rolled up and a hearse emerged and parked in front of the vans. More Pollos Locos appeared, ducking through the rain to their vans, yellow blurs through the smeared windshield.

A guy came out of the funeral home, opened a large black umbrella.

"*Hola, Indio,*" another Pollo Loco said to him. "*Ella esta bien?*"

The man nodded. In Colombia, *Indio* was the name used on the streets to refer to indigenous men, sometimes in good humor, other times not so much. The deference showed to the tall, dark figure standing in the rain suggested the former in this case. A woman emerged from the funeral home and ducked under the umbrella as the guy escorted her into the first van behind the hearse. I couldn't see her face but knew it was Laura. That head-high posture and the long legs of a filly.

I started the Shark. The funeral home was on the other side of traffic-ridden Roosevelt Avenue, so I U-turned to follow the procession and fell in behind the last van of the cortege.

CHAPTER 18

The cemetery was a few poorly tended acres in the shadow of the elevated Long Island Expressway—a dismal site even on the best of days, rendered all the more somber in the drizzling rain.

Its rows of tombstones were a necropolis that blended with the surrounding low buildings, growing taller until culminating in the distant city spires of the metropolis.

I parked a distance away from the vans. Another car was parked near me, unmarked, with a telltale whip antenna. The law, probably staking out Laura.

The mourners filed through a density of vaults and mausoleums to a pile of loose earth alongside a new gravesite. I kept my distance and circled around the gravesite, coming up behind it and concealing myself behind a stone virgin.

A priest was delivering a benediction as the casket was lowered. Laura stood with hands clasped, looking at the casket. The Pollo Loco guys had taken their caps off and lowered their heads, the one holding the umbrella standing tallest among them. He had the chiseled dark features, jet hair, and silent aura of an indigenous Colombian, and although he didn't move, his gaze cut around purposefully. Eye Patrol, the professional drugsters call it. I don't think he saw me, or if he did, he didn't show it.

The priest perfunctorily drew an air cross. The Pollo Loco guys started away. Indio said something to Laura. She nodded and he left with the others. Alone, Laura stood looking down at the grave for a long minute. Then she tossed a wet, dark flower into it and turned toward where I was concealed, staring.

I realized she had spotted me, so I emerged from the shadow of the virgin.

"What do you want?" she asked.

At the *quinceañera*, Laura had shone, a fresh young queen among the gussied-up older women. In the dim funeral parlor, I'd been captivated by the perfect planes and hollows of her face and elegant bearing, the epitomes of womanhood. Now, her wet hair stringy, her face damp in the gray daylight, she looked younger. Nineteen, twenty?

"For you to tell me everything," I answered.

"You're *Martin's* lawyer," she said angrily.

"I'm my own person. *A* lawyer."

She looked me up and down: from Mama's classic Hermès boots to the adorable Fendi rainhat I'd discovered in a vintage shop.

"You don't even look like a lawyer."

"Tell me everything," I urged her.

She blinked back a tear and a single streak of mascara ran down her face, bifurcating her features to a Janus of opposites, one of which knew of my complicity, I thought.

"It's better if you tell me," I tried again, this time gently.

"I've nothing to tell." She wiped her eyes then frowned at her fingers, blackened by mascara. "*Dios mío*, I'm a mess." Suddenly, she smiled self-deprecatingly—a naïve, vulnerable girl only beginning to bloom into womanhood.

"The police who arrested Pacho are watching you," I said. "You need a lawyer."

She drew herself up. "I'm not afraid of them," she said defiantly. "And if I need a lawyer, it won't be you."

"Then let's be friends," I said, surprising even myself as I spoke.

Apart from Pops and Gino Moskowitz, I'd never had friends. Being Mama's caretaker had been a full-time job, one that cut short my childhood and isolated me from others. My "intimate" relationships were anything but, beginning as ten minutes in the front seat of a car, where something may or may not have happened with some boy I don't remember, and continued sporadically but never memorably through my cocaine binges, culminating in an all-too-memorable experience—in the worst way.

Thereafter, lawyering satisfied my social appetites. Professional relationships are structured, controlled, predictable—everything that social interactions in the "real world" were not.

Until now. Had I suddenly morphed from a loner to a lonely gal reaching out to make a friend? At a funeral, no less?

"I don't think so," she said, and walked away.

I watched her go, realizing I'd just tapped into a part of myself I'd never known existed: a knight-like Joan of Arc, attempting to rescue a damsel in distress. It didn't feel like a random act of altruism—something had shifted inside me. And, beyond that, there was the shadow hovering over me that I needed to bring into the light.

Had I killed? Yes, or no?

The gravediggers began working. I peered into the grave as spaded earth dappled the mahogany coffin. The flower Laura had thrown atop it wasn't dark from the rain. It was a black rose. A symbol.

Anger, danger, sorrow, vengeance? All or some or none? Whichever, I thought the black rose was not Laura's declaration to others, but a resolution to herself. I wondered what it meant.

I heard vehicles start in the parking lot, and when I looked, saw yellow vans leaving. One remained. Waiting for Laura, I assumed. Indio got out of it and crossed the lot to where the cop surveillance vehicle was still parked. It seemed as if he was about to confront the watchers, but when their window lowered and he bent to it, his body language bespoke familiarity.

I put on my phone's magnifying app and zoomed closer. The cop Indio was talking to was the big, older DEA who'd been top gun at Pacho's arrest.

Aha! Laura's valet, bodyguard, confidante—whatever the hell Indio was—was also an informant. Laura would be used until she was no longer useful, and then they'd lock her up and throw the key to her youth away.

I had to warn her.

Where the hell was she, anyway? I climbed atop the virgin's

pedestal and scanned the cemetery, finding her kneeling before a stone Jesus.

I started toward her but stopped when she stood and headed to the parking lot, where Indio was now holding the van door for her. She got in and I watched as it left the lot. The cop car followed it.

My phone buzzed. Its screen said, "Unknown Caller."

"What did the *chica* tell you?" a man demanded.

"Pardon me," I said. "Who is this?"

"Vizcaino. What did she say at the *funeraria*?"

"Pacho's sister? I expressed *mis condolencias*."

"You were in there for fifteen minutes."

"There was a line. Why do you care?"

"She has much to answer for," he said. "*El señor* wants to see you tomorrow."

"Tomorrow he's being extradited."

"He wants to see you before."

"He'll be here in two, three days," I said. "I'll see him soon as he arrives."

"Tomorrow, he insists," he said. "It's of the utmost *importancia*."

If Montez had an issue with Laura, I wanted to try and straighten it out, but I wasn't thrilled by another flight to Colombia. So many hours in reconditioned air was drying my skin; I made a mental note to reorder *Biologique Epiderme* moisturizer.

At eleven that night, I was just settling into my first class 1-A nest when Arias called me.

"*El señor* has another cooperation," he said. "It's a laboratory in Amazonia that processes five hundred kilos a week. I've texted you the coordinates."

"I'll take care of it. Good night."

Sure enough, the coordinates were on my phone. Hmm. I needed to pass the information on, but didn't trust calling from Colombia, which was rife with bugged listening devices. At this hour, Wilkinson wouldn't be available, so I figured I'd display my *bona fides* by leaving a voicemail saying Montez had more cooperation to give, then phone in the particulars when I got back, then *finally* get off the case.

But Jenna Wilkinson, bless her ambitious heart, was working late. She picked up on the first ring. I told her my client had more information. She asked me to hold on.

Rain streaked my window as the plane began to taxi. A red-caped attendant pointed at my phone and cutely wagged a no-no. From Wilkinson's end I heard a door open and sensed another presence had entered. Standard operating procedure. I was the subject of an investigation and might be upgraded to a target, or possibly a defendant, and Wilkinson wanted another AUSA overhearing me so that if I incriminated myself, she'd have a witness.

Nasty night, nasty business. Made me doubt whether my considerable income was worth it ... nah, it was.

Wilkinson came back on, and I gave her the lab details.

"Got it," she said. "Anything else?"

"The Honduran information work out?"

"I'm not at liberty to comment."

"My client has more info."

"Text it. No promises."

"Texting now," I said.

"Right. Got it. Okay."

"It's late," I said. "Go home."

"You should too, Ms. Electra."

"On my way as we speak."

CHAPTER 19

My fellow passengers were a mixed bag: people with battered luggage availing the cheapest flight, others with faces averted from recognition. Everyone was running to or from something. I reclined, facing the window and the darkness beyond, thinking I didn't know what I was running from, or to where.

ETA was dawn. The next day would be long, and I needed to be at my best. To avoid brain fog, I planned to sleep through the trip. I declined dinner, dropped a blue valium the shrink had prescribed, and washed it down with a vodka.

Then, hoping perchance to sleep, I closed my eyes.

Instead of knocking me down, the combined intoxicants kicked me up a notch.

The Montez case had escalated to a situation fraught with danger, and I'd been too preoccupied dealing with its sudden twists and turns to step back and see the forest from the trees.

Now I did.

Whether due to the orphan drug or not, much of my memory gap had begun to fill in. I thought I recalled most of what had happened before I sniffed the burundanga, and all that followed after I'd awakened. But what had occurred in the interim still remained in utter darkness.

Was it possible that in my addled state I'd been a left-handed killer? Would the incriminating photograph someday emerge, enabling DiMaglio to nail me?

Most troubling of all: would I be corroborated as the killer by Laura? Although my sudden appearance at the grave obviously had disconcerted her, I sensed no hostility toward me personally, rather at my being Montez's lawyer. I shared her antipathy.

The red-eye droned through the night.

Arias picked me up at the airport.

This time his ride was a Chrysler 300. We climbed into the back. "*Música*, Carmencita," he said to the driver.

Bad enough I had morning-after headache, now I had to endure Colombian pop. But to my relief, the driver donned headphones, and the only sound was of her elaborate fake nails tapping a beat on the steering wheel.

"Now we may talk privately," he said.

I'd assessed Arias as a dull errand boy for the precise Vizcaino, but now reassessed him as a kiss-up, kick-down type who had his own agenda. Should have known. He was a lawyer.

"Pacho ran a formidable enterprise," he said. "He is no longer with us, but the work must continue. Perhaps new leadership is required. There are things to be decided. Business."

"Like whether to keep wings on the menu or switch to nuggets?"

He chuckled. "You have the unique humor only we lawyers understand. Between us, I think Pacho would have cooperated," he said. "Can't say I'd have blamed him. One's priority is one's self."

The driver's head nodded to her fingers' beat. I wished he'd get to the point.

"Nowadays, we lawyers earn our money from cooperators," he said. "Easy work, eh? Plenty to go around, and more to come, I think. The new leadership will be inexperienced and prone to mistakes. Perhaps one day you and I may share another client. Who knows?"

I didn't know that, but knew Arias was a snake whose allegiance depended on which way the wind was blowing, and he was wondering if my sails were set likewise.

"*El señor* is preoccupied with a developing situation. I imagine that's why he asked you to come. No doubt it's very important to him."

"I imagine it has to do with Laura," I ventured.

"He's very fond of her. Taken, one might say."
"Is he really? She's quite young."
"Ah," he said. "We've arrived."

CHAPTER 20

The police precinct was an island in a slum.
Its compound was enclosed by barbed wire and manned by soldiers. Under their gun barrels, those about to be extradited commiserated with their families.

Vizcaino and Arias stood aside as Montez and I spoke. His expression was composed, but a vein throbbed in his temple. "It is *imperativo* that you stay close to Laura Grajales," he said.

"I don't know where to find her."

"She'll find you, *Doctora*."

"I hope by then I'm paid."

"I've given the order."

"The check's in the mail, eh?"

"*¿Discuple?*" he asked, unsure.

"The postman better ring," I said.

"You and your *gringaísmos incomprensibles*," he said. "You're a serious woman so talk seriously. I have an *estratagia* for my case; with your help it will be achieved. The work will be difficult but well worth it. Forget about our fee agreement. Guide me as required and you will become so wealthy you can retire. I assume you know I have such resources. One million or ten million or fifty million means nothing to me. *¿Me entiendes?*"

"Got it. I'll stay close to Laura," I said. "It might help if I knew why."

Montez chuckled. "I need her to help me. Moving on, I know that when one cooperates it must be this thing called, 'first party,' meaning that it is something the cooperator knows of personally. This is to ensure that the cooperation is not purchased. ¿*Correcto*?"

"Yes," I said, thinking, *Not really*. Montez had the rules down pat but was unaware that ambitious cops and prosecutors ignore them if the cooperation is substantial.

"I have personal knowledge of a cooperation so grand it will begin an investigation that will continue for months," he said. "I am correct that my knowledge will make me an important witness, and thus my trial will be put off?"

"If it is what you say."

"Oh, it is," he said. "There is a freighter presently docked in Cartagena. Below its mundane cargo are ten thousand kilos of cocaine. The reason I needed to tell you today is that the freighter is sailing at midnight."

Ten thousand kilos were an agent's wet dream, pardon the vulgarism. Sounded like another one of the fantastical rumors that abound in the drugster culture.

"The freighter's name?"

"The *Blue Atlantic*."

Montez snapped his fingers and Vizcaino gave me a phone. We were in the middle of a police station where half the inmates had illegal phones that were tapped by the fuzz.

Montez smiled. "*Tranquila, Doctora*. It's a satellite phone."

I cupped the receiver and called Wilkinson. Her demeanor was receptive, and I guessed that was because the previous cooperations had been fruitful.

"One thousand kilos," she said. "Nice."

"No, *ten* thousand," I said.

"What? Are you serious?"

"Check your messages."

I texted Wilkinson the *Blue Atlantic* info and handed the phone back to Vizcaino. He was staring across the yard, frowning. I followed his gaze and saw armored trucks parked nearby, presumably to ferry those about to be extradited to their flights.

"The *cabrón* is back," he said angrily.

The trucks were manned by a mix of Colombian cops and soldiers and some guys in jeans I made as DEA. One of them was an older, bear-like guy. I remembered him at the scene of Pacho's arrest, telling DiMaglio to back off me, and surveilling Pacho's funeral.

He saw us looking at him and waved both hands at us with fingers bent at mid-knuckle, as if saying bye-bye to a child.

"Kesey," Montez murmured.

"You know him?" I asked.

Vizcaino cut in, changing the subject. "I've been told they believe this threat business is serious," he said disapprovingly, as if it was my doing.

"It is serious," I said. "But if you keep the cooperation coming, I think all will go well."

"Think?" Vizcaino said. "You're being paid to be sure."

"*Tranquilo*, Victor," Montez said. "The so-called threat is a falsehood easily explained. When I was first arrested, I was put in general population. Not very pleasant. Long days confined in the Combita yard, huddled beneath eaves against the rain. I was angry, because my two lawyers had promised I'd be treated as a guest."

"The intake guards were not paid," Vizcaino protested. "The fucking *commandante* pocketed all the money. You can believe the *Xs* straightened him out."

"A lack of communication," Arias said. "Quickly corrected."

"While these two *genios* corrected the problem, I lived for a week like an animal among savages," Montez said, an edge in his tone. "One day lightning struck nearby. Foolishly, I vented and said I hoped God struck my prosecutor dead with lightning. My words were stupidities meant for no one. But those who heard me have since conspired to elaborate my meaning. Encouraged by their greedy American lawyers to cooperate, they told the prosecutor. Surely my lawyer is an expert at uncovering such lies."

"She had better be," Vizcaino said.

"How many heard you?" I asked.

Montez shrugged. "Four, five."

I figured the truth of what had occurred was somewhere between opposing versions. All such tales invariably are.

"Get me their names," I said.

Footsteps creaked above. A woman with an XL ass implant descended the steps. Her lipstick was smeared.

"Threw him one to remember you by," she said to a second woman ascending the stairs.

Montez smiled. "How I love the smell of perfume in the morning. Excuse me, gentlemen. The joy of sex awaits me."

He went up the stairs. "*Hola, mi amor*," I heard the second woman say, then a door closed.

Arias chuckled. "*El señor* likes his ladies. The more the merrier."

"Fool," Vizcaino snarled. "He closes his eyes and pretends they're the one he dotes on."

"Hard to blame him," Arias said. "She's such a pretty young thing."

CHAPTER 21

Two days later, Montez was arraigned in the Southern District of New York.

Since the events of 9/11, its courthouse at 500 Pearl Street is within a restricted enclave among the tall buildings that loom above Chinatown.

I parked the Shark in an exorbitantly priced lot outside the no-vehicle zone, then entered it and crossed Police Plaza. The surrounding buildings funneled a stiff wind across the space. The anger and resentment Montez had felt when hunched and hiding from the rain in Combita, I felt now—bulldogging the vagaries of life.

I left the plaza and went down the narrow alley bordered by St. Andrew's church, the U.S. Attorney's Offices, and the poured concrete walls of the federal Metropolitan Detention Center. Above, a maze of covered walkways connected the buildings, conveying the imprisoned from justice to confession and, if they were good rats, to salvation.

I entered the courtroom a minute before the appointed hour.

Judge Graff was already on the bench. He glared at me as if outraged at my timely brinksmanship. The rest of the cast was present, and Graff's deputy clerk Brunhilda called the case.

I heard metal clink and saw Montez being led in. He was not only cuffed but shackled. His expression was an odd mixture, somehow both bemused and amused.

"I'd like a moment with my client before arraignment," I said. I'd already told Montez what to expect, that he need not say anything—I would do all the talking. I wanted to establish a modicum of presence at the appearance.

Trouble was, in this courtroom, Judge Graff alone ruled. "I'm to assume you haven't already had an opportunity to prepare him prior?" he said. "Really, counselor?"

AUSA Mizrahi snickered quietly. He was seated between two marshals. What a pompous prick. Him, with 24/7 protection for an exaggerated threat, the better to enhance his station.

"I have, your Honor," I said. "But I'd like to talk to him now as well."

"Application denied," Graff said. "Begin."

AUSA Mizrahi stated that he had moved to be recused from the case. "Application granted," Graff said.

"Thank you," Mizrahi said, and he and his bodyguards left.

AUSA Jenna Wilkinson announced her appearance on behalf of the government. She was a trim young woman: blonde hair in a severe bun, large glasses obscuring much of her face. Her voice was low but firm and self-assured.

Graff began the arraignment. He summed up the necessities in a few boilerplate sentences, then asked how Montez pled.

"On his behalf, he pleads not guilty," I said.

"That right, sir?" Graff asked Montez.

Montez didn't reply. He was staring past the bench at the high window and the lower Manhattan skyline beyond.

"Did you hear me, Mr. Montez?" Graff asked.

"Sorry, your Honor," Montez said. "I've never seen New York before. Magnificent, I must say. As my attorney said, I plead not guilty."

"On my client's behalf, not guilty," I said.

"So entered," Graff said. "Bail?"

"The government seeks detention," Jenna Wilkinson said. "There exists both a danger to the community and the risk of flight."

"I assume you are not seeking bail," Graff said to me.

A no-brainer. Although Montez had been extradited, technically he was not legally in the country, and even if he was, the charges were light-years beyond the possibility of bail.

"Not at this time," I said. Nor any time, I might've added.

"This being an extradition case, I expect the government already has its evidence in order," Graff said. "One week to provide full discovery. Two weeks for the defendant to respond. Trial, thirty days from today."

Graff banged his gavel.

Montez seemed distressed, but before we could speak, he was whisked away. Good. Let him wonder and worry. Not that there was reason to, for the thirty-day trial date was just a control date to keep Graff apprised of any interactions between the G and the defense, and the trial date would be extended at that time.

"My client is ready to proffer," I said to Wilkinson.

"We're considering it," she said.

"I assume your reluctance to accept his cooperation is due to an alleged threat," I said. "Why not afford him an opportunity to address that issue?"

"We're considering it." she said.

"The *Blue Atlantic* happen?"

She smiled. "Considered."

CHAPTER 22

I was sure Jenna Wilkinson would proffer Montez, at least to hear his take on the alleged threat to Mizrahi, at most to delve into the source of his information.

I wanted to update Montez and prep him on what to expect. Probably would take an hour or so for him to recross the rat maze and go through Metropolitan Correctional Center intake. Rather than wait in the MCC lobby for him to be cleared for my visit, I walked over to Chinatown and lunched while checking my email. It was mostly PACER bounces regarding my other cases, some of which required responses. I told myself I'd do them tomorrow, just as I'd been telling myself for the past few weeks.

When I got to MCC, I signed the attorney-visit book. Standard operational procedure was that no one may check the previous sign-ins. Still, when writing my name and the inmate I was visiting, it was in a deliberately unreadable scrawl. Defense lawyers are notoriously prone to poaching clients, and Montez was a big fish. Not my style, but I couldn't help but notice the two sign-ins directly above mine listed Montez's name and inmate number.

Very interesting.

One signature was in the elaborately unique script Colombians devise to protect against ID theft. I deciphered its convoluted scribble as Adolfo Arias. Since Colombian lawyers are only allowed in the MCC if accompanied by American attorneys, I assumed his co-visitor was one; additionally, that lawyer's signature was an illegible scrawl, much like mine.

I'd been right.

I'd suspected Montez was meeting with another American lawyer. But if the lawyer—an experienced pro like me, judging by his unreadable sign-in—was talking to Montez, why was I being kept in the dark about it?

Did Montez want a second opinion?

Did he want us as co-counsel?

Was he planning to dump me?

Good questions, but I wouldn't ask them. It would only elicit an evasive response; no need for Montez to know I was onto him. Forewarned was forearmed.

Montez wore an orange jumpsuit with SHU—Special Housing Unit—lettered across the back, IDing high-profile inmates. The stated rationale was to isolate them from general population inmates; the reality was that the SHU was a punishment designed to break a man's spirit.

Twelve-by-eight cells. Cold, windowless concrete boxes, fluorescent-lit around the clock, bare but for a stained mattress and a hole-in-the-floor toilet. Meals slid through a slot in a steel door, no contact with anyone except attorneys.

The SHU attorney visit area was several small, wire-glass walled rooms visible from the guard-patrolled corridors. They were studded with cameras in all four corners—ostensibly for security but also for lip-reading, I thought.

Montez seemed unperturbed by the indignities of the SHU. The opposite. He was composed just as he had been in El Modesto. I suppose he was acting out that big boys don't cry.

"I view my stay here as a learning experience," he said.

I arched a sarcastic brow. "I'm happy for you," I said.

"Skepticism doesn't serve you well, *Doctora*. It's counterproductive. Experience is a teacher that broadens one's perspective. A crystallization of life, so to speak. For example, without being obvious, look in the adjoining visit room."

I cut my eyes sideways. In the adjoining room, an inmate was arranging documents in front of a computer. He was well-known as an accomplished jailhouse lawyer who'd strung out his case for years, during which he'd become somewhat of a legend. He still carried himself like the Mafia *capo* he used to be, back when his street name was Tony Handsome. Not only did he seem uncaring of his isolation, he looked like a man happily at work before a computer where his discovery was stored.

"Three years they hold Tony H here because they say he threatened a judge," Montez said. "A lie, as with me. But they have not broken him. The lesson? That's how a real man behaves."

"I spoke with your prosecutor," I said.

He listened calmly as I told him about my exchange with Jenna Wilkinson, and what to expect if she proffered him.

"Proffer means?" he asked.

"An interview, sort of."

"Kesey will be there?"

That was the second time he'd mentioned Kesey by name. The first time Vizcaino had changed the subject.

"How do you know Kesey?" I asked.

"They say this Wilkinson prosecutor is ambitious," he said. "She defers to the Day-ahs. I was told this DEA Kesey has a vendetta for me. Why, I have no idea."

"Who told you this?"

He smiled. "The shitters are connected by sewage pipes. We communicate through them. Tony H and I often talk."

Toilets as phones? I knew that incarceration stimulated ingenuity, but this was a new one I'd never heard.

"As for this ridiculous threat, I will tell the prosecutor what I told you," he said. "That it is a fabrication of those who falsely seek cooperation credit."

"I asked you to get the names of those who say they overheard you making the threat. Have you?"

"I made inquiries among my former Combita inmates. I was given four names. Juancho. Beto. Kiko. Fercho."

"Their real names?" I asked.

"Those in Combita share many secrets but their true identity is not among them," he said. "Sometimes there are disagreements—best not to let them affect their families."

"Keep trying," I said. "And get more cooperation."

"Vizcaino is away, doing so as we speak. But one thing greatly troubles me. The judge says my trial is in thirty days, but that will not be sufficient time for my people to provide cooperation."

"The trial schedule will be put on hold for cooperation."

"What if they don't accept my cooperation?" he asked.

"Clear up the threat and they will," I said.

"If they want my assistance, this Wilkinson woman must show good faith and remove me from the SHU to general population. There I can use phones. Here I cannot communicate."

"I intend to make that request," I said. I didn't add that a request would be a waste of time. The G would let him rot in the SHU for however long they wanted to.

"Excellent," he said. "I'm pleased with your work and have instructed my friends to increase your forthcoming fee payment. I want you to enjoy the fruit of your labors, but before that, there is something you must understand."

He reached across the table and put his hand atop mine. His fingernails needed trimming and I felt their sharp edges.

"*Doctora*," he said. "Stay close to Laura."

CHAPTER 23

There were still red half-moons on my hand where Montez's nails had bitten me.

How did Laura fit into the picture?

Maybe he believed she knew where Pacho's stolen money was, yet his intensity seemed personal. When Arias had said Montez was obsessed with Laura, I'd taken that to mean it was a two-way thing. It had sparked a defensive instinct in me, making me want to warn the impressionable young girl that sleeping with wolves will get you eaten. Or perhaps Laura was Montez's daughter ... then again, Montez was of pure Spanish blood; a womanizer who feasted on darker flesh, doubtful he'd allow his mistress to bear a mixed-blood child. So maybe Laura really was his lover? A typical scenario: an older, powerful man and a young, defenseless girl ... who now may have a degree of control over his fortunes. Possible, perhaps even likely.

I processed these thoughts while crossing Police Plaza and exiting the no-go zone. I reached the parking lot where the Shark awaited and patted my pockets for the lot receipt. Where was it?

Ah, my lapel pocket. I handed it and a Grant to the attendant. He took the fifty but handed back the receipt.

"This may be Chinatown but we ain't no Chinese restaurant," he said.

Huh? I realized the receipt I'd given him was not paper issued by the lot, but a blank white plastic card. Oh.

I was wearing the same suit I'd worn when Pacho was arrested. DEA had left the card on top of a freezer, and now

I remembered picking it up, assuming it was part of Pacho's personal effects. I put it back in my lapel pocket. Hopefully, the rest of my fog would lift soon, and the card would take on meaning. I fished the parking lot receipt out of my breast pocket, handed it over, got in the Shark, and—

My phone *pinged.* It was a text from still another unfamiliar number with a Colombian prefix code. All it said was "GAA 23, LGA 5:00 PM." When and where to pick someone up, I assumed.

A Mr. Green, I hoped.

A search ID'd GAA as Great America Airlines. LGA was the airport shorthand for LaGuardia Airport. Another search revealed GAA 23 was an incoming flight from Akron, Ohio.

Montez had said Vizcaino was away, and Akron was likely a flight pit stop, so there was a good chance Vizcaino was the pickup. I was still smarting from his sneering tone. Stranding him in LaGuardia was a satisfying thought, but self-defeating if he was bringing my money.

That concerned me.

Vizcaino wouldn't be carrying the money, so picking him up meant accompanying him to the safe house where the money was stashed. I didn't know what Vizcaino was up to but had the strong feeling he had his own agenda. Could well be that he resented my alliance with Montez and wanted to sever it; if so, the safe house he'd take me to could be decidedly unsafe.

Only one way to find out.

Great America Airlines had one counter in a far corner of the terminal.

A sign above it confirmed Flight 23 was on time. I went to another far corner and sat down with a cup of black Joe and called Gino Moskowitz.

"Guy gets busted on an extradition warrant in Bogota," I said. "Gets processed into the system before they ship him to Combita. Question. How long does it take to process him?"

"Like, do the trains run on time?" Gino asked. "I dunno. A day, maybe three?"

The extradition warrant listed Montez's date and time of

arrest. I told them to Gino. "Figure the next couple days he gets to Combita," I said. "He's in general population for a week until he buys an upgrade to a private suite with unrestricted legal and conjugal visits."

"Yeah, that's Martin Montez. Mister Money. Very smart guy. Kept one partner up on the Mosquito Coast doing the product transporting."

"Don J," I said.

"Kept the other in the jungle running leaf-to-powder labs."

"Lucho," I said.

"Montez stayed in Bogota," Gino said. "Maintained control over the money. Only he knows where the money is."

"Knowing he was being extradited, wouldn't he want someone else to access it if he needed money?" I asked.

"If he trusted anyone," Gino said. "Guys like him tend not to."

Except a younger woman too naïve or frightened to buck him, I thought. "I'm looking for four guys who were inmates in Combita from the day Montez arrived through the following week," I said. "Jail yard names were Juancho, Beto, Kiko, and Fercho. I need their real names."

"Thousand-something dudes in Combita," he said. "Must be a bunch with those names. Gonna be difficult, Electra."

"Which is why it's lucrative."

"Getting stateside skinny is doable," he said. "Getting Colombian info is difficult, putting it mildly. But I'm thinking about a way. Combita was built by us, right? From the nuts and bolts to the computers. Find a guy who knows the guy who installed the computers, pick his brain for a back door into them. How soon do you need the names?"

"Yesterday would've been nice."

When I returned to the Great American gate, Flight 23 was just disembarking. Some midlevel business types, some people with the stunned expressions of escapees from the Rust Belt, a bunch of young guys with whitewall military haircuts looking eager for a fun leave in New Yawk.

No Vizcaino yet. More passengers to come, I hoped. Yes. A gaggle of Gen Zs with rainbow-dyed hair, piercings, and tats. I think myself an open-minded, tolerant person, but thought self-mutilation and deliberately weird eccentricity were the marks of lemmings marching like clockwork beneath an orange flag toward the edge of a cliff. And *Z* being the last letter of the alphabet, I harbored serious doubts about humanity's future, which was why I wasn't saving for my old age.

Still no Vizcaino. No more passengers came.

I've learned not to be offended by the rudeness I encounter during my intercourses with clerks and minor functionaries. But being stood up by a cartel lawyer was beyond the pale. The disrespectful dog....

A young woman with green hair paused at me.

CHAPTER 24

"Hello, Laura," I said.

"Hello, Ms. Electra," she said demurely. I sensed a wariness in her manner.

"I thought I was waiting for someone else," I said. "I didn't recognize you."

"What? Oh. The hair is, um, camouflage," she said.

I nodded as if understanding although I didn't. If she was here to deliver my fee, I got that she wanted to stay under the radar. But green hair in Akron, Ohio? Was she delivering my fee? She wore a backpack much too small to fit a million, even in Franklins.

"Shall we pick up your bags?" I asked.

"Don't have any," she said. "Your package is already here. You know what I'm referring to?"

I knew all too well, but why was she asking? Was she wired? Trying to get me to acknowledge that the package was money? But her tradecraft was weak and easily deflected.

"Aw, you brought me a Christmas present," I said.

"What? Oh, right. I'll take you to it."

"Well then, my chariot awaits."

I put her backpack in the Shark's trunk. Her fingers traced its big fins. "I love Cadillacs."

A covert message? There are many terms for cocaine in the drugster lexicon: *yeyo,* snow, flake, and the old standby Cadillac, describing top-notch product. Was Laura referring to my car, or cocaine? Another attempt to elicit a confirmation that I was hip to the drug money?

Troubling for many reasons.

Maybe Laura was working for Montez. Maybe his stern order for me to stay close to her was because he didn't trust her. That fit. She'd denied being involved in Pacho's business, but if that was so, why was she on the Clinton List and delivering money for Santa Fe—and why had he asked me to stay close to her?

Unless it was her own errand and the delivery was not money, but baited payback to the woman she believed had killed her brother.

I missed my silver Sig.

We drove in strained silence.

Without speaking, she pointed directions: Turn there, take that exit, stay right. The first time we doubled back on a roadway, I thought she wasn't certain of our route. But when it happened again, I realized she was deliberately squaring blocks to be sure we weren't being followed.

By *Los Xs*? By the DEA?

We ended up on a potholed cul-de-sac in a crummy south Queens neighborhood, littered with empty lots where, years ago, Hurricane Sandy had washed homes away, save for a dilapidated few that seemed empty.

She pointed at an intact house. It was dark. A rusted swing hung above an overgrown lawn. Behind it, a midsize sedan was parked in the driveway. She'd arrived from Akron and the car had Ohio plates. I wondered if Laura had lured me to a secluded place with bad intent. I raised my guard to DEFCON 2.

The street was dark. There was a streetlamp, but its bulb was shattered. I didn't like the set, but I followed her to the house. The front door was triple-locked. She had the keys and knew which keyholes they fit. Yeah, she was a player, all right.

When we were inside, she relocked the doors and lowered blackout shades before switching a lamp on. Except for an old sofa leaking stuffing, the room was empty and looked as musty as it smelled.

"I've got a priority to deal with," she said.

With that, she left the room. I heard a door open and then close, and a lock snap shut. Now what? Get to it, woman. Show me the money, or whatever you really have planned.

I looked at the old couch. Poor thing was on its last legs. Hell, I might be too. There was another door. It was unlocked. I opened it and saw a laundry room with a large washing machine and dryer unit.

Hmm....

I went back to the first room and peeked through the edge of the black window shades. The street was quiet. I paced around the couch.

Laura returned. She'd rinsed off the green dye and her hair was now dark. She went to the couch and took out a cheap metal suitcase from beneath a cushion. She unlocked the lid and opened it, revealing banded bricks of bills bearing the wise face of Benjamin Franklin.

I riffled through a brick, eyeballing bills that flashed by as if in a primitive card-flip movie. In my business, I've counted as much cash as a veteran bank teller, and had acquired a rough but decent-enough correlation between size and total: figure a twelve-inch brick was ten thousand bills. I eyeballed ten bricks. One million. Montez had kept his word. I closed the suitcase.

"Thank you," I said. "I'll leave now. I see you have your own vehicle, so no need to drop you anywhere."

"Need ..." she said, trailing off. "I can't stay here and want nothing to do with that car."

So she knew the car was hot. Maybe the DEA had told her to leave it because they were waiting to snatch whoever came for it. Or maybe she knew that the car, like the house, was Santa Fe property best avoided.

She didn't lock the house as we left. I put the suitcase in the Shark's trunk; she got in and locked the door. I got behind the wheel and drove off.

"Could you drop me where I can find a taxi?" she asked.

"You won't find one around here," I said. "I'll give you a lift. Say where."

She shrugged. "Hotels by the airport. One of them."

"The week before Christmas, may not be any rooms."

"Doesn't matter," she said. "I'll catch a flight."

"At this hour? Where you headed?"

She didn't reply. The Shark was built before armrests

were *de rigueur* and she perched in the far side of the seat with her hands wrapped around her knees, her face turned to the window.

I felt a pang of sympathy. She was just a kid who probably had no idea of what she had gotten into. She wasn't the first and sure wouldn't be the last.

"Why do you care where I'm going?" she asked without turning.

I shrugged. "I don't. Small talk."

"Like all of Martin's lawyers, you say what he tells you to."

"That's not true."

"How can I believe you?"

I pulled to the curb and turned to her. "Look at me."

When she did, I saw her cheeks were wet. Tears?

"I will not do anything to hurt you," I said.

"That's what Mar—what he said, before, before...."

I didn't speak. I knew what she was about to say.

She sobbed. "He made me, he...."

A wellspring of empathy burst within me. Without conscious awareness, I'd been drawn to her because we shared a history—she was the lost waif I'd been before Gino Moskowitz righted me. I drew a breath. Lord knows I'm not a giving person. The only donations I make are to myself and Gino's cut—yet I wanted, *needed,* to help her.

"Where're you going?" I asked.

She shrugged. "Anywhere."

What goes around comes around. Do unto others and all that jazz. Gino had been my Good Samaritan. My turn now. Yet for Gino there was no downside; if I had failed it would have been on me. But my downside to helping Laura was considerable. Consorting and conspiring are different words with the same root prefix and too-similar meanings for DEA, an org that preaches guilt by association.

We were stopped at a light on a Queens Boulevard corner and the flashing neon of a nearby restaurant alternately lit her face: red ... green ... stop or go?

"I know a place," I said.

CHAPTER 25

We didn't speak until entering my apartment.
She looked around, taking it in. "It's large," she said shyly. "You live here alone?"
"I do," I said.
"*Minimalista.*"
I wasn't sure if she intended "minimal" to be disparaging or complimentary, but it was true. I lived minimally. After Mama passed, I'd renovated the apartment. Cordoned off Mama's bedroom and its vast closets. Left the rest as one large room. I'd always envisioned myself surrounded by fine things when I could afford them, yet now that I was flush, I couldn't seem to find time to acquire any.

My big room was spare but for essentials: king-sized futon atop a platform, bedside table supporting connections to the outside world: clock radio, multi-pronged device charger, many-buttoned remote for the big flat screen fixed above the footboard.

The rest was empty but equally necessary: ample floorspace for thoughtful pacing, windows offering naked city views for stark contemplations.

"*Muy* Zen," she said approvingly.
She was smiling. Lovely.
"Hungry?" I asked.
"Starving."
I pulled up my favorite take-out menus on my device screen. "Say which," I said.
Her smile grew. "*El mínimo.*"
"Japanese, then," I said, approvingly. As we polished off

our feast of sushi, I was increasingly aware that we were in perfect sync. I even liked the way she ate. *Con gusto, pero delicada.*

Sated, she propped a pillow and leaned against it and looked at me.

"I really can trust you?" she asked.

"Trust is a two-way street," I said.

"You don't trust me? Why?"

The obvious answer was that I suspected she was working with either Montez or the DEA, and one of them was pressuring her to entrap me—and she might. Still, Montez was my client and I was duty-bound to honor all that entailed, including not aiding and abetting his accusers.

"I know what you're thinking," she said. "You needn't worry. I won't cooperate against Martin."

Gino had drilled a business rule in my head: Trust no one. Neither clients nor the government nor the go-betweens. Yet Laura seemed a potential exception to the rule; I wasn't sure why, but instinctively went with my gut rather than my head.

"I trust you, Laura," I said. "All I ask in return is that you trust me. No deceptions, no omissions, no half-truths. Deal?"

Her eyes met mine; she nodded ... then yawned. "Sorry," she said. "Long day."

I dimmed the lights and went into Mama's room. Her bed was as she'd made it on the day she flew out the window; whether it had been in search of her future or to recapture her past, I wasn't sure. If that sounds confusing, it was, and still is.

Her clothing was neatly stored by seasonal use. Oh, Mama, how I missed her. Every day she dressed to the nines in a different outfit, although she never left the apartment. I moved aside her collection of silk scarves, a veritable curtain of Hermès silk—and for a moment a thought hovered: *scarf?* Then it was gone.

I pressed the wall behind the scarves and a panel slid open. There was a steel combo-locked safe, empty except for my passport, fifty thousand in getaway money and, until recently, my dearly departed silver Sig. I spun the dial, opening the safe and sliding the suitcase of Franklins inside it. Then I locked the safe, straightened the scarves, and lay on Mama's bed.

A low ringing sound awoke me.

I opened the door and saw Laura with her phone to her ear. She saw me and put a finger to her lips, then put the phone on speaker, and I heard a man's voice, all-too familiar.

"*El negocio?*" Vizcaino asked. "It is done?"

Hmm ... *If,* as I suspected, Vizcaino's agenda was out of sync with Montez's, *if* Vizcaino was making a move to snatch Montez's crown, could be that Laura had cast her lot with the lawyer, an enemy-of-my-enemy-is-my-friend kind of partnership. That explained the dichotomy between Laura bringing me Montez's fee despite his not knowing her whereabouts. But it raised another supposition: why would Vizcaino pay Montez's fee? Didn't add up, but one of Gino's maxims did: *When the client puts money on the table? Take it off.*

Laura looked at me as she spoke. "*Si, todo está bien,*" she said.

"*Donde estas?*" Vizcaino asked.

"*Un hotel,*" she said.

"*Cual?*"

Laura looked at me. "*No es asunto tuyo.*"

Good girl. None of his business was right.

"*Donde esta ella?*" Vizcaino asked.

"*No sé,*" she said. "*¿Mi mami está bien?*"

"*Buenas noches, chica,*" he signed off.

She stared at the dead phone, shaking her head. "Martin forced my brother to work for him. My mother is unwell, and he holds her to get what he wants from me."

A light bulb lit my mind. Montez believed she knew where the money Pacho had filched from Santa Fe was. But if true, why hadn't she given it up? Whatever Laura was or was not, she did not seem the thieving kind.

"I hate Martin for what he's done and for who he is," she said. "But you did not know any of this, and I forgive you for working for him. There, I've confessed my feelings, as it should be between us. If you've privacies to admit, do so now. I want us to be transparent."

"For better or worse, I am what I seem," I told her.

"Why does *Doctora* Electra have just one name?"

"My father left my mother before I was born," I said. "I chose not to honor his name."

"My father is dead," she said. "They killed him."

My phone rang. I didn't answer it. The ringing stopped, and a moment later, I got a voicemail alert. I put my phone on speaker and played the message.

"Sleeping, *Doctora*?" Victor Vizcaino asked. He whinnied a high-pitched laugh. "Good that you rest, you will need to be acute tomorrow. After *el señor* talks to the prosecutor, he wants to talk to you as well."

Weird. Why did Vizcaino think Jenna Wilkinson was proffering Montez tomorrow? Wilkinson hadn't told me. Or had she? I'd muted my business alerts.

Now I looked at my email. It was true. Wilkinson had notified me Montez was being proffered tomorrow—which was now today as the sky beyond my window was lightening.

"You're going to see Martin?" Laura had loosened her collar and at her neck I saw a flash of gold. It was a gold locket inscribed with a name: Cleo. Pacho's daughter. "My brother intended to give it to Cleo at the *quinceañera*," she explained. "What will happen when Martin and you meet with the prosecutor?"

I shrugged. "Depends on Martin."

She nodded. "His game begins."

CHAPTER 26

The fifth floor of 500 Pearl, a.k.a.. the Southern District of New York, is a condensed story of the typical federal criminal case.

The elevator opens mid-corridor. To the left lies Pretrial Service offices, where the newly arrested are printed and pedigreed. In the center is the Magistrate's courtroom, where they are formally arraigned. To the right is the proffer area, a green door behind which obscenities are confessed in the hope of forgiveness.

I arrived for the proffer on time. Waited in the anteroom while people came and went. Suited FBI agents and DEA guys in jeans and sneakers. Pinky-ringed drug lawyers who eyed me. Ugh. A few lawyers were women. A primped blonde glared at me as if we were competing cougars.

I waited some more. Dialed Jenna Wilkinson but hung up when the call went to voicemail. An hour later, Agent Kesey came to fetch me.

Up close he looked even bigger. A big, beefy guy, a wrestling fan type ... yet his greeting was unlikely: "Lest auld acquaintance be forgot," he said theatrically. "Hey, nice scarf."

"Thank you," I said. "An hour?"

"Your guy took his time coming down," he said. "Probably wanted to spiffy-up before his big moment."

Probably, I thought. Montez ... so vain he believed looking good would do him good. Maybe at a bar, but not before *the* bar. He was cocky now, but by the time all was said and done, he'd be begging the G to accept his cooperation. Even with cooperation, he'd be locked up for eight or ten years, minimum. Time may not heal all wounds, but it marches on, and whenever he got out of jail, he'd be too depleted to revisit me.

"Spiffy client, spiffy lawyer," Kesey said. "That really is a nice scarf."

What was he insinuating? "Tell you what," I said. "Let my guy cooperate, I'll give you the scarf."

He grinned. "Nah, I already got one just like it," he said. "Come on, let the festivities begin."

The proffer room had black-out shades because its windows were just across the rat-maze alley from curious eyes inside the MCC. Overhead fluorescence paled the faces of the people in the room.

Kesey. DiMaglio. Jenna Wilkinson. A Secret Service Agent named Leeds I remembered having been with Kesey at Pacho's arrest. I wondered what Secret Service had to do with the case.

They sat in a circle facing Montez.

Cue the blinding interrogation light, I thought. Of course, there wasn't one, but Montez was in the spotlight. SHU inmates are issued one-size-fits-all overlarge orange jumpsuits that make them look like kids in grown-up clothing, but Montez had wangled one that fit him as if custom-made. He was freshly shaved, his salt-and-pepper hair brushed, his expression earnest as a Boy Scout's.

"At the outset, I want to be clear," Wilkinson said. "This discussion is strictly limited to the threat Mr. Montez is alleged to have made. After we hear him out, we'll decide whether or not to elevate to a cooperation agreement. All right, Mr. Montez, tell us your version of what, if anything, happened."

"Thank you for the opportunity," Montez said easily. "I have no idea what others may have told you, but I'm quite sure it's a fabrication based on a remark I foolishly made. I should have known better, but I'd just arrived in Combita. It is not a nice place, and I was out of sorts when I spoke."

"Get to it," Kesey said gruffly.

Montez rested his elbows on the table and leaned forward, speaking quietly. He was playing Mr. Sincere well, I had to give him that.

"It was a stormy day," Montez said. "I and a few others

were gathered beneath eaves taking protection from the rain. They were ignorant thugs who smelled of the streets. Never in my life had I felt so downcast and, yes, angry. When lightning struck the mountain I said—quietly, as if thinking aloud—that I wished it struck my prosecutor. There you have it."

"You didn't say prosecutor," Wilkinson said. "You spoke his name."

Montez nodded. "Mizrahi, yes."

"How did you know his name?"

"My lawyers told me."

"That's all, sir?"

"All," he said.

Wilkinson stood. "I'm going to confer with my supervisor. While we do, if you recall anything else, tell your lawyer."

They left me alone with Montez. As if removing a mask, his demeanor changed. "Laura left her vehicle and went with you," he said grimly. "While I was locked in a concrete box you were with her. In a hotel."

"Not true," I said. That he knew I and Laura were together meant he and Vizcaino were still communicating, and that the lawyer had not yet revealed his ambitions. "You told me to stay close to her, so I put her up in a safe place."

His gaze was locked on mine. Ye olde inquisitor's stare-down. I'd been on both ends of it many times and knew how to appear honest: I kept my expression neutral and didn't blink. Not that I was supernaturally able to control the involuntary; more that I was telling the truth—we had not been in a hotel.

"If you fail to obtain a cooperation agreement, *el final para ti*."

A typical client threat; his ultimate victory or my final defeat. Succeed, he gets to wear the laurels. Fail, he thumbs-down the lawyer. I wasn't overly concerned. When—not *if*—Vizcaino took over, Montez was powerless and wouldn't have a button to push.

"Another thing," he said. "Laura. If you give into your depravity and touch her? I will kill you."

WTF? He actually thought Laura and I had been intimate. His unflappable veneer had given way to an anger obviously fueled by jealousy. Now I understood the nature of his relationship with Laura and why he viewed me as an obstacle to it. Sexism at its crudest: if two women are in one another's company they must be gay. I said nothing.

The door opened and Kesey leaned in. "Like a word with you, counselor," he said.

CHAPTER 27

Kesey and DiMaglio were in the corridor. Wilkinson was still meeting with her supervisor.

"You okay, counselor?" Kesey asked me.

"Why wouldn't I be okay?" I snapped.

"You look pissed," DiMaglio said.

"I am," I said. "How long does it take for a yes or no?"

"Ah, they'll cooperate him," Kesey said. "Leeds's D.C. pals already put the fix in. Fucking Secret Service morons put their agenda first. As if counterfeiting is the number-one problem."

Counterfeiting? This was an element previously unknown to me. But it explained why Leeds was there: counterfeit investigations were run by Secret Service.

"Pricks in sunglasses," DiMaglio said. "Earpieces, lapel pins, Uzis in attaché cases. Twenty-eight-year-old kids—gimme a break. They lie to inflate their importance."

"Not to worry, counselor," Kesey said to me. "Brian and me are running this situation. By the way, we don't give a damn about the bonus I'm sure you negotiated."

Bonus? A stab in the dark, I thought. "You're out of line."

"Ain't we all," he said. "Occupational hazard. But you can relax because your prints didn't match any at Pacho's house. Lucky you. Prints don't take on silk scarves."

Scarves again. "You a forensic haberdasher?"

"Funny," he said. "Y'know, I really do have a Hermès blue scarf just like yours. In fact, it is yours, or was. Somehow it ended up at Pacho's house."

Good grief!

I'd used my scarf to wipe the coffee table, then tossed it aside and forgotten to take it.

Although I grumbled at the outrageous price of Hermès scarves, they now proved more than worth the money if, as Kesey said, silk didn't take fingerprints. Of course, there probably was DNA on it: mine and Pacho's and maybe some from an *X*, too. But a mix like that made it impossible for a DNA test to function accurately.

Jenna Wilkinson returned. "Green light," she said. "We'll proffer him on everything, starting tomorrow. But no cooperation agreement unless his information proves valuable."

"Why not continue today?" I asked.

"Some sort of lockdown situation in MCC," she said. "The marshals have been told to bring all defendants back, stat."

Even as she said this, a pair of marshals appeared to take Montez back. As they cuffed him, he looked at me. I wanted to flip him the bird, but my better half prevailed, and I gave him a half-hearted thumbs-up.

Ordinarily, the situation would have merited my visiting Montez to review and refine tomorrow's proffer, but since the MCC was in lockdown, that wasn't in the cards, a twist of fate that pleased me.

Surprising myself, I wanted to spend my time with Laura.

Midtown was crowded and bright. Two days to Christmas Eve and angels were harking. Growing up the way I had, my holiday season had never been particularly festive, but now I felt the spirit move me. I had no cares and worries to put aside, but for one: Had I killed Pacho? Yes or no?

All else was well. Montez would cooperate. I was no longer in the shadow of Pacho's murder because his revealing the photograph of my holding a gun to Pacho put him in the mix. The case would end, I was flush, and had a kid sister for the holidays.

I glided the Shark up Madison Avenue. The sidewalks were filled with people who had money spending it.

Presents…. I'd never gotten nor received a present, but now I wanted to give Laura one.

I pulled over outside a shop that specialized in antique

jewelry. I knew less than nothing about that—my tastes were more contemporary—but had walked past the place a few times and admired its window display.

A ring seemed too betrothal-like. A brooch too flashy. A bracelet too intimate. Then I saw the perfect gift.

A pair of gold-wire earrings, artisanal looking, with tiny emerald chips. Supposedly pre-Colombian—I wasn't sure about that—but clearly old. Cost a small fortune, but this was what money was for, right?

For a moment, I thought I'd walked into the wrong apartment.

The moment passed and I saw my *minimo* flat had been transformed into a fantasy land. Candles flickered. Violins swooned and sighed. Wine chilled in a silver bucket I'd once bought on a whim but never unpacked.

From the kitchen I never use came the rich scent of dinner cooking. Laura leaned out. She wore one of my white shirts, its sleeves rolled up, its long, swaying shirttails her skirt.

"What do you think?" she said.

"It's grand. No one ever...."

My voice trailed off, choked by a feeling I'd never experienced rising in my throat. Lord help me. How many thousands of times have I stood in a courtroom not having the slightest idea of what I was going to say until I spoke? Now I knew exactly what I wanted to say but couldn't.

"No one ever what?" she asked.

"Made me so hungry," I said.

Dinner was superb. Chicken stewed with sweet yams dusted with cilantro. When I praised the meal, Laura sheepishly confessed that the chicken had been delivered by one of Pacho's Pollo Loco trucks.

"I thought the restaurant was closed," I said.

"It is. But the kitchen's open for takeout."

"Mmmm," I said. "Their chicken is still tops."

"Pacho spices it with our *mami's* secret recipe," she said brightly, but her eyes were disconsolate.

Something going on there, I thought. Behind those eyes, was there an image of me murdering Pacho? Was the charming smile an elaborate ploy for revenge? Then again, maybe I was wrong. Maybe her thoughts had to do with her ailing mother.

I refilled our wine glasses, and when she drank, her good mood returned and my suppositions vanished. After dinner, we sipped brandy at the window while looking at the shining city beyond. It was snowing.

"I hope it snows ten feet," I said. "I bet you've never been in snow, have you?"

"There's snow in the high Andes, but you're right, I've never gone up there."

I slid the terrace door open. Barefoot, we tiptoed across the snowy terrace.

The snow muffled the traffic sounds from below, but just after we entered the winter wonderland, there was a sickening, loud crash that made us both jump. I looked over the edge: ten stories down a van had run up on the sidewalk and struck a building. The van was bright yellow with a red logo I couldn't make out but had a pretty good idea what it was.

"What happened?" Laura asked.

I was wondering myself. The Pollo Loco people had delivered a bird hours ago. The upper East Side wasn't home to their type of clientele, so why were they still here?

"It must've been the icy street," I said, reassuring her. "Let's go back inside."

That night we had a pajama party.

Girl stuff. When I showed her Mama's closets, she nearly swooned. She'd never seen such classic clothing, but she had a natural eye for finery. Her fingers lingered on a Carine Gilson silken kimono.

"Try it on," I said.

"Oh, I can't ... it wouldn't be right, it belonged to your moth ... moth...." Her voice broke.

I shuddered at the pain she must feel. Sequestering her mother and controlling her meds was Montez's way of controlling Laura, but there was nothing I could do about it except lend a sympathetic ear.

"It must have been very beautiful on your mother," she said.

"I'm sure she'd want you to try it on," I said.

She did. Draped in silk she was regal.

We opened another bottle of wine and sat cross-legged on the futon and giggled about toenail polishing and how to endure the monthly curse and the clumsy ways men came on. The wine got her sleepy and she closed her eyes.

I went to do the dishes and discovered a knife she'd used to cut the chickens. Strange, I thought. Years earlier, Mama's fantasies had devolved into weeping. I'd feared she might kill herself and had thrown out the kitchen blades. Obviously, I'd overlooked one, and Laura had used it.

It was an old folding knife with a serrated blade of the sort used by sport fishermen, which got me to remembering that Mama had a deep-rooted aversion to fish, and I reasoned that the blade must have belonged to my father. I cleaned it and left it to dry. When I returned, Laura was fast asleep. Snow whipped past the terrace door. The TV murmured something about the city shutting down tomorrow.

I felt strangely peaceful. Since Mama passed, I'd never entertained, much less had an overnight guest. I'd convinced myself that I liked being alone, but Laura had disabused me of that. It was good having a like-minded spirit around, and I wanted to enjoy it for a while.

I padded to my laptop and went into PACER, cancelling my pending court appearances, then phone-texted cancellations of my upcoming office appointments.

Then I went to the futon and listened to Laura's gentle breathing and to the gears in my mind meshing. She'd given me a gift after all—friendship, or perhaps companionship—whose duration was probably limited. I put a blanket over her, padded to Mama's bedroom, and fell asleep.

When I awoke, it was morning, and Laura was still deep asleep.

I dressed quietly and left. The snow had stopped and was already melting to slush. When I got downtown, I parked the Shark and went to Chinatown, breakfasting on pork buns and coffee. The other patrons were locals who had purchased the morning tabloids, taken out the horse racing programs, and left the rest behind. Their yammering was sing-song to my ears, and to drown them out I scanned the morning news.

A headline caught my eye: a shooting had left one person dead, an unknown Latin male. Beneath the headline was a picture of a van halfway smashed through a storefront I recognized as a restaurant across the street from my apartment building. The van was a commercial vehicle. Part of its sign was visible. It said "LOCO." The van driver had disappeared. He was a person of interest described as dark-haired and complected, about thirty, trim.

I thought of Laura's indigenous escort; not only had he survived a cartel hit but had whacked his would-be whacker.

He must have delivered our dinner to Laura. I wondered whether that was the extent of their relationship. I hoped not, because if he was an informant, my damsel in distress might well already be damaged beyond repair.

CHAPTER 28

"Mr. Montez, before we begin, these are the rules," Jenna Wilkinson said.

Montez nodded like an obedient choir boy.

"Successful cooperation requires two things," Wilkinson said. "The first is substantial assistance. You clear on that?"

"*Sí, Señora Fiscalía de la Nación.*"

"Ms. Wilkinson will do," she said.

"I hope my cooperation will be more than merely substantial, Ms. Wilkinson," Montez said humbly.

A sincere touch of resignation there, I thought. Perhaps Montez thought displaying defeatism was the right tone. Or maybe he was just tired. Probably hadn't slept during the lockdown. Got rousted from his cell and stood shivering in the underheated corridor while his few belongings were inspected. Toothbrush, jail-issue Bible, roll of toilet paper. The guards probably kept him there half the night. Underpaid correctional cops taking out their resentments on rich criminals was a fact of daily life in prisons.

"The second requirement is that your cooperation must be complete and truthful," Wilkinson said. "You can tell us ten things, nine of which are true, but the cooperation fails if you lie about or omit the tenth thing."

Montez nodded. "I understand."

Don't involve Laura, I prayed. I'd already told him the rules, but he'd suavely brushed me off, saying he'd deal with them when the time came. Now that dreaded time had arrived: when bad men bury their former friends.

"Another thing," Wilkinson said. "What you say here

cannot be used against you. But if you choose to go to trial and testify, they can and will be. Clear?"

"*Claro*," Montez said easily.

"Let's begin," she said.

"Santa Fe had a nice run," Kesey said. "Vertical combine. Turning leaf into powder, transporting it up here, sending the money back to your country. How was that done?"

I pictured a salt-bleached hollow sphere of compacted Toyotas and Fords bobbing in a tidal wash.

"I don't know," Montez said. "I was notified when money arrived. My job was keeping it secure."

I wondered why Montez was low-keying his participation. The more cooperation the better. So why not reveal everything? Or was his lie motivated by not wanting to ID who had assembled and sent the spheres?

Kesey was a vet whose Q&A style was rat-a-tat. Ask a question, get an answer, shift the subject.

"Your role was keeping the money secure until it was distributed, that right?"

"True," Montez said.

"Who distributed it?"

"I don't know," Montez said. "I'd get an anonymous message asking where it was."

"You were just a middleman who knew nothing from nothing, that what you're saying?"

"No, sir," Montez said. "I just didn't think it wise for anyone, including myself, to know everything. I believe it's called compartmentalization."

"Your Honduras information was correct," Kesey said. "But you get no credit because we already knew about it."

"From Don J, I imagine," Montez said. "Honduras was his territory."

"The cocaine laboratory information was also right, but we already knew about it too."

"From Lucho," Montez said.

"Speaking of the devil," Kesey said, his eyes drilling Montez. "Lucho died last night."

Montez winced. "I saw that coming," he said. "The poor fellow had heart problems."

"Like a jail-made shiv stuck in it," DiMaglio added.

Aha. So that was the incident that had triggered the lockdown. I had no illusions as to who had paid for the hit. Montez was eliminating the competition. But there was nothing I could do about it; I couldn't turn on a client based on mere suspicion.

"Any ideas as to who did it?" Kesey asked Montez.

"By cooperating, Lucho made many enemies."

"Including you, Martin," Kesey said.

"Oh, I know Lucho sat on me, but he was an old friend I'd never harm," Montez said. "I hear various people are arguing over who will run Santa Fe. I imagine one of them eliminated Lucho from consideration."

Leeds leaned forward. "Only you know where your money is hidden, correct?"

"Correct—before I was arrested," Montez said. "I don't know where it is now."

"What about your other assets?" Leeds asked.

"I assume you're referring to the counterfeit printing plate?" Montez asked.

A printing plate? That explained Secret Service's dibs on the case.

Leeds eyes were bright. "Where is it?"

"I have no idea," Montez said.

"Does Pacho's sister know?"

"She knows nothing at all."

He was protecting Laura. But no telling whether for love, or for love of money.

"The lab and Honduras," Kesey said. "You knew about them because you knew what Lucho and Don J were doing. But neither ever said anything about the African route that's the gateway to the European market. How'd you learn about the *Blue Atlantic*?"

"Santa Fe moved money for other groups too. In doing so I met many people."

"Name them," Kesey said.

Leeds cut in. "Stay with the money. You only dealt with people who delivered or picked up money. You know how to turn street tens and twenties into hundreds. You know whether it's real or counterfeit."

"I do," Montez said. "Counterfeiting is a growing problem that threatens the security of your country as it did the success of my former business."

"How did it threaten your business?" Leeds asked.

"The money I received often included a few counterfeits," Montez said. "But once a shipment of money is received, it's mixed with other shipments before being delivered to its owners. I have no way of knowing who gave the counterfeits. Even if I knew the source, they would deny it. I had to make good for it."

"What did you do with the money before it was picked up?" Leeds asked.

"Safeguarded it until the owners invested it."

"Invested it where?" Leeds asked eagerly.

"You people think my people are backward," Montez said. "The opposite is true. We don't trust the monetary system. People in Colombia invest in tangible things."

"Things?" Leeds asked. "Such as?"

"Land. Cattle. Emerald mines."

"So all you know about counterfeiting is that sometimes poor-you were victimized?"

"That's not all," Montez said. "I know who the actual counterfeiters are."

"Why didn't you say so before?" Leeds demanded.

"I was waiting for you to ask," Montez said.

CHAPTER 29

Kesey had suggested we break for lunch.
I had no appetite. Neither did Montez.
"Then chew on what you got for us," Kesey said, as he and DiMaglio followed Leeds and Wilkinson out. The door was locked. Montez and I were alone.
I was simmering. What to say to a man who was blackmailing both me and a woman I cared about? A man who'd threatened to kill me if I touched her? I wanted to knock his capped choppers out. To expose the stained stubs beneath. To humiliate the arrogant jerk. But I kept a lid on. I wanted to know how deep Laura was in it.
"What's with the bogus-money thing?" I asked.
"Secret Service does money cases," he said. "I knew that was why Leeds was in on my case. He wants a missing printing plate."
"But you waited until he asked."
"He's hungry, and I wanted him to salivate before feeding him."
"I advise you not to toy with these people," I said, although I wished he'd try because he'd fail. El Jugador thought the game was on his home field. He mistook the way Kesey jumped from topic to topic as an indicator that cooperation was a walk in knee-deep water. He had no idea Kesey was lurking beneath the surface, ready to bite his ass if he prevaricated.
"Sincerity without substance won't cut it," I said.
"I know missteps are fatal," he said. "Lucho forgot that."
"They'll be asking you more about Lucho."
"You're thinking I gave the order to kill him," he said. "I

didn't. Lucho may have been cooperating, but he was already plotting to regain Santa Fe when he got out. There are others with the same aspirations. Out with the old, in with the new, they think."

"Name them," I said.

"Don J, for one."

Hmm.... Was Don J still a rival, much less a witness, if Montez and or Vizcaino had his family? "There was a related murder last night," I said.

"I heard a Pollo Loco truck was at the scene," he said.

Forget about 5G cellular. The Colombian grapevine was 6G.

"The Upper East Side," I said. "Pollo Loco delivers that far?" I knew they didn't but was trolling him. I was curious about the indigenous dude. Was he DEA or Santa Fe? Was he keeping an eye on Laura, or about to harm her?

"You live there," he said. "Laura's staying with you."

I had no idea how he knew that; in my head echoed Gino Moskowitz's oft-repeated maxim about never underestimating a criminal mind. "Is she involved?" I asked.

"She's Pacho's sister. I care for her."

"Let her mother go."

He laughed. "Another victim of Laura's many charms. She's a changeable woman. Love me, love me not. *Te amo, no te amo.* You understand, *Doctora*?"

"No," I said.

"I don't have her mother. It's a fabrication of her mind. You see, Laura's quite ill. I've sent her to the finest clinics in the world. The diagnosis is always the same."

I didn't reply.

He laughed. "Always the listener, you. Always patiently waiting. Laura also keeps others waiting. Not intentionally, as you do. She doesn't even realize it."

"What's that supposed to mean?"

"She's severely bipolar."

CHAPTER 30

The afternoon proffer session was mostly show-and-tell.
Kesey fanned more photographs face-down on the table. "Turn them over one-by-one and tell us what you see," he said.

My take on Kesey had been of a bull in a china shop. Now I realized the brawler was meticulously purposeful. By having Montez react unprompted, he was testing his truthfulness. I was certain Montez would understand this and react with some semblance of truth—not the whole truth because doing so was not in his nature.

The backs of the photographs were exhibit-marked.

"Start with number one," Kesey said.

Montez turned the photograph. It was a mug shot of a middle-aged man whose expression was deadpan.

"Jorge Jaramillo," Montez said. "Don J. We grew up together."

"Skip the nostalgia, jerkoff," Kesey said. "That one."

It was another mug shot—a sad-eyed small man.

"Lucho," Montez said. "God rest his soul."

"Doubt he will," Kesey said. "That one."

The shot was slightly tilted as if taken surreptitiously by a phone camera. In it two men were seated at an outdoor café.

"The fat one is my lawyer, Arias," Montez said.

"What's his role?" Kesey asked.

Montez shrugged. "A butler."

"The other man?" Kesey asked.

"Victor Vizcaino. Another of my lawyers."

"All he does is lawyer?" Kesey asked.

Montez shrugged. "Victor's ambitious."

"Go to the next one," Kesey said.

It was a photo of two women. Slightly blurred as if a blow-up of a long-lens framed shot. One woman was Laura, smiling happily, with one arm around the other woman, an older version of her.

"Pacho's sister and their mother," Montez said.

"Tell us more about both of them," Kesey said.

"I haven't seen nor heard from Laura for some time. I believe her mother is living in the countryside outside of Bogota. She's ill, I hear."

"The last photograph?" Kesey asked.

The man in the photograph was behind the wheel of a yellow Pollo Loco van. It was the indigenous man who might or might not be an informant for the DEA, or for Santa Fe.

"Don't know him," Montez said.

Leeds held up a crisp new Franklin. "Let's get back to what's important."

Kesey rolled his eyes. Again, I divined the rift he and DiMaglio had spoken of. The usual federal inter-agency rivalry.

"This bill real, or not?" Leeds asked.

Montez considered. "It looks real."

"It is real because it was printed by a real U.S. mint plate," Leeds said. "You can tell that, can't you?"

"Yes, I can," Montez said.

"What else can you tell?"

"It's a counterfeit."

"The serial number?"

Montez nodded. "It has the same sequence ending in six-eight as on all the counterfeit bills."

"Finally," Leeds said. "This is your one and only chance, Martin. You need to get us the plate."

"I'm working on it," Montez said. "It's hard for me to communicate from the SHU. Take me out of the SHU so I can use a phone and I'll find it."

"Communicate through your lawyers," Wilkinson said. "Get the plate and *then* you're out of the SHU, and maybe on your way to a cooperation agreement."

Before leaving 500 Pearl, I made a restroom pit stop.

My mirror image had changed. Despite the stressful day, my features looked … softer. Or maybe it was just my self-perception which had mellowed. Because of Laura. Montez had lied; she was not bipolar. I knew the real person and trusting her felt good.

The gorilla was waiting for me in the hallway.

"*El Jugador* played Leeds good," Kesey said.

"You think so?" I said. "Here's hoping."

"Bullshit. You don't wish him well."

"End of conversation," I said.

"Here's a head's-up, counselor," he said. "We both know silk scarves don't take prints, but the cotton labels on their back do. There was a faint print on your scarf's label. Not enough for DEA forensics to clarify, but the spooks in D.C. have magical mystery devices that can pick up an impression we can't. Even as we speak, they're scoping your scarf for a print. What do you have to say about that?"

"Have a nice day," I said, starting away.

"Regards to Laura," he called after me.

My heart leapt into my throat—I hadn't seen that coming. Bad enough my every step would be under a microscope. Worse now that Kesey hinted Laura was among the tawdry suspects.

What should I do? What could I do?

CHAPTER 31

The proffer left me depressed.
I saw the world through a dark fog. In Chinatown's restaurant windows, dead ducks hung like omens of misfortune. Little Italy tenements, where secret oaths were once sworn, were now condos occupied by people who made fortunes dealing, wheeling, and often stealing money that didn't really exist. Soho and Noho and NoMad were just tired old 'hoods with glitzy new cachet. In midtown's high towers, suited scoundrels overlooked the city they looted.

"Cool it," I told myself. Stay positive. Ignore the insignificant. Forget the sad state of society. Chill.

My phone buzzed. It was Arias.

"We must meet now," he said.

I didn't want to. Could be I'd pushed Montez too far and he was planning to push back harder. Adding to that, Arias and I were both under investigation. If our meeting became known, it could be taken as collaborating with illegal intent. Conspiring.

"I'm unavailable," I said.

"It has to do with her."

"Where are you?"

"Outside your office," he said. "I don't like being in the street. Buzz me in."

"I'm not there," I said. "Wait, I'm on my way."

"*Rápido, Doctora*," he said.

I was on Midtown Madison Avenue, my office just blocks away. But then I ran into traffic backed up behind a truck, its flashing caution lights reflecting off a "Dig We Must" sign. My office was on a westbound street on the other side of the truck.

Frick it.

I wrong-wayed an eastbound street, turned at the corner and wrong-wayed a downtown avenue. I saw the startled look on a bus driver's face. I veered around him and turned into my street, passing a guy seated on a cycle idling at the corner. He wore a black visored helmet and a black ski mask.

I pulled to the curb and cut my lights.

Down the street I saw Arias outside my office building, looking toward the far corner he expected me to round.

I was troubled. Somewhat by Arias's urgency, more so by the biker. The classic Colombian hit was a drive-by cyclist.

My phone buzzed. Arias again. "¿Qué pasó?"

"Traffic," I said. "Just wait there."

I saw the biker cross the street to a car parked opposite my office building. When he bent to the driver's window, it rolled down. Victor Vizcaino was behind the wheel. He listened, nodded, motioned for Arias to remain at my building.

It was the classic assassination set-up; Arias the bait, the biker the fisherman, me the fish.

I'd ditched my Sig, but not all my resources. Taped in the back of the Shark's glove compartment was a little .25 semi-automatic that a client had left in my office, a throwaway gun with a taped grip and a filed-off serial number. Seven rounds in the clip and a tracer in the chamber to show them the way home.

If I proceeded to the office, Arias would text the biker to do me. If I backed up, the same result. I called Arias.

"I'm nearing the corner," I said. "You'll see me come into the street in a couple seconds."

Moments later the bike started up. I flicked the .25's safety off. Then called Arias.

"Almost there," I said. "Turning in now."

I saw him make a call and lowered my window, positioning myself. From behind I heard the motorcyclist burn rubber. The .25 was notoriously inaccurate past ten feet, but he would pass hardly a foot away.

I aimed at his center mass, but at the last moment, I lacked enough malice and instead fired at his motorcycle. Didn't matter. The tracer round was a green streak that ignited an orange explosion, sending him head over heels and the now-flaming, overturned bike scraping along the street, showering sparks like fireworks....

CHAPTER 32

Fireworks....
I remembered a long-ago summer evening. Pops, my sometime surrogate father, had taken me to the Fourth of July extravaganza above the East River. Eagerly, I'd perched atop a railing with Pops's strong hands securing me as I gaped at the rockets bursting in air, their reflections splintering on the dark water. Pops. I hadn't seen him in years until I'd consulted him, and I wanted to see him again, get to know him better. I'd run away from my past, and he was the only link to it.

Fireworks ... sparks shot up from the bike, still ablaze down the street. The biker lay still. I backed up to the avenue and entered its traffic flow.

I sped past my office—Arias gawking at the wreck—turned onto the uptown avenue, pulled over to the curb, cut the Shark's big V-8, got out, and began walking. After making sure I was alone, I wiped the .25s butt on my pants, let it fall from my hand, and kicked it into a sewer. I continued to my office's street, and paused at the corner, peering around the edge.

No sign of Arias. Vizcaino's car was gone.

The street had been empty when I'd shot the cycle, but now people were staring at the scene: the still-smoking bike, the cyclist sprawled as only the dead can lay. I walked to my building and elevatored to my floor, unlocked and entered my office, and locked the door behind me. Silence but for my inner voice: you just killed a man—a*gain.*

Shaking and shook, I downed two valiums. Impatient for them to kick in, I rummaged in an odds-and-ends cabinet, found a gift-wrapped Buffalo Grass vodka a client had given me on a long-ago Christmas, and drank straight from the bottle.

Better. But not totally. I kicked back on the couch where visiting clients sit. *Criminals, like me*, I thought. The valium joined the vodka, and I closed my eyes.

I had a dream.

It began in a dark limbo that gradually became a gray haze. From somewhere beyond my depth of field, a hand appeared and moved to my face. Behind it a gold pendant hung.

I bolted awake.

Something had disturbed me—a sound?—from the hallway. I put my ear to the door. Heard water splash and a squeegee squeak. It was the cleaning woman, mopping.

The dream was still fresh in my mind, and now I realized it wasn't a dream, but my fragmented memory reconsolidating. I'd seen a hand, Cleo's gold pendant around Laura's neck ... and realized it was Laura who'd put cocaine to my nose, Laura who'd awakened me from my burundanga haze, Laura who'd saved me from being arrested for Pacho's murder....

The orphan drug was working its magic after all. I sensed more lost moments would soon surface. Wanting to hurry them along, I swallowed the second orphan pill and glanced at my watch.

After ten.

Laura would be wondering where I was. I tried calling her to say I was on my way home, but her phone was off. Like me, she liked to isolate.

We were so alike.

When I left my office, the street was deserted again.

All that remained of what had happened was a charred spot on the roadway. I stepped around it.

I drove home with one eye on the rearview. Squared a few random blocks. Concluded I wasn't being followed. When I reached my street, above the bare treetops my terrace was lit as if by a candle in a window. Laura's vigil for me, I thought.

CHAPTER 33

From outside my apartment, I heard Christmas music within.

Laura must have seen me from the terrace, for the door was ajar, as if inviting me in. I took out the gold earrings—her gift. I'd doubted she'd had time enough to get me anything, but that was alright; all I wanted for Christmas was her friendship. I entered the apartment and stopped, gaping.

"Jingle bells, jingle bells ..."

The music was coming from my radio. It was lying on its side, cracked but still croaking. The kitchen cabinet doors yawned, their contents strewn. The place looked as if torn apart by a hurricane.

Or by searchers executing a warrant.

Or Vizcaino, for darker reasons.

"Laura?" I said. "Laura...?"

"Jingle all the way ..."

Mama's bedroom door was closed. Was Laura in there? Was she okay? Was she alone? I went to the door and stood there listening.

"On a one horse open ..."

I lowered my shoulder and slammed it against the bedroom door.

Unlocked, it swung open and I rushed inside.

No Laura—or sign she'd been there.

The only signs were of a struggle.

Or a frenzied search? Or both?

The bed was turned over, the mattress ripped apart, Mama's precious wardrobe strewn. If the DEA had executed a search warrant, they'd have taped a copy to the front door. Maybe they had, but in my haste to enter, I hadn't seen it. I went to the front door.

No warrant.

While I'd been dreaming in my office, Vizcaino had snatched Laura. But given how the place was ransacked, they'd wanted more than her.

I went into the closet and removed the wall panel, opening the safe behind it. The suitcase was still there. I unlocked it and opened the lid. The money remained.

Had they been searching for it? It didn't make sense—just days ago they'd given it to me. But if not the money, what else were they searching for?

They. Was Laura among *them*?

Had she been playing me all along? Did she, too, think I possessed Pacho's secret? Did she want it for herself? Or for Montez, in exchange for her mother? She'd promised to tell me all, but had she lied?

My heart said, "no way," but my head said, "count the ways."

Laura knew I'd be occupied proffering Montez. Afterward, they'd have taken him across the rat maze to the SHU, where he'd use the toilet grapevine to ask for someone with telephone access to call Vizcaino and say I'd just left.

Vizcaino would've told Arias to arrange a meet at my office while he set up the cyclist to hit me. Knowing I wouldn't be returning, Laura had ransacked my place.

I didn't want to believe it. But whatever the truth was, I had to know why they'd wanted to kill me. More importantly, I had to make myself scarce, then figure out what was going on and what to do about it.

"Have yourself a merry little Christmas …"

I figured I'd bunk in a hotel until things blew over.

Hole up there and stay away from the office. Catch up on my other work via Zoom. Where to begin?

I had a pending motion to dismiss on a 500-kilo case; the government's response had been weak, and a strong reply might gain a dismissal … or maybe concentrate on pressing for a concession on a stash house plea negotiation, or, or—

Who was I kidding? The only important thing on my agenda was untangling myself from the Montez case—and maybe Laura as well, whoever or whatever she was. The angry girl who'd shunned me at the cemetery? The sweet kid who'd danced on my snowy terrace? Or was she really both, with a bipolar smile that suddenly transformed to bared teeth?

I was about to check into the hotel when my phone rang. The caller didn't say his name and didn't have to. I recognized Vizcaino's snicker.

"You're fast," he said.

"Where's Laura?" I asked.

"With you in a hotel? Maybe I'll be your room service." He whinnied a laugh and the line went dead.

I left the hotel lobby. As always, New York was bustling, and I knew Vizcaino might be a hidden face in the crowd. I needed to go elsewhere. A place he'd never find me.

But first, to Gino's apartment.

"We'll use these to communicate," I told Gino, handing him one of two throwaway phones. "I'm forwarding my personal phone to you," I said. "Be my answering service. As a rule, just say I'm out of town you don't know where—with one exception. If a woman named Laura calls, three-way her to me."

"You running, or chasing?" Gino asked.

"Running in circles chasing my tail."

"Must be tiring. You look like shit."

"Up to my chin in a sea of it."

"My advice? Don't make waves."

I looked out the window. I'd scanned the parked cars when I'd entered. No new ones had arrived.

"All clear, I take it," Gino said. "Are you thinking they'll be back?"

It wasn't a question, and I didn't reply.

"You don't know where you're going," he said.

"No," I said. "So long as its elsewhere."

"Stay in touch. Don't just nod, say it."

"I'll stay in touch," I said.

"If you don't want to be found, your phone's not the only thing you need to change," he said. "Toll and highway cameras are part of Big Brother's tracking system, which is easily hacked by those possessing the know-how. I assume the folks you're concerned with are technically sophisticated?"

"They're still in the Middle Ages," I said. "But they buy what they lack."

"Check your wheels for a GPS," he said, taking out a used car license plate. "That there's my last year's plate." he said. "The year tag's too small to be recorded."

The license plate had a handicap imprint.

"It's a wonderful life," Gino said.

CHAPTER 34

I drove by night.

I took I-95 South through New Jersey. Kept below the speed limit to avoid a stop, fearing Kesey had verified my print and put out a BOLO—be on the lookout—alert for me, although it seemed unlikely a verification would've triggered a warrant so quickly, and even if it had, my plates wouldn't match. And I'd carefully checked—no GPS had been planted in the Shark.

Ahead, red bubble lights flashed. For a moment I thought it was a cop stop for me, but as I neared, I saw a generic midsize pulled over, a Black family inside while a NJ State Trooper wearing the shiny tall boots and visored cap endemic to the Waffen-SS wrote them a citation. I would've bet the million stashed in my trunk that they hadn't broken any law except Jim Crow's.

Unlike me. The orphan drug was working sporadically. Between the intermittent red bubble flashes that lingered on my retina, I saw Pacho's vacant face, his leg dripping the same too-vivid red.

Once past suburban Jersey, the interstate was unlit, and the Shark's beams ate up the inky blackness. I kept glancing in the rearview. Traffic was light but my guilt weighed heavily.

After an hour, I exited the interstate for state and county roads less traveled. Passed towns I'd never heard of and continued toward a place I knew not, so long as it was far from the demons I was fleeing.

As the first gray of dawn seamed the sky, I ran out of road. Ahead was Delaware Bay. All around were the depopulated remainders of what looked to once have been a bustling community. But hard times and a polluted fishery had reduced it to a near-empty strip mall and an old gas station, a one-pump affair outside a dilapidated frame house. A frayed sign taped to the pump advertised a fishing cabin for rent.

No one was around. After a few minutes, I tooted my horn and a towheaded, large-eared kid came out of the house.

"Please fill me up," I said.

"Fill up," he said. "Yah."

I thumbed at the cabin for-rent sign. "Tell me about it," I said.

"Yah," he said. "Tell."

I asked him if the proprietor was around. He nodded like a bobblehead doll, and I saw a five-finger-shaped slap mark on his cheek. I thought either the kid was dumb, or someone had slapped him so hard his brain was scrambled.

I knocked on the door. Waited. Knocked again. The door opened and a man with the slurred speech and snaggle teeth of an oxy-junkie glowered at me.

"I'm interested in your rental," I said.

"End of the road," he said. "Ten a day."

I peeled off a couple of hundred in twenties—flashing a Franklin hereabouts would draw attention—and drove a half-mile to the rental, which, both figuratively and literally, was at the end of the road.

The cabin was a falling-down shack whose sole amenity was an equally collapsing outdoor john. Both were perched above the high-water line of a pebbly beach where a jetty was crumbling into the murky bay. There was no electricity or hot water but there was a wood stove, and the place was broom-clean, somewhat.

All in all, none of the comforts of home but none of the discomforts of being home either. And a perfect place to hide.

I went to the strip mall and provisioned-up with canned goods and detergents. There was a general store with a closed sign on the door, but a light was on inside. When I knocked, a teenage kid let me in. I bought a sleeping bag, flashlights, candles, and some other stuff I thought I might need. I wasn't an outdoorsman, but hoped to qualify as a survivalist, so I asked the kid if they sold guns.

"Long rifles only," he said. "But hunting season's over."

"Rifle will do me fine," I said. "I like plinking."

"Sold all the rifles during the close-out sale," he said. "Maybe Billy will sell you his BB gun, but I doubt it. Don't think he gives a shit about the gun, but he likes saying "Beebee, beebee, beebee."

A pellet gun wasn't much of a weapon but at least it looked like one, and who knew what lurked in the night outside my lonely place?

"Who's Billy?" I asked.

"The duh-duh-dummy whose old man owns the gas station," he said.

I thanked him and left.

I spent the rest of the day shack-cleaning. I gave the john a twice-over. It was propped up on cinder blocks and the crawl space beneath apparently was someone's hidey-hole: a ragged Easter bunny, a faded photograph of a woman holding hands with a big-eared little kid, an assortment of other mementos, and a cigar box filled with BBs.

Billy's stuff.

Almost done. Before kicking back, I had one more thing to do, but wanted to be sure I wasn't a blip in someone's long lenses, so I waited until dark.

I needed a place to hide my million.

The Shark was too obvious. The shack was devoid of nooks and crannies. The john was too spare. But the jetty's broken timbers were jumbled, and doubtful a searcher would think I'd hide money amidst damp decay that would eventually turn it to mold.

There was a gibbous moon that night.

Dim enough for me to see close-up, but too dim for me to be seen from a distance. I'd purchased a shovel and waterproof trash bags. I took them and the suitcase to the jetty. I set the suitcase down and began transferring the Franklins from it to the trash bags. It took a few minutes, but I wanted to be sure they were secure. One packet had become loose, and I put on my phone light and straightened the bills—

"Same, same, same," a voice said.

Startled, I turned. Saw Billy, the slow kid from the gas station, looking at the bills in my hand from over my shoulder. My instinct was to chase him away, but I didn't want to escalate the moment to something memorable.

"Yes," I said. "All same."

"Same all bad." His gaze, fixed on the bills, was intense. "Same bad."

"No, all good," I said.

"All bad," he said.

"Why all bad?"

He reached to the top bill and put his finger on the serial number. "Same bad."

"It's a serial number," I said. "All the bills have one." I riffled to the next bill. "See?"

"Same," he said. "Bad, bad."

"No, each bill has a different number," I said. "See, this one ends in six-eight, the next one ends in ... six-eight...?"

Disbelieving my eyes, I turned to the next bill. Its serial number ended in six-eight, and so did the next ... it was inescapable. The Franklins were printed by the same plate with the same serial number as the counterfeits Montez had acknowledged when proffered.

My million was in bogus money.

Los Xs had killed Pacho and drugged me to face the consequences. Had Montez—with or without Laura's knowledge—tried to frame me as a counterfeiter to enhance his cooperation? A catch like me would satiate Agent Leeds's obsession with counterfeiting.

"Same number, bad," Billy said.

I dug myself a hole close by the shack, filled it with the not-so-funny money, and set it afire. In the reflected firelight, Billy's eyes no longer seemed vacant, but possessed of an immense intelligence. The boy was not disabled, I realized, but blessed and cursed with a mind different from most; a mind his father lacked the heart and mind to accept.

The bills burned brightly. A bonfire of my vanities, I thought ruefully. I'd been a blind fool.

"Bad," Billy said.

CHAPTER 35

"You promised ... stay ... in touch," Gino said.
 A storm was raging, and its atmospheric disturbance segmented Gino's telephone voice. "Say again," I said.
 "A month since ... left ... but haven't."
 I hadn't called Gino because I didn't want any distracting discussions; he'd call if he thought it necessary. I hoped that was the case. It was.
 "The exception to your rule occurred," he said.
 Laura called? "Why didn't you three-way us?"
 "Sounded as if her failure to communicate earlier was dictated by untimely circumstances. Just a hello, then hold on a minute, then can't talk now, and a hang up."
 Untimely circumstances? DEA? Vizcaino?
 "Did she say she'll call back?"
 "Keep your phone close," he said. "You also got a lot of other calls. Angry clients wanting to know why you abandoned them."
 I sighed inwardly. The practice I'd taken so long to build was now in freefall.
 "Also, a call from a DEA agent named Kesey," Gino said. "Said you'd know what about."
 I sure did. Kesey wouldn't call if the CIA's super-secret scanning device had come up negative-me on the scarf's label print. Good fellow that he wasn't, he'd let me twist in the wind. Ergo, he'd called to flaunt my print as a positive.
 Or had he?
 The CIA bowties were using their secretive tech scanning device for arcane security work; doubtful they'd allow their

cowboy cousins to use it in a cockamamie drug murder case. There was no deep analysis. Kesey had conjured it to con me.

And if the scarf's label actually bore my print? Easily explained. See, for Pacho's daughter's *quinceañera*, I'd given it to him as my gift to her, okay? *Sigh.* Interact with criminals and by osmosis acquire their mentality.

"By the way," Gino said. "I got the real names of the four parties you mentioned."

I was so relieved knowing Laura was reaching out to me that it took a moment to refocus on the four inmates I suspected were cooperating about the alleged threat Montez had made against AUSA Mizrahi.

I couldn't care less. Montez had tried to frame me and, failing that, to kill me. I no longer felt obliged to help him. The opposite. I wished him the worst. Hoped he was losing his mind in the SHU—just as I was losing mine in the bleak middle of nowhere.

Five in the afternoon and already dark. Quiet except for wind whistling through the cracks in the ceiling. Last person I'd seen was Billy on the night I burned the million bucks that weren't. I wondered how the kid was doing. Same old same old I supposed. Getting poked and slapped around, but too focused on minutiae to notice the world was dumping on him.

Me too, Billy.

I went out to the Shark, started it up, turned on the heat, and plugged in my phone to be sure it was fully charged. Then I reclined the seat and waited, my mind a blank slate, eyes wide shut.

Lightning veined the darkness, its sudden crack jolting still another unit of lost memory—the crack of my Sig, Pacho's final, disbelieving expression as—

My phone rang.

"She's on the line," Gino said. "Talk, I won't listen."

"Laura?" I said. Silence. "Laura, you there?"

"I'm a fool," she sobbed. "I believed in you. You weren't there when I needed you. I went to your office. People were saying there had been a shooting and there was a body on the street. I nearly died thinking it was you."

What could I say? That I'd been cooped in the office trying to regain my memory of her brother's murder?

"I thought maybe you went home but you weren't there, and everything was torn apart, and I thought they took you and it was my fault because I put you in danger. Suddenly, you were lost...."

"And now I'm found," I said.

"It's me who's lost," she said.

"Tell me where you are," I said. "I'll go to you."

"No. Yes. I don't know," she said. "I won't be able to call for a while."

The connection broke. Whether by electromagnetic interference or Laura's unwillingness to continue, I had no idea. My first thought was to find her. Then I reconsidered whether I should try. Whether Laura worked for Santa Fe or was their unwitting dupe, she well might be bait in a trap set for me.

The wind was gusting and the Shark gently swayed, like a cradle. Beyond its streaked windows, the world was pure chaos, but as the heater's air washed over me, I fell asleep.

It was still dark out when my phone rang again.

"Montez sent you a CorrLinks," Gino said.

Didn't make sense. The CorrLinks system allowed federal inmates to email with approved persons, and as Montez's lawyer, I was one. But that amenity was only available to inmates in general population. SHU inmates were strictly incommunicado. And Wilkinson had made it clear that Montez was remaining in the SHU unless and until he provided actionable cooperation.

But I was his lawyer, and without my consent—which hadn't been requested, much less given—Montez could not be proffered unless I was present, and without proffering he could not pass the cooperation info I knew Arias was feeding him. Yet if he was in general pop he had. Somehow.

"Tell me what he wrote," I said.

"'Come see me. I'm not pleased with my new attorney. I want to fire him and rehire you.'"

I *knew* he had another lawyer. The guy must have emerged from the shadows, poached Montez by making promises he couldn't keep, then proffered him, obviously successfully, since Montez was out of the SHU.

"The rest is kinda cryptic," Gino said. "Return to me."

"Reply," I said. "Tell him, 'Yes.'"

CHAPTER 36

That night, I couldn't sleep. I lay awake listening to a buoy bell ringing out in the shipping channel. When the water is choppy, the bell rings clearly, and I would count the peals as if they were sheep leaping a fence until I lapsed into slumber.

On nights when the bay is calm, the bell is so faint that I wonder if it is real, or a subconscious warning for whom it next would toll.

But tonight, a storm roiled the bay, and the bell was so distinct I knew it was real, its bobbing rhythm a lure leading my leaping sheep to slaughter.

I bolted awake.

There was a car nearing on the county blacktop. Strange in this forgotten place at this early hour. I stepped into my jeans and went out on the porch. In the dawn light, headlamps shone, their beams growing brighter. This did not augur well.

Only two entities might be looking for me: Kesey's DEA group, coming to arrest me, or Montez's *Xs,* coming to kill me.

Barefoot, I ran across the pebble beach and hid beneath the jetty. I heard the car turn into my shell driveway. Its engine stopped; a door opened and closed. An older man got out and took shape in the dim light as he approached the shack. I could not see his face, but the open way he revealed himself suggested neither cop nor criminal, but someone familiar to me.

He stopped by the Shark and trailed his hand across its fins. Then he turned toward the house and called my name.

I emerged from beneath the jetty. "If I'd have known you were coming, I'd've baked a cake, Pops."

"If I had known you were living like this, I would've brought one," he said. "Handicap license plate?"

"Subterfuge," I said. "What's your reason for coming to the middle of nowhere, Pops?"

"Just a follow-up visit on a patient," he said. "Old times still forgotten?"

"I thought I was making progress, but not really," I said. "How did you find me?"

"I'm vice chairman of the Society of Honorary Police Surgeons of the City of New York," he said. "A cop doc. When fellas in my waiting room talk trade, I hear things."

"Cut the sphinx act," I said. "No cop would know where I am. I didn't even know I'd be here until I was."

He shrugged. "Checked your Caddy for GPS bugs?"

"Double-checked," I said. "Talk to me, Pops."

"I have a cop patient who knows where you are," he said. "There's an AirTag in your car."

"He shared its tracking with you?"

He winked. "When he stripped to be examined, I looked at the memo pad in his jacket."

I opened the trunk and there was the backpack Laura had toted from Akron. An AirTag had been tucked into a side pocket. But the DEA wouldn't have known about it unless Laura had told them—maybe inadvertently via Indio?

In any case, the DEA had not come for me, probably to give me rope enough for me to tie myself to Santa Fe. I wouldn't. After burning the bogus money, I'd gathered the ashes and dumped them in the bay, so conspiring in a counterfeit beef was unprovable.

Still, DiMaglio had a wild hair up his tush about nailing me. Would he find another link between me and Pacho's murder? Failing that, would he manufacture one? Maybe.

"Let's move on to why I'm here," Pops said. "Before your present client became *jefe* of Santa Fe, he commanded a paramilitary *bloque* financed by wealthy landowners to protect people from Marxist guerrillas. They did so by wiping out entire villages of peasants, supposedly to deny the guerillas safe haven, but in truth to take over their drug routes. Your client and his number two personally executed hundreds of people. After one such incident, a stream ran red with blood for days."

"That's what you came to tell me? Why?"

"So you know what you're up against."

"How do you know this?" I asked.

"The blue grapevine," he said.

I didn't buy that. Beloved cop-doc or not, the DEA wouldn't share this with Pops. But they were quite capable of planting the story in Pops's mind and sending him to share it with me just to get me nervous.

"How's Kesey?" I asked pointedly.

Pops shook his head. "Forget him. There's only one thing that should be on your mind."

"Enlighten me," I said.

"Should you continue to be involved with this matter, you're going to find yourself doing things you never anticipated."

"I'm no longer involved in it," I said.

But I knew he was right. I was.

CHAPTER 37

When I got to New York, Gino had been asleep before I invaded his home, fractured his peace, and spilled my feelings.

"You haven't been reading your ECF bounces because you left your phone with me," he said. "If you had, you'd know that Montez did in fact retain another lawyer."

"But in his CorrLinks message, Montez said he wanted to fire his new lawyer and rehire me."

"Newsflash," he said. "Criminals lie. In any event, since you never asked to be relieved, you're still Montez's counsel of record. Or I should say, co-counsel?"

"Who's the bottom-feeder that came in?" I asked.

"Guy with the unfortunate name of Smukler."

"Never heard of him," I said. "A nobody."

"Well, he knows about you. Left a couple voicemails asking when you'd be available to visit your client with him."

"When I visit Montez, it'll be alone."

"So you are staying on the case?"

I nodded morosely. I was staying because I needed to know if Laura had witnessed Pacho's murder. Aw, heck, I was also staying because she really did need someone to look after her.

Gino handed me a sheet of paper on which four names and corresponding inmate numbers were typed. "These are the true names of the guys Montez said overheard him threatening Mizrahi. So do what you need to do. Me, I'm going back to sleep."

"While you do, let me use your computer," I said.

"So long as you don't accept cookies," he said, rolling

into his bedroom. The door closed and then reopened, and he gave me a thumbs-up.

"Nail the bastards," he said.

CHAPTER 38

I contemplated the world as Gino saw it on his wide, curved-screen monitor.

Compared to my old, outmoded computer, his machine was a sixth-gen stealth fighter. The screen was covered with unfamiliar icons, portals to worlds I couldn't imagine; its keyboard studded with buttons resembling a control panel that directed mysterious functions.

Intimidating.

Took a while, but I managed to hunt-and-peck my way into the PACER system, and from there into the SDNY site, where I searched Montez's case. Its caption now included Montez's new lawyer, Morton Smukler, Esq.

I went into Google and got a visual of Smukler's office building. It was a forlorn two-story affair whose ground floor was occupied by a bodega. I magnified and saw a sign on the second-floor door with lettering that said, "Law office of Morton Smukler," and beneath that, "Personal Injury Cases," and below that, "Notary Public," all in Spanish and English.

My puzzlement grew. Why would a smart operator like Montez retain a jerkwater lawyer who probably had never done a federal criminal case before? To be sure, I went into the PACER site and searched Smukler.

I had pegged him wrong. He had four pending cases in the Eastern District of New York. Brooklyn.

Still, I figured they were nothingburger cases. Smukler wasn't even close to the major leagues.

Wrong again.

His four pending cases were fairer than middling. He

represented mid-level players in multi-defendant indictments that alleged trafficking impressive numbers of kilos and dirty money.

Hmm. I was in a business where everybody knows, or knows of, everybody. Yet I'd never heard of Smukler. Could be he'd haphazardly connected to a source of work, a referrals-for-money source. That happens. But why would a productive source choose to work with a low-level lawyer?

Then it hit me.

The names of his four active clients were more than familiar: they were the same four who'd been with Montez when he'd allegedly threatened Mizrahi.

I don't believe in coincidences, but I do believe there are lawyers who will do anything if the price is right. Like sell clients' cooperation. Like coordinate phony remembrances of Montez having voiced a threat.

I thought on this until a plan blossomed.

Wilkinson was ambitious. She knew scalping a dirty lawyer was a major win. She'd hear me out, say nothing, but quietly activate Kesey to take Smukler down by breaking the four. The threat would be gone, and Montez would get his cooperation agreement.

I had mixed feelings about that. The lawyer in me was all about winning, but it ate at me that I was saving Montez's ass. Something else nibbled at me: who was the source who put Smukler in the cases?

I reviewed each of the four defendants' dockets. Their co-defendants were represented by the usual suspect: high-priced lawyers. In fact, a well-known and largely despised Miami-based thief named Joachim Paz repped the lead clients in all four cases, clients who were the four guys' bosses.

It was a too-familiar scam. Paz had not only sold himself as the bosses' lawyer, he'd convinced them it was in his interest to control their co-defendants by having him select their lawyers. Probably he'd charged a hefty fee for each, pocketed most of it and hired grunts—like Smukler—to do his scut work. Still, he'd personally rep a *jefe* like Montez. So why had he given him to Smukler?

That stumped me. Re-think time.

I went back into Montez's case and found the answer. Paz couldn't represent Montez because he already represented one of his partners, Don J. A clear and present conflict, so he had made Smukler Montez's lawyer in name only, but Paz was Montez's shadow counsel.

Aha!

Paz's ultimate score was representing Montez. Of course, he couldn't so long as Don J was in the case. But maybe, just maybe, Don J would end up like Lucho—knifed in the back.

I saw Paz's grand scheme now.

He'd initiated the alleged threat in order to exacerbate Montez's situation. Then planned to squeeze a big fee from Montez by promising to deflate it.

He could do so with a single call. He'd instruct Smukler to undercut the four hapless fools accusing Montez. Then he'd secretly continue mentoring Montez, lengthening his cooperation, while I remained his lawyer in name only, thereby also becoming a fall gal if things went south.

I wasn't about to let that happen.

I met with Kesey, DiMaglio, and Wilkinson in her office overlooking Police Plaza.

I'd prepared a simple Venn diagram. Boxed each of the threat witnesses on the perimeter by name and nickname. Drew lines connecting all to an interior box labeled MORTON SMUKLER. Drew a line connecting Smukler to another box labeled JOACHIM PAZ. Drew lines connecting all.

I handed them the Venn, then set down PACER-generated documents that were the captions and lists of retained attorneys in each of the four witnesses' indictments.

"The four witnesses are all midsize players in large indictments," I said. "All are represented by Smukler. Their bosses are all represented by Paz. It's obvious Paz put Smukler in the cases to coordinate the witnesses' threat testimony."

"That's *your* conclusion," DiMaglio said.

"It is what it is or isn't," Wilkinson said. "I'll take it to my supervisor. Up to him to decide whether to have another AUSA look into it."

"No way," Kesey said. "Why delegate part of our case?

We can find out if the threat's phony on our own. If it is, we'll take Paz down. Guy knows where a lot of skeletons are buried; it'll be us who gets to dig 'em up."

"I dunno, dude," DiMaglio said. "Dirty lawyers are a sideshow. Let somebody else deal with them. We got our hands full with Santa Fe."

Wilkinson seemed unsure. She had enough on her plate with the Santa Fe case. But the last thing she wanted was to overrule a senior DEA supervisor.

"You sure you want this, K?" she asked.

"I'm ..." Kesey launched into a paroxysm of deep coughing. His face tuned red, and for a moment he seemed on the verge of passing out, but then he regained himself and drew a deep breath. "... fucking positive," he said.

CHAPTER 39

I took my time signing the visit book at MCC.
Pretended my pen was dry and fumbled for another. The duplicity was overkill because the correction guard manning the front desk was too busy dealing with family visitors to check on me. I looked through the sign-in book and found the sign-ins two pages back when Smukler had visited Montez with another lawyer whose name was deliberately scrawled, but I now recognized three letters: P-A-Z.

My visit was to curb Montez's enthusiasm with doubt. Let him know he was being played. Tell him Paz wasn't there to help him but was spying for his client, Don J.

But I had to be careful. It went against my grain to inform on other lawyers, but I was duty-bound to protect Montez. It wasn't the kind of thing I wanted known and hoped that when the crap hit the fan, I'd be out of sight and mind.

But Kesey had other plans for me. After our meeting he buttonholed me on the way out of the building.

"We're going to nail Smukler and Paz, sis," he said.

"We? That's your job, big guy," I'd said.

"You're right. I misspoke. Not we, you."

"Had a late night at Montecristo, huh?"

"Every night. But I'm serious. You."

"Why the concern for those creeps?"

"Same as you," he said. "Laura."

Ow. Sucker punched by a palooka.

"I'll be in touch," he said.

Montez wasn't happy.

"I sent you a message," he snapped.

"Got it," I said. "You want me."

"Do not disappear on me again."

"I want Laura," I said.

"I don't have her."

"I don't believe you."

"You're a woman, yet you chase her as if you're a man," he said. "I feel sorry for you."

It wasn't easy but I let the slur slide. "Joachim Paz is scamming you," I said.

He shrugged. "So what? You think I don't know he's a snake? Like you."

"So why take me back?" I asked.

"I like the way you think."

My butt is beautiful, but I don't like it being kissed. I knew Montez had another reason: he wanted the unknown something he thought I had or knew about.

It was my ante in his game.

"Paz told you about Don J's Honduras cooperation," I said. "That gave you credibility enough to get your foot in the cooperation door even though the government wanted to slam it."

"With your help. Thank you."

I made an educated guess: "Paz isn't just spying for you. He's also spying on you—for Don J."

"Of course he is. Paz loves taking money from everyone," he said. "The point being, I have far more money than Don J. When this is over, Paz is a dead man. For now, I keep my enemies close. I'm beginning to think you may be among them."

"I want Laura."

"Maybe she doesn't want you," he said. "She's unpredictable. The bipolarity. One day she shares your bed, the next she won't share a word. One day I ask her for the help I need and she claims, quite convincingly, that she doesn't have it. I ask again the following day and she insults me by saying you have it. I didn't think that was true. But now I'm wondering. Do you have it?"

"I don't know what you're talking about."

He gave me a long, hard look. Nodded as if he'd decided something. "Laura will help me. Just like you, she'll have no choice."

His veiled threats were seriously pissing me off. I couldn't let him slide home safely. I had to establish my own protocol. He throws me a curveball; I kick him in the gonads.

"From now on, I want my money wired to my bank," I said. I knew he couldn't wire it because he'd have to legalize the money, and doing so would reveal its illegitimate source.

"That's very difficult," he said. "You understand."

"I don't give a rat," I said. "Sell some cattle."

"You're nothing but a *gringa* bitch," he spat.

"Who holds your future in her hands," I said.

CHAPTER 40

Once more, I reexamined the whole megillah.

Montez: What hold did he have over Laura? He'd said she would do his bidding. She already had done so by keeping me on his case by delivering his bogus money from Akron.

Akron, Ohio: Small city an hour south of Cleveland. Population 189,000. Median income $24,530. Once known as the Rubber Capital of the World because both BF Goodrich and Firestone had started there. Home to a university. Birthplace of LeBron James. All in all, a typical city inhabited by typical people in the heartland of America. So how and why was it hooked up with the Santa Fe cartel?

Vizcaino: Montez called him ambitious. As in, taking over Santa Fe. Outwardly they amicably worked together, but beneath the surface there was a deadly struggle. It's possible, even probable, that Vizcaino wants to kill me because I'm helping Montez.

Kesey: Until now he'd been concentrating on Montez and Vizcaino. DiMaglio was right about Smukler and Paz being a sideshow, so why was Kesey shifting his focus to them? Was it really to help Laura? I had no idea. Or choice.

As Kesey instructed, I telephoned Smukler.

He was delighted to hear from me. "I'd hoped you would be sitting in on during our client's proffers."

"I had some other matters to deal with," I said.

"From what I've heard about your practice, I'm sure they were extremely important," he said. "But don't worry, the proffers went well. Very well."

"The counterfeiting information, I assume?"

"Yes, indeed," he said. "They resulted in no less than four takedowns. Printing presses, tens of millions in counterfeit hundred-dollar bills. Agent Leeds is extremely pleased."

"Excellent," I said.

"Leeds said they were the best quality counterfeits he'd ever seen. Indistinguishable from the real thing because they were printed from a real plate. Our client is diligently trying to find the plate. Leeds said if he did, a formal cooperation agreement would be forthcoming."

"That's if the threat problem is resolved," I said.

"I believe that issue may soon be resolved."

"Really? What leads you to that conclusion?"

"Instinct," he said. "And prior experience."

"I'm sure you've had a bunch. Goes with the territory. The business we're in."

He chuckled. "Yes, it certainly does."

"The DEA guy, Kesey. His position?"

"Skeptical. But it's Leeds's show."

"It's a pleasure dealing with a colleague like you, Mort," I said. "Speaking of colleagues, I've been trying to get in touch with Joachim. He doesn't seem to be in his office. I know you two visited our client the other day. I was hoping he was still in New York."

"You know Paz. He moves around. Could be way down south. If he calls, I'll let him know you want to talk."

"Thanks, Mort. Great speaking to you."

"The pleasure was mine."

Smukler had confirmed that counterfeiting was a focal point of the case. Montez's cooperation effort was in limbo until and unless he found the printing plate. I wondered why he hadn't yet. Surely, he knew its whereabouts. Maybe his problem was trusting someone to get it. Vizcaino was too lean and hungry to be trusted. Arias was a bumbler. Laura an enigma.

So it came down to the last woman standing—me—but I'd already gone above and beyond my ethical obligations, and besides, had no wish to help Montez.

But Kesey had said the gambit was to help Laura.

The following day, an unexpected visitor came to my office.

I don't get many walk-ins, but when I do, they never look anything like the woman who came through my door. She was plump, rosy-cheeked and gray-haired, and spoke in a slight but not-quite southern accent that I, who had once tried a case in Cleveland, pinned as what linguists call Ohio Inland North—a regional dialect in which verbs are somewhat elongated.

"Not many high-rises in my neck of the woods," she said. "Your elevator took so long I felt tree-apped."

"Uh-huh. How can I help?"

"I haven't the faintest," she said. "I was just told to deliver this to you."

"This" was a roll-on suitcase. "Well, that's that," she said. "Nice to meet you, but I must be going. It's a long drive back to home sweeet home."

"Say hello to Cleveland for me," I said.

"Close but no ci-gar," she said. "Akron."

"Lot of green-haired folks there, huh?"

"Tsk. The things you New Yorkers say."

Her roll-on was identical to the one Laura had taken from the couch. Not many luggage shops in Akron, I thought. Maybe a Walmart.

Scary.

The cartels had not only infiltrated mid-America, they were using it for their own purposes. Akron. Walmart. God-fearing middle-aged ladies. Nothing was sacred anymore.

When she was gone, I opened the roll-on.

Sure enough, it was filled with banded packets of Franklins. Montez's revenge. I'd spoken down to him, and in return he was playing down and dirty with me. I'd told him I wanted to be paid by wire, but he'd sent me another batch of fake bills. I got so mad that I punched the packets hard enough to burst one open. I looked closer at the scattered bills.

When Laura made the delivery, I'd received crisp, uncirculated bills with the same serial numbers. But these were used bills—or had been crumpled to seem used—as if they'd been literally laundered and dried.

I remembered the washing machine and dryer in the house

where Laura had given me the phony money. Wondered if she knew it was bogus. Heard Billy's voice: *Same, same, same.*

I riffled through a packet of Franklins.

Their serial numbers were random.

Wonder of wonders, it was real.

Not surprising that Montez had both real and counterfeit money in the States. Pacho had stolen the real and Laura had delivered the bogus. I drew a blank as to where they were stashed, but figured they were with the plate.

In Akron?

CHAPTER 41

Understanding the Akron link was the key.

Pondering, I paced my office, looking for inspiration but seeing only files filled with documents, the uninspiring paper trails of my life's work.

I left the office. I didn't want to go home. I'd find no answers there; understanding lay elsewhere. Not in Akron. Akron was for transactional business and Laura was transient. Was she in Colombia? Here?

I pointed the Shark toward Queens.

The house where Laura had kept my phony fee looked as before: a falling-down reminder of better days. The lawn was knee-high weeds. The rusted swing was dappled with bird droppings. Behind it the driveway was empty. I wondered who had removed the car with Ohio plates, and whether it had been registered in Akron.

The street was still. The door was unlocked, just as Laura had left it. Whoever had taken the car with Ohio plates apparently didn't intend to return. I switched on my phone light and went inside.

No one and nothing but the now-depleted old couch. Then I heard a small sound from the bathroom. I froze, listening. I heard another sound from the bathroom. I switched my light off. My left hand groped for the bathroom door. I took my brass knuckles from my bag and slipped them on my right hand. Paused. The sound was louder now.

A scrabbling?

Possibilities flashed. A breeze through an opened window

rattling a shower curtain? Someone or something digging into a wall. Searching?

I clenched the knuckles tightly, its jagged teeth as cold as my intentions. If hand-to-hand combat was what it took, that was fine with me. I was done being bodily punched—time to knock someone's block off.

I held up my phone light, cocked a leg, and kicked the door open. Something darted into the shadows. It was a rat. I laughed aloud. First, I'd been spooked by a cleaning lady, now by a rat. The irony. My business was cleaning up messes and making rats squeal. The dank bathroom was empty save for a reminder: green streaks of hair dye staining the sink.

I went into the other room. The washing machine and dryer were still there. A scrap of paper lay on the floor. A strip with adhesive edging. Like those used for banding money. An insight came to me that I should have realized much earlier:

It was about washing money, stupid. Removing the crispness from new counterfeits so they looked like crumpled used bills.

Was Laura the laundress?

I gave the Shark free rein.

It meandered the side streets. The Queens 'hoods: Jamaica. South Ozone Park. Maspeth. Neat small houses. Bluish TV lights behind curtained windows. Evening in America from sea to shining sea, mom and pop watching game shows, the kids out getting zonked.

From behind a siren yelped. Bubble lights brightened the rearview mirror. I pulled over to let the cop or ambulance or whatever pass. It did but then stopped, blocking my way. It was an unmarked car, an antenna on its trunk. Law.

Kesey? If so, he was crossing a bright line. Surveilling me was part of the game but harassing me was out of bounds. I set my phone on the seat, switching it on to VIDEO. First thing tomorrow I'd have Gino file a complaint, maybe sue the DEA.

Forget that. It wasn't the hulking Special Agent Kesey.

The cop was a string bean in a denim jacket. DiMaglio.

He shone a flashlight in my eyes. Blinding.

"License and registration," he said.

"You reassigned to night patrol?"

"License and registration."

I gave him the docs. He looked at them and laughed. "You changed plates to avoid detection?"

Shit! I still had Gino's plates on the Shark.

"Using another's plates is a Class A misdemeanor," he said. "Stealing handicapped plates might kick that up to an E felony."

"Not stealing," I said. "Borrowing. With permission."

"Borrowing with bad intent, maybe even a D felony."

"So write me up and find a streetwalker to roust."

"I could," he said. "Or offer you another option."

"How much you want?" I asked. "Fifty? A Franklin?"

"Shit on your money, Dirtbag," he said. "Tell me about your green-haired girl from Akron."

I didn't reply.

"Make it easy on yourself," he said. "Give her up and I'll keep you out of it. Where is she?"

I didn't reply.

"Cover her up and you'll be charged with obstruction."

"See you in court," I said.

He handed my docs back. Then his expression softened, and he spoke quietly. "Helping us is helping both yourself and Laura. We need to know where she is and whatever they think you both have."

"Can't help you with what I don't know," I said.

He shook his head as if at a child.

CHAPTER 42

I was back to minus square one.

Why would Montez and the DEA believe I had or knew something important to both? Had someone falsely pointed at me? Paz? Don J? Laura?

Thinking cap time.

DiMaglio had been tagging me in the hope I'd lead him to Laura. Meaning he thought she was still in the city. Via another wiretap? An informant? Point being he didn't know where she was but thought I did.

I couldn't find her but knew I wouldn't have to. When the mood came over her, Laura would find me. I didn't know why I thought that, but felt certain she would, sooner or later. I'd just have to wait for her. And make sure my followers weren't there when she showed. To shake them from my tail I'd have to move.

I reserved a room at one of the West 57th Street businessmen hotels that throw their shadows across Central Park. Parked the Shark in a far corner of my garage and draped its tarp. Disabled my phone GPS.

From behind, a black COVID mask was yanked over my eyes. Strong hands gripped my arms. My wrists were bound. I was fast-walked into a car. When it screeched up a garage ramp, I slid across the seat. When it turned onto the street, I slid the other way.

Talk about being shaken, rattled, and rolled.

I was taken to a place that smelled like a hospital.

My mask was lifted. I blinked away the fluorescent glare and saw white walls bejeweled by colored lights on machines trailing wires to a bed half-hidden by a curtain. I was in a hospital. Its stringency was tinted with cheap aftershave.

Arias swam into focus.

"Forgive the harsh procedure, *Doctora*," he said. "Vizcaino's people were nearing you. Therefore, *necesario* to leave immediately, no time to explain why."

So Arias and Vizcaino were, in fact, working opposite ends. That validated Montez's claim of a power struggle for his throne.

"Who's in that bed?" I asked, pulling the curtain aside. A nurse interposed herself between me and the person in the bed.

"Are you a relative, ma'am?" the nurse asked me.

"A sister," Arias said. "She don't speak *Inglés*."

The nurse was a graying woman who looked as if she'd seen it all and wasn't afraid to say so. "Tell her something for me," she said to Arias. "She should be ashamed of herself. She should've taken her to a clinic. Allowing a young woman to abort herself? Do you realize she nearly died? Five minutes, then go."

I went to the bed. Laura was so pale she appeared translucent. But she had a gleam in her eyes and a hint of a smile on her lips.

"*Dame un abrazo*," she said to me.

Frowning, the nurse left. I hugged Laura; she kissed my cheek. Her breath was warm against my ear.

"Don't trust Arias," she whispered.

"Privacy, *por favor*," I told Arias.

"Of course," he said, leaving.

"They say women used to use wire hangers but I couldn't find one," Laura said weakly. "The moment I realized I was pregnant all I could think of was to get the incubus out of me immediately. I mean, I freaked. Guess what I used."

She was babbling. Still fogged by sedatives.

"A chopstick. *Mínimo*, huh?" She laughed.

"It's not funny," I said.

"You're right. It's awful. But better than bearing Martin's spawn. I hope he rots in jail forever."

Montez was the father?

But he'd languished in Combita for six months before

being extradited, and had been in the MCC the next, what, four months? So how?

"The first time you met Martin," she informed me. "Remember how he shooed you out? It was because I'd come for the conjugal visit he demanded."

I remembered the woman who'd visited Montez when I'd left Combita. "Demanded?"

"He refused to allow my mother her medications unless I became his puta. The one time I did and look what happened. An incubus. That day in Combita Martin thought it hilarious that you were disappointed about not being retained. He'd already decided he wanted you, but it pleased him that you felt rejected."

"Why did he want me?" I asked.

"Pacho recommended you," she said. "He told Martin you could be trusted. Martin went along with the recommendation because he believes he can control women and thought you might be useful. He had no idea that you would prove to be vital because it turned out that you possessed something he badly wanted."

There it was again. I had something everyone wanted.

"That day," she said. "The moment I saw you, I knew you were the one I was waiting for. Don't ask me why because I don't know. A friend, an ally. Someone to trust. But can I really?"

"Get some sleep," I said.

"Aw, I hurt your feelings," she said. "By now you should know not to take all I say seriously," she said. "Martin thinks I'm crazy. Do you?"

"Yes," I said.

She clapped her hands, like a little girl. "Good. I am crazy. So are you. It's us against them."

"Which side are we on?"

"Arias is loyal to himself. Vizcaino wants to replace Martin. Pacho had his own designs. We're following Pacho's blueprint."

"Let's take a break from New York," I suggested. "Go somewhere we can figure things out."

"There is no leaving them. They'll find us."

"What is it they think I have?"

"Put your finger on your forehead and try to remember what happened the night Pacho was murdered."

"The black Porsche was yours. It was there when I arrived, but you left before …"

"No," she said. "I saw everything."

"Everything?"

I swallowed hard.

"I'm not the woman you saw that night," I said. "They drugged me. I can't remember what happened. I understand if you can't forgive me."

"There's nothing to forgive you for. You had no choice. What happened was meant to be."

"No," I said." I believe in free will."

"So did Pacho," she said. "He cared for you very much, but he cared for his plans more. My poor, naive brother didn't know they were there to kill him to frighten you into giving them what you have. When they realized the police were coming, Martin told them to leave you."

"Mental telepathy?" I asked.

"Martin was on the phone with them when Pacho was killed. He thought you'd be arrested. He would have sent Arias to tell you he could save you if you gave him the thing."

"Save me how?"

"Martin knows I was there," she said. "He'd have me tell the police I witnessed everything. I'd say it was *Los Xs* who killed Pacho."

She took my hand and pressed it to her lips. She still wore the leather necklace, Cleo's golden pendant glinting above her breasts.

Another lost memory clarified.

The person who had used cocaine to rouse me from my burundanga-drugged stupor had worn the gold pendant. That person had seen everything.

Laura.

The nurse entered. "That's enough for today," she said.

Ignoring her, I put my ear to Laura's mouth. "What is it they think I have?" I whispered.

Her reply was so faint I couldn't hear it.

"She needs to sleep," the nurse said. "Sister or not, you'll have to leave."

I kissed Laura's forehead. "Be back tomorrow."

"You do speak English," the nurse said.

"I'm a quick study," I said as I left.

CHAPTER 43

Basic survival skills:
 Know thy terrain: Forget hiding in a hotel. Live at home.
 Be tactically aggressive: offense is the best defense.
 Analyze intelligence: On the night Pacho was arrested, I found a white plastic card, seemingly meaningless. Could it somehow be the obscure object of everyone's desire? It made sense: The card's the thing. And Laura knew it.
 Define short-term goals: serve and protect myself and Laura from ostensible friends and obvious foes alike.
 Strategize the big picture: The beginning is over. I'm somewhere in the middle. When the end comes, I'll survive but others won't.
 I rented a car paid for with a rarely used credit card, one of the many I have for no particular reason.
 My next stop was a curbside sewer where I ditched that credit card. Kesey would be tracking it, but now I was off his radar, and to stay off I'd spend cash only.
 Then I visited a sporting goods store on lower Broadway and used cash to buy a watch cap, XL Mets hoodie, and cheap shades. So costumed, I drove past my apartment building.
 Saw no watchers as I drove around the block. Put on the shades, raised my hoodie, pulled the cap low, then turned into my garage. Parked and shrouded the Shark. Forsook the elevator—cameras in it—and went up the fire stairs to my apartment.
 It was as the searchers had left it. A mess. They'd gone through my closet and my clothing was strewn. I picked through it and found the suit I'd worn to Elmhurst Manor. I'd

stuffed Pacho's things in my pockets. They'd pulled out its flap pockets, now empty, but had overlooked the lapel pocket.

The white card was still there.

It was just a blank piece of plastic the same size as the credit card I'd just ditched. No writing on its face. Useless and unknowable but meaningful. Somehow.

I took the fire stairs to the sub-basement. My venerable building had been erected back when coal was used for heat. Where the old ovens and boilers had operated was a neglected and long-forgotten side entrance for coal delivery.

I went through it to a narrow alley that ran between and behind adjoining buildings. Halfway down the block, I emerged in the street. Still no sign of watchers.

I told Gino everything.

"First off," he said. "Give me back my license plate."

"It's still on the Shark," I said. "Forgot. Sorry."

"They didn't take the bogus million from your place. Why not, you think?"

"Probably for the same reason they framed me as Pacho's killer," I said. "Because they could drop a dime on me and I'd get busted for possessing counterfeit money. Sound right?"

"Montez," Gino said. "Show me the card."

He held it beneath his lamp.

"It's imbedded with a metallic strip," he said. "Looks like an ATM card but it's not."

"Then what is it?"

"A key," he said. "You shouldn't be walking around with it."

I gave it to him along with two envelopes. "The big one is my fee from Arias. Hold onto it for me. The small one is twenty-five for legal services, past and future, that are above and beyond the call of duty ... and for your thoughts as to what I should do next."

"Attend if Montez is still proffering. When you speak alone, he'll circle around to the thing you have. Flash your know-it-all look but don't say what it is you know. And being the devious fellow he is, he will conclude that indeed you have it."

"I don't know if he's still proffering," I said.

"Ask Smukler if there's a proffer scheduled."

I phoned Smukler but the call went to voicemail. I left a call-back message.

"If there's a proffer, the agents may turn the spotlight on you," Gino said. "If so, you know the drill."

"Keep my big mouth zipped," I said.

"What if Vizcaino finds you?"

"I'll deal with it," I said.

"Sure you want to stay on?"

"Surer than sure."

"Then you'll need this." From a drawer he took a gun and handed it to me. It was a small, flat, semi-automatic Beretta 950. It felt good in my hand and fit my pocket without a tell-tale bulge.

"Take Laura from Arias and go underground until everything blows over. Or, I should say, explodes, because cartel soldiers don't fade away."

"What if my other problem doesn't blow over?" I asked.

"If the feds had actionable evidence on you, this conversation would be in the MCC," he said.

My phone rang. It was Smukler, returning my call. I asked him if and when Montez was proffering again. He replied and I thanked him and hung up. Gino looked at me.

"Next week," I said.

CHAPTER 44

That night I was restless and could not sleep.

In retrospect, I regretted allowing Laura to remain with Arias. She'd said not to trust him, yet did not seem otherwise concerned by his presence, and I wondered if she thought him a useful idiot; a tool in the plan I knew she had.

But there was no telling with Laura. About anything.

Had she really been impregnated by Montez? Or did she have a secret lover? Perhaps the sleek indigenous man who'd escorted her at Pacho's funeral and fit the description of the shooter outside my apartment?

I put the Beretta under my pillow.

Then laid my weary head to sleep.

At first light I left by my building's basement door.

The hospital Laura was in was several miles downtown. It was a brisk day, but it was early so I walked there, hoping the wind would blow away my misgivings.

The hospital was a beehive of activity. Another long winter, another viral strain. Ambulances bringing the newly afflicted in, morgue vans carrying previous victims out.

Laura's room door was open. It was redolent with flowers. Who had sent them? I moved the curtain aside. A woman lay in the bed, dark hair spilled across the sheets.

"Good morning," I said. "Feeling better?"

The woman looked up. She wasn't Laura.

Fearing the worst—ICU?—I went to the nurse's station. The nurse frowned. "Against doctor's orders, she insisted on leaving," she said. "Headstrong, that one. Told her to at least wait for the doctor to write scripts for antibiotics. 'Mail it to me,' she says."

My phone buzzed. I didn't answer it. "She has several addresses," I said. "Did she say which one?"

She sighed. "She didn't. No phone number, nothing. Just got dressed and left alone. Maybe she's with the Spanish gentleman who brought her here. Likes his aftershave, that one. And no, we don't have contact information on him, either."

Strange, I thought. I looked at my phone; I had a voicemail. I hoped it was from Laura.

But it was from a person I despised but I had never interacted with. Yet.

Joachim Paz was a small man prone to frequent smiles that did not conceal his saturnine nature.

He so resembled an elf that I was tempted to see if his ears were pointed, but I couldn't because he was wearing headphones. So was I. A wire connecting us drooped atop the small table where we sat facing one another. Splices led from it to our throats where vibration-activated mics were taped. He cupped his hands around his mouth when he spoke, despite the .0001 percent likelihood of being lip-read in a felt-lined closet-sized room in the sub-basement of the unpretentious building we were in.

And I thought I was paranoid.

His voice was tinny through my earphones. "The volume is okay?" he asked.

"Fine," I said. "Try content."

"Ha ha." His thin lips parted in a mirthless smile revealing pointed canines. He shot his shirt cuffs over the sleeves of his ice-cream-colored suit. I knew the elaborate set-up and his fastidiousness was intentionally meant to divert from the fact that he was recording us.

"Let's negotiate, Ms. Electra," he said.

I removed my headphones and throat mic.

He leaned over the table and cupped my ear and whispered sotto voce.

"From one professional to another," he said. "This case

can be the mother of all scores. Let's work with, not against, one another. I'm talking partners. Interested?"

I nodded.

"Forgive my obscenity, but tit for tat," he whispered. "You get the girl, I get the card, we split the score."

So he knew about the card, and that it had to do with the money Pacho stole. Had Don J told him? Montez? No matter. He knew.

"I get sixty points," he said. "Your end's forty."

I shook my head.

"No? What then?"

I air-sliced a stiff-edged palm.

"Fifty-five, forty-five," he said.

I shook my head.

He sighed. "Okay. Fifty-fifty."

"Montez?" I mouthed.

"Fuck him," he said. "He won't be in a position to do anything. He's headed for life in a Supermax. Trust me, they won't take his cooperation."

"Don J?" I whispered.

"Montez can't touch Don J," he said. "Wilkinson put him in a safe house. Marshals around the clock. They play pinochle with him. I told the moron he's in a halfway house. He thinks that means he's halfway home."

"Won't he come after the score?"

"He won't even know we have it."

I shook my head, mouthed "no."

"What do you mean? Why not?"

"I don't have tat," I said.

"I don't believe you.

CHAPTER 45

Joachim Paz had me questioning my faith in humanity.
Not that he was a valid specimen. He was an inhumane parasite. Honorable to none and disloyal to all. An acolyte of avarice. I really wanted to fuck him up.

Another week until the proffer.

I spent it slogging through the cases I'd neglected. On Monday, my 5,000-ton weed guy, who despite his prior convictions I'd managed to get bailed out—and had a bad-search motion to suppress pending that I actually thought winnable—fired me.

"You're a procrastinator, Jack," he said to me.

"Jill, you mean," I replied. "Good luck."

On Tuesday, my fifty-kilo coke trafficker opted not to pay the balance of his fee. "No work, *sin dinero*," he said.

On Wednesday, my real estate lady who rented stash houses in Little Colombia, for whom I was close to getting a no-jail deal, was unappreciative. "*Te gusta el dinero*, but not to work," she said. "*Adiós*."

On Thursday, I went to jail where I pitched a newly arrested guy to whom I'd been highly recommended, but he didn't swing at it. "Word in here is that you're bad news," he told me.

And so it went. By Friday, my active-case cabinet was empty. The practice I'd spent years building was collapsing like a house of business cards.

Saturday night I had a drink or three. Sunday, I slept it off. Monday, I went to the Southern District Courthouse, elevatored to the fifth floor, and right-turned toward the proffer rooms.

Wilkinson sat between Leeds and Kesey, facing Montez.

I sat on one side of the table. Smukler sat on the other side facing me, watching those in the middle playing ping-pong.

Kesey served first, low and hard. "Since when you got religion, Martin?"

Montez fingered the wooden rosary beads looped around his neck. He smiled like the choir boy he wasn't and said, "A gift from my *mamá*. I feel her spirit in it, talking to me."

"I hope she says the truth will set you free," Leeds said. "Let's begin with the printing plate."

"Let's bypass that and get to the major dope," Kesey said.

"A threat to America's economy is the major dope," Leeds said.

Kesey sighed. "For Chrissake, there's eleven billion Franklins in circulation. Maybe one in ten thousand is bogus. No one notices them anyway."

"One in nine thousand," Leeds said.

"You want to talk numbers?" DiMaglio said angrily. "How about every year fentanyl kills a hundred thousand people? How about Mr. Montez here, a major distributor of fentanyl, giving us leads on his *compadres* in death?"

"Ask and I'll gladly answer," Montez said. "I was under the impression my partners already told you everything about that end of the business."

"What your partners may or may not have said is none of your business, sir," Wilkinson said to Montez. "If we decide to offer you a cooperation agreement, we'll discuss everything."

"If?" I asked. "It was my impression that putting my client in general population indicated an agreement was forthcoming."

"Mine too," Smukler chimed in.

"We've reconsidered and the issue is on pause," Wilkinson said. "Where's the plate, Mr. Montez?"

"On my mother's life the truth is that I know approximately, but not precisely," he said.

I knew Montez wasn't acting. Whether a cartel boss or a street punk, *mamacitas* were off the table, and swearing on one's mother's life was simply not done. Never. Ever.

"Approximately?" Leeds said.

"My people are close to finding it," Montez said. "If they

see Day-ahs they'll run. Let them be. As soon as they find the plate it shall be yours."

"We're pleased with the counterfeit information you've already provided," Leeds said. "I mean, four printing presses, over twenty million in counterfeit bills, that's pretty significant."

"Making zero arrests and not finding the plate is even more significant," Kesey said.

I bit back a smile. Kesey was dead-on. I figured Montez had given up fifty thousand bucks worth of presses and worthless bogus bills yet had kept his most valuable resources—his fortune and the authentic printing plate—out of harm's way. The seizures were obviously sham cooperation. Little wonder Kesey was skeptical.

"Where's Victor Vizcaino?" Kesey asked.

"Colombia, helping me," Montez said.

Kesey looked at me. "Counselor?"

"I have no idea," I said.

But the question gave rise to a realization: Somehow Kesey knew Vizcaino had tried but failed to off me. Vizcaino was likely now a fugitive and Kesey was tagging me in the hope he'd snag Vizcaino when he surfaced to finish the job.

"Where's the fat guy, Arias?" Kesey asked Montez.

"Also in Colombia," Montez said. "Also following my instructions to find the plate."

"Excellent," Leeds said. "How close?"

"Very," Montez said. "If I'm able to communicate with them they'll find it. Let me out of the SHU and I can expedite the process."

Wilkinson closed her file. "Tell your American lawyer when your Colombian lawyers find it," she said.

"Stay on top of this, Martin," Leeds said, leaving with Wilkinson.

Kesey started out but then pulled a *Columbo,* pausing to ask Montez one more thing. "By the way," he said, "who killed Pacho?"

"I don't know who or why," Montez said. "Pacho was a good person. He was like family to me."

Marshals entered, cuffed Montez, and led him out. I started out but Kesey blocked my way.

"What was Pacho to you, counselor?" he asked.

"Started as a client. Became a friend."

"I'm your only friend, El."

CHAPTER 46

Kesey was not my only friend.
"He's playing with my head," I told Gino.
"Cops tend to do that," he said.
"He wants Vizcaino," I said. "And Vizcaino wants me. Which is why Kesey's watching my ass. I'm bait."
"Were," he said. "Vizcaino's gone."
"Maybe Montez just wants me to think so. I let my guard down, Vizcaino shows, case closed."
"Not if you don't give up the card," he said. "Anyway, let's hope he shows and Kesey grabs him. Until then, be smart, stay under the radar."
"I'm not smart. I go with my gut."
"Heart, I'd say," he said.
"I want Vizcaino to find me. I'm not afraid of him."
"Be very afraid," he said. "He'll be with his X-men." He handed me a spare clip for the little Beretta he'd given me. "There's a lot of them."
Time to go proactive.
I went to the garage via the back alleys, uncovered the Shark, and hit the streets. Vizcaino was a professional. I knew he'd leave eyes on my apartment 24/7 just in case I appeared. He got his wish.
I drove slowly, squaring blocks as if in search of a parking spot, not looking behind but sensing a trailing presence.
I cruised aimlessly for a couple of hours. Gray sky became pale twilight that faded to the dark of night. Traffic on the avenues thinned, and I stuck to side streets that were nearly empty. The closer to Fifth, the more pedestrians, so I drove

around the farthest east side of Manhattan, where the sidewalks were nearly deserted.

All the way I felt eyes on me.

Nine o'clock on the Shark's clock and all was going well.

Four hours since I'd begun playing street-driver. About as long as it would take Vizcaino to assemble and prime his crew for action. I knew how it would go down. There'd be two or three cars. Shooters in each. Maybe including some *Los Xs,* maybe augmented by local talent. They'd be communicating via speakerphones.

Vizcaino would be in command, parked in the middle of the rough circle I was driving, wondering what the hell I was doing. Why had I reappeared, and so obliviously? Perhaps he'd think I was relapsing into a burundanga state of mindlessness. Didn't matter. I was there for the taking, and he would. Alive. At least until he tortured me into divulging what I was now certain was the object of his desires: the white card.

I had other plans. My taxi-driving days had left the Manhattan grid embedded in my mind. Catch me if you can.

They'd already begun trying.

They were taking turns tail-sitting so I wouldn't be spooked by the same pair of headlamps—whoa! In my sideview mirror the car behind me turned off the avenue just as another car turned into it behind me. These guys were good.

So was I. It was a match between quantity and quality. My adrenaline was pumping and the hairs on the back of my neck stood up, but not because I was frightened, rather because of the cold air rushing through the Shark's open windows. Leave them up and they'd be shattered if things deteriorated to gunplay; be hard to find outdated Shark-sized windows to replace them. Not that I thought it would come to that.

I had a plan: Operation No-Exit.

I tooled north on York Avenue. Passed the hospital-zoned quietude where people spent their last dollars on overpriced medicines and short-term lodging. Passed the taverns whose cocktail hours attracted lonely singles. Passed stretch limos double-parked in front of Sotheby's where uppity fools spent their fortunes on artless crap.

I was pissed off at the whole world. That was a good thing—it would fuel me—but I needed to channel my anger.

North of 72nd, traffic on York Avenue was sparse. Side streets were empty. On my left, odd-numbered westbound East 70 streets. Nah.

On my right, even-numbered eastbound streets that dead-ended at the FDR. Yeah.

I slowed. Unbuckled my seatbelt and made a hard right, flooring the Shark and speeding down the street. Dark storefronts flashed past until I stood on the brakes and screeched to a stop where the street dead-ended above FDR Drive.

I quickly got out and closed the door, darting onto the shadowed sidewalk, then crouched as I ran back up the street toward York.

They'd think I was trapped.

I wasn't. Soon they'd be.

A car slowed to a stop behind me. No one got out. They were waiting. Vizcaino would appear to direct the action, leading from the rear. That's when I'd make my move. Sneak up behind him and introduce my presence with the Beretta barrel in his ear: "Where's Laura?"

A light shone from behind me. I turned as the interior dome light on the first car went off. A man had gotten out; I couldn't make out his face. Briefly, he was silhouetted against the traffic on the FDR, and I glimpsed a gun in his hand. Then he was on the shadowed sidewalk. Walking toward me. Had to be Vizcaino.

My bad.

I'd figured Vizcaino would do what bosses do and leave harm's way to his underlings, enjoy the product of their labors. I'd neglected to account for him being a hands-on type.

I free-styled a move.

The guys in the first car remained inside. Vizcaino was approaching me alone. In Montez's video, I'd seen Vizcaino's face when he'd murdered a helpless boy, heard him laugh, like killing was a thing for him alone.

Now it was mine too. Imagine that.

I crouched in a shooting stance and two-handed the Beretta at Vizcaino's center mass.

Cold steel jammed the back of my head. From behind it another man spoke.

"Put the cap pistol down, Dirtbag."

CHAPTER 47

Strange how during the worst of times, your thoughts are of your best old times.

A teenage brawl in which I bloody-nosed a bully. My first trial win. Drinking with Gino while telling crime war stories, him advising me not to make waves when up to your chin in a sea of shit.

I wasn't about to. For now, mum was my word.

Strong hands roughly patted me down. Took my brass knucks and my gun. Spun me around and planted my hands atop a car.

"Consider yourself Mirandized," Kesey said. "Now that you know your rights, anything you care to say?"

I didn't reply. Kesey didn't look well. Pallid, gaunt, weary. A battle-scarred old bull who'd seen it all and was on his way to pasture. But his eyes were bright as a rookie making his first collar. Figured. It was his last major case, and he wanted to go out a winner ... but I sensed something more was driving him, some deep-down fierce need.

"Defendant declines a statement," DiMaglio said.

"She's considering the scenario," Kesey said. "Is this a federal bust? Answer: no. So now she's thinking it's a state case. Also no. So now she concludes it's a city misdemeanor for which a person cannot be arrested unless the police saw the act, or the evidence is overwhelming. And since law enforcement didn't see her do anything, she's okay because there is no overwhelming evidence."

DiMaglio laughed. "Don't know about that."

Kesey cleared his throat and hawked up a gob. His phlegm was spotted with blood.

He's not just sick, I thought, *he's terminal.*

DiMaglio verbalized the clipped words of a hypothetical arrest affidavit.

"While investigating an unrelated matter, I noticed a vehicle operated by a female. Over a period of several hours, said vehicle circled the same blocks. I observed said vehicle to frequently slow when passing private homes. Officers were aware of numerous recent burglaries and attempted robberies in the area by an individual who drove similarly. Said individual was believed to be involved with narcotics dealers. Hence, said vehicle was surveilled. When it made a turn without signaling, it was stopped."

Suddenly, Kesey was seized by a convulsive cough. He put his hands atop his knees and hunched over, hacking as if a frog was caught in his throat.

Concerned, DiMaglio put his hand on Kesey's shoulder. "Easy, bro," he said to him. "Breathe."

Kesey brushed DiMaglio's hand away. "Keep going," he said.

"Officers observed a small backpack on the front seat of said individual's car," DiMaglio said. "An AirTag was attached to it. Officers were able to identify the AirTag as having been attached to a backpack that had been reported stolen."

A lie too far. I'd dumped the AirTag when Pops had alerted me.

"Continuing," DiMaglio said. "When asked for license and registration, defendant opened a glove compartment and I observed a Beretta pistol. Its serial numbers were filed off. Officers ran a carry license check and discovered the defendant, although licensed to carry concealed, had not registered that weapon."

"It gets worse," Kesey said. "Show her."

DiMaglio dug in a cargo pocket and took out a plastic baggie filled with white pills. He held the baggie with two fingers, his expression filled with disgust.

"Subsequently, defendant's vehicle was searched and a

plastic bag of pills was discovered," DiMaglio said. "Officers performed a field test which came up positive for fentanyl."

"Defendant then called the arresting officers two pieces of shit," I said.

"Hmmm," Kesey said. "We got us a schedule-one drug felony."

"Mandatory minimum ten," DiMaglio said. "Plus the gun rap."

Keeping my big mouth closed no longer was a problem because these guys would lie to their heart's content. Protocol was cuffing me and whisking me off to a holding cell until I was arraigned.

Yet they hadn't done either.

Instead, they chose to taunt me.

I knew why. It's the classic approach to recruiting an informant: sign up with the law or be consigned to jail. But I knew they were bluffing. I took my hands from the car roof and turned and shoved Kesey.

"What the hell do you want from me?" I demanded.

Kesey returned my guns and knuckles and smiled. "Just to talk things over, El."

CHAPTER 48

I'd often passed Montecristo Cigar Bar but had never ventured inside.

I didn't smoke cigars, but even if I did, this joint was not my style. There were always pricey sedans double-parked outside, many with city agency placards on their visors insulating the cars from no-parking rules. The people who owned the vehicles were also above regulations: fat-cats and A-listers and assorted bigshots, all of whom knew the key to success was ingratiating oneself with deputy mayors, assistant Police Commissioners, ex-cops who did favors—all of whom frequented Montecristo.

Kesey was known here. Welcomed, and with me in tow, he was welcomed and led to a private room. In no time flat, a bottle of Johnnie Walker Blue and a box of illegal Cuban Cohibas appeared. Kesey indulged in both. I declined.

I was seeing Kesey in a different light.

I'd thought he was a bit rough around the edges for a federal, but now I respected him as a shrewd operator. A go-getter who got because he bent rules, a true son of law enforcement family tradition—scratch my back, and I'll watch yours.

Guys like that don't hesitate to play dirty. And he was obsessed with Montez and Vizcaino. Was it the men he hated? Or did he care more about the card that was the key to a printing plate and, just maybe, a trove of Santa Fe money? Was he planning for his last hurrah to include an XL golden parachute?

He finished his drink in a swig and poured himself another. Fished a gold guillotine from a pocket and clipped the cigar, held a torch to the end until it glowed, then inhaled so deeply that smoke streamed from his nose.

"Talk to me, counselor," he said. "Don't be shy. No listening devices in this joint."

"Inhale those things you'll die real soon," I said.

"My ex-wife used to say that," he said.

"Ex?" I asked. "So this is a date?"

"Funny," he said. "You're a funny lady. But maybe you break like a little girl. Afraid I'm gonna nail you for Pacho? Don't be. I already know about what happened to him. Far as I'm concerned, that door is locked and the key's thrown away."

Sincere? I thought so, but it was pointless to reply.

He shrugged. "The question's simple: you want to work with or against me?"

"I'm a lawyer, not an informant," I said. "Not to mention I have nothing to inform about."

"Correct," he said. "I already know what you know."

"So why the charade? Why pull me over for bullshit? Why take me to this stink-hole?"

He finished his drink and poured another. "I told you why. To talk. Not about what we know. About what we're gonna learn."

"Is that so?"

He sucked his cigar until smoke hazed his face. "Tell you a story."

"As long as it's short," I said wearily.

"Short and sad," he said. "Goes like this ... when you disappeared, I thought you'd been offed. Then I learned about the AirTag."

From Laura? I wondered.

"I decided to let you go on playing hermit until you couldn't deal with it and came back. We knew you'd go to Moskowitz. But when you returned, you didn't make any moves with the *misterioso* thing you got, so we figured you'd stashed it in the shack. We went down there. Struck out. Misterioso, huh?"

Misterioso, my tush. He knew it was the white card. Again, from Laura? Had she seen me pocket it when Pacho was arrested?

I trailed my finger around the rim of my glass. It emitted

a thin, flute-like sound. "I thought this was going to be a short story," I said.

"It is. Which brings us back to me and Brian DiMaglio looking for it in Lower Shitsville."

Interested now, I sipped Scotch while he spun his tale.

"We looked through every nook and cranny of the fishing shack and the john. Was about to give up when we heard a strange noise outside. Went out but saw nothing, and figured the sound was waves shushing on the pebble beach. But then we heard the sound again. Not a wave but a moan. We followed our ears to the jetty. A kid had crawled beneath it. He was beat up pretty bad and blue with cold. Was incoherent except for one word he kept saying over and over. 'Daddy, daddy, daddy.'"

Billy! I thought. *Oh, that poor boy.*

"We took him to a hospital. They knew who he was because he'd been there before. An obvious case of child abuse but the kid's father denied it and there were no witnesses. Sad, but none of our business, we thought, and were about to leave. Then the doctor told us they might have to amputate the kid's toes. Frostbite. Gangrene. They'd called the kid's father, but he'd said he couldn't leave the gas station unattended."

"Sonofabitch don't work," I said. "The kid does. Did."

"Brian said we should go see the father. I knew what he was thinking, but he was my partner, and it was his play. Same reason he went ballistic on you for giving Pacho his home address."

"That being?" I asked.

"Protecting kids."

I didn't reply. Took another sip. Getting buzzed now.

"Brian knows you didn't intend to put his family in danger, but you did. His family is his life. He lost a big part of it when his son OD'd on fentanyl. Reason he's still a fucking berserker about taking Santa Fe down."

I filled my glass with booze and drained it. The liquor felt like fire in my veins. At that moment, I no longer viewed Kesey as an enemy. More like a kindred soul in commiseration. I wanted to get sloshed. Poor Billy. Poor Brian's son.

"Brian took a baseball bat from the trunk," he said. "It was his son's. He smashed the kid's father's head over and over until it was a broken watermelon, only the seeds were teeth.

"We cleaned up the scene and checked on the kid before we left. Some dimwit in the hospital told him his father was dead. He didn't cry but began repeating a word over and over again."

Bad, bad? I wondered.

"Daddy, daddy?"

He shook his head. "Orphan, orphan."

I gulped a shot. Fire in the hole.

"Would you kill for your kid, El?"

"I don't have any children."

He chomped his cigar and all at once I remembered a childhood day at the zoo. With Pops? Probably. We were in the big cat house watching an old lion pace back and forth. When he snarled, his teeth were worn, and Pops had said he no longer tears meat apart but crushes it with his molars. Like the lion's, Kesey's gapped teeth were worn down.

Gee, I'm ripped, I thought. *I'm. Totally. Plastered.*

"These people want to hurt Laura," he said.

"No bat for them," I said. "My bare hands."

"Figured you right," he said. "Stand by."

He stood and departed, trailing smoke and leaving me wondering: stand by for what? It was hard deciphering Kesey. He was a self-educated brute who communicated with a mix of military jargon and literary paraphrasing. Stand by who? Stand on my feet? Stand at the ready? Stand by my friend? My ally?

Kesey was now mine, just as I was his. He'd defrocked and deconstructed me, just as I had decoded and understood him.

I raised the last of my Scotch in an imaginary toast:

"Okay, I'll stand by," I said. *Until it's time to kill.*

CHAPTER 49

I was still smashed. Blotto.
All I knew was that things had changed, but not what the things were or how they'd been altered. I had a vague recollection of leaving the cigar bar—Kesey telling me to stand by—suited old johnnies veiled in blue smoke. But that was all.

I couldn't recall walking home or entering my apartment or anything. Shedding my clothes along the way, I staggered to the bathroom. I got into the shower and stood beneath it for long minutes with my head raised, swallowing what cold water didn't drum against my head.

Slowly, clarity returned, and with it a headache. I gulped a handful of aspirin, found my way back to bed, and lay there, still tipsy but somewhat coherent.

My phone pinged. I had a CorrLinks message from Montez. It was a cut-and-pasted document written by a Bogota psychiatrist. Lot of mumbo-jumbo but for a highlighted phrase, "CONCLUSION: PATIENT LAURA ESMERALDA GRAJALES SUFFERS SEVERE BIPOLARITY." that jumped out at me. A lie, I thought. A forged manifestation of Montez's envy, a spiteful message fueled by his having lost her. Laura didn't need help.

But I did.

Bile rose in my throat at the thought of Laura and Montez—whoops!—I beelined to the bathroom and vomited.

Tasted like Scotch. Ugh. My stomach felt raw.

In search of soothing, I went to the kitchen. I'm an eat-out or take-in gal and my cupboard's eternally bare, but the weekly maid I never see likes her coffee. I filched her milk carton from the fridge and drank a glass. Felt a degree of instant relief the way I used to during my once-upon-a-time days and nights as a drug abuser. I poured a second glass. Milk was a good thing. Like mother's milk....

Orphan, orphan.

The words resonated. I had no father and my Mama had been more akin to my little sister. I was a *de facto* orphan and somehow Kesey knew it, and that Billy's story would get to me. I'd dropped my guard, as he'd segued to DiMaglio killing a man, and from there to whether I would kill—and I'd been stupid-drunk enough to say that I would. With my bare hands, no less.

Judge Graff ordered the Montez case to be conferenced.

Energized by sudden purpose, I put on my mom's prized fall collection 1990 Bottega Veneta pantsuit, stepped into her vintage Versace velvet low heels, and went to court.

Montez on my right, AUSA Wilkinson on my left, we stood before the bar.

"Status?" Graff said.

Wilkinson's reply was *pro forma.* "Negotiations are continuing. The government requests a four-month adjournment."

Graff looked at me. "Counselor?"

"Defense agrees and consents."

"Adjourned," Graff said, pausing. His poker-faced brief rulings were legendary, but I'd pickled up a tell—the 'stache of his white goatee curled ever so slightly before he added a caveat. Now his 'stache rose above a wicked smile and I sensed a problem coming. "For thirty days," he added, "at which time trial shall commence."

Montez let out a low gasp. "No...."

"The negotiation is of great import," Wilkinson protested.

"You people have been negotiating for months," Graff said. "The government wants to offer an agreement, then do it now. The defense wants to accept it, schedule a plea with Brunhilda. If not, see you at trial."

Graff banged his gavel. Black robe swirling, he left the bench.

Sotto voce, Wilkinson said, "I'll speak to my supervisor, but I don't foresee a cooperation agreement."

"Come on, Jenna," I said. "Montez gave you the skinny on Paz. How can you not reward him?"

"The printing plate's still out there. He's holding back where."

"No, I'm not," Montez said to her. "Just a little more time."

"Discuss it with your lawyer, Mr. Montez."

Montez turned to me, but the court security marshal gripped his arm. "Let's go, pal," he said to Montez. "Counselor, I'll give you a minute in the pen before he goes to intake."

I followed them into the pen. The marshal stood aside as Montez and I spoke between bars.

"Listen to me," he said. "My people are close to finding the plate. You have to help them."

"I want Laura."

"I'll tell you where she is."

His eyes were moist and I knew it wasn't an act. Without a cooperation agreement, he'd either be forced to go to trial in a month and he'd lose and get life, or plead to the indictment and, if lucky, get twenty-something.

"But you have to trust me," he continued. "You're the key to my problem. Please, meet my people in Colombia."

"Vizcaino will be happy to see me there," I said. "Afraid I'll have to deny him the pleasure."

"Don't worry about Vizcaino," Montez whispered. "I have my own plans for that dog."

"Okay, time's up," the marshal said.

"Arias will lead you to Laura," Montez said. "Together you can get the plates."

Huh? Had I heard him right? *Together? Plates, plural?*

"Time," the marshal said.

CHAPTER 50

Leeds appeared at my office unexpectedly.

I'd disliked him at first sight and on second look pinned down why. With his slim-cut suit and narrow tie and too perfect hair, he was a Jared, the G version of a male Karen; a me-firster.

"Here's the deal," Leeds said. "Get the plate, and your client will get his cooperation agreement. I'll make a submission to his sentencing memorandum that the government recommends a very significant sentence reduction."

Coming from Leeds, the promise seemed an overreach. "Says you," I said.

"Says the Treasury Department after consulting with Main Justice," he said. "As an added incentive, you can continue your practice, tawdry as it is."

"Spot-on observation," I said. "You wouldn't believe the types who visit me. Pull up a chair." I think he smirked, but maybe it was the customary angle of his thin-lipped mouth. He about-faced and left.

"Leeds's father has major connections in DC," Gino said.

"He sees his son as a rising star. The kid wants to make a big splash by turning Montez from a drug dealer to a counterfeiting mastermind who threatens the nation's economy. Apparently, he sold it, because if the plate's recovered, Main Justice will overrule the Southern District, and Montez will not only get an agreement, he might even be released into the Witness Protection Program."

Just as Leeds had intimated. "You know this how?" I asked.

He shrugged. "My own old-boy network," he said.

"Don't jive me, Gino," I said. "What really freaks me? Leeds lifted his 'economic disaster' fantasy from Montez."

"Told you Martin was a smart boy," Gino said. "He knows the plate is Leeds's Holy Grail because he knows the backstory."

"Which is?"

"Currency plates are closely guarded. Particularly Franklin plates. About twenty years ago, Treasury did a routine inventory and discovered a Franklin plate was missing. It was a big deal for a while, then went hush-hush. Six months later, the Bureau of Engraving and Printing issued a press release saying the confusion had been resolved. The missing plate was one that had been damaged and destroyed. Should have been deleted from inventory but wasn't. The schmuck who screwed up was canned."

"There's a moral to the story?" I asked.

"An *im*-moral. It was never destroyed."

"How do you know that?" I asked.

"Trust me, Electra. I know."

CHAPTER 51

Home alone.
Beyond my terrace window, March was a raging lion. Wind whined and rattled my windows. The apartment was dim but for a red light winking on my landline. Like the red light that had winked on Pacho's phone before the message from his Pretrial Supervisor that had motivated my leaving the scene, pronto. Doubtful the present winking would be so pivotal. Probably was a voicemail from one of my few remaining clients wanting to rant about my absence, or Gino Moskowitz, checking in on me.

But I didn't want to speak to anyone. Hadn't since I'd cooped up and began waiting, for what I didn't know—but feared it was for Godot, who never arrives.

"Out, damn light," I commanded, but it winked on. "Okay," I told it, "if you won't stop winking on your own then I'll do it for you." Savagely, I punched the red button.

A voicemail came on from a guy I couldn't place about something I didn't know.

And then I did. It was the forensic lab hermit. I'd forgotten all about the lab test. He said that the powder he'd analyzed, as I'd suspected, was scopolamine.

"You were in a hurry, then forgot all about it," he said. "You got a short-term memory problem?"

Yeah, I did. And long-term complications: short circuits in my brain that had influenced the true north of my moral compass. I needed to right myself. Shed ill-advised forays to the dark side. Quit Martin Montez. Forget Laura. Pick up the pieces and start all over.

But I couldn't, because, despite everything, I was still waiting for Montez or Vizcaino to come at me again, so I could take them down. Because of Laura, peaceful me had taken a savage turn. Saving her was a belated way of saving myself. Long weeks had passed without a word from, or about, her. At first, I'd fretted whether she was okay, but then dismissed that thought. Laura was a survivor.

Kesey had disappeared. He'd used me until I was useless. He was following his own agenda. At Montecristo, booze had loosened his tongue.

"About Laura," he'd said. "I'd heard she was Montez's skirt and figured her as a former Miss Bogota second runner-up, whatever. But I figured wrong. She's one hell of a young woman and she hates Montez worse than I do. I'm gonna help her get payback."

Then he'd hacked a laugh which became a cough and he'd patted his lips with a napkin that came away blood spotted. I wondered what he meant by payback. For Laura's lost innocence? Or for some private memory of his own? His Rosebud....

I wanted payback too.

I got my wish.

The steam bath was hot and humid but gave me the shudders.

Droplets beaded on the ceiling and trickled down its walls and sheened the tiled bench. I hoped a terry robe and three folded towels under my ass would insulate me from the bodily fluids of previous Korean Delight 24-hour Massage customers who'd taken post-sex steam there.

The room was a petri dish. I shivered. *Yuck.*

"Mother of pearl, Smukler, you couldn't find a better joint?" Joachim Paz asked. He turned roaming eyes to me. I tucked in my robe.

"She ain't wired, Joachim." Smukler said.

Paz looked at me. "You look under her robe? The way she got it wrapped so tight nothing shows but an inch of ankle."

"You don't ask a lady," Smukler said. "I mean, I wouldn't mind if she chooses to, ah, expose, but I doubt she will. Right?" Smukler asked, eying me hungrily.

I wasn't wired—no need to be—Kesey had already wired the steam room before renting it for our exclusive use. But there was no way I would flash my goodies. Not for anyone, but especially not for these creeps. Smukler was repulsive; his teats were bigger than mine and his belly was so big I doubted he'd seen his pecker in years.

"You lied," Paz said to me. "You do have something."

"Lawyers lie," I said. "Maybe I do. Or not."

"Let's get down to business," he said.

"Vizcaino contacted me," I said. "He wants to deal. He'll exchange the plate for Montez's stash."

"Make the deal," he said.

"I don't trust Montez. You and him are old buds. Broker a treaty. I get a one-third finder's fee. You get one-third of my one-third."

"One-ninth?" Paz said. "I don't do one-ninths. I do fifty-fifty. It's not negotiable."

I pretended to consider. "Okay," I said. "If you kill this phony threat crap."

Paz looked at Smukler. "Have your clients repent about overhearing Montez threaten anyone."

"Consider it done, Joachim," Smukler said.

Paz looked at me. "When?"

"I'm working on it," I said.

March had departed silently as a lamb, and my window glistened with the first April shower.

My phone buzzed. Unknown Caller. I held it to my ear. "April fool," Kesey said. "Pick you up in ten."

The rain had backed up traffic.

Kesey held a cigar with one hand, the other on the wheel, casually driving his unmarked car through and around traffic, occasionally whooping cars out of our way, ignoring red lights, wrong-waying streets. He drove like Vizcaino, I thought. Cops and robbers.

"Why the hurry?"

"Because the guy we're about to see is a creature of habit. It's five-thirty. At six sharp, the guy locks up his office and blows up a snowstorm with the secretary he's dicking."

"DEA to the rescue, huh?" I replied. "Pull over and let me out or I'll open the door and jump."

Smoke streamed from Kesey's mouth as he spoke: "Before you parachute let me tell you what's up. You'll like it."

CHAPTER 52

The waiting room of Morton Smukler's law office looked like the lobby of a hot sheet hotel.

When we entered, Kesey flashed his badge and thumbed the secretary out the door; her butt implants jiggled as she left.

Smukler was taking his tie off when we entered his room. When he saw Kesey's badge, he began blinking as if trying to make the image disappear.

"Don't say one fucking word, counselor," Kesey said to him. "Just listen hard, because the next couple of minutes are going to determine the rest of your life. Understood?"

Smukler nodded pathetically. For a dirty lawyer, he wasn't a bad guy. I felt sorry for him because I knew what Kesey was going to say, and was equally sure how Smukler would respond, and what it would lead to.

"I'm gonna keep it simple," Kesey said. "Joachim Paz fed you four drug cases in Miami. These same four guys are cooperating in an investigation of a threat made to a federal prosecutor. Their stories match because Paz instructed you to tell them what to say. So now you have to decide whether you want to fight us and get your ass kicked or give up Paz and maybe get a walk. Give you one minute."

A tear ran down Smukler's cheek.

"I'll give you Paz," he said.

Back in the car, Kesey relit his cigar.

"Enjoy the scene?" he asked.

"Great fun watching a man grovel," I said. "Lock him up, whatever, he deserves it. You needed an audience?"

"You," he said. "You're still in the game, sis."

"If I choose to be," I said. "Supposing I am, what's my role?"

"Skinning a snake," he said. "A smart snake who hides behind cutouts like Smukler."

"Joachim Paz," I said. "Hip-hip-hooray for humanity. Again, why me?"

"Smukler's an evader," he said. "Not the best witness. Which is why you're gonna corroborate his testimony."

"Wrong. No way I'm gonna testify as a rat," I said. "What's the real haps anyway? Like DiMaglio said, Smukler and Paz are minor players."

"Smukler is. Only thing minor about Paz is his height."

"You're getting your rocks off nailing them because you ran into a stone wall with the lead characters."

"Actually, Smukler and Paz are the warm-up act for the principal thespian's final appearance."

"Between your stogie and your bullshit, it stinks in here," I said. "Lower your window and stop talking in other people's tongues."

"You know the rules. Rats can't choose how they cooperate; they cooperate about everything. Smukler will give up Paz, who knows he's looking at major time. Paz knows all about Montez's past. He'll vomit everything up and he'll nail Montez's coffin shut. Slam dunk."

"I thought Don J already was the nailer."

"Yeah, well, that remains to be seen."

"The jury will hate Paz. If he's all Wilkinson's got, a good lawyer might walk Montez."

"No fucking way that happens, Ms. Electra," he said. "Montez is going down to where the Unabombers and Chapos go. The supermax. Alone in an underground box, losing his mind."

"Not," I said. "Montez will give up the plate and get a cooperation agreement."

He laughed. "You really think so? Don't."

"You don't care about the plate, you just want to hurt Montez," I said. "Why do you hate him so much?"

"Do I? Free country, you're entitled to your opinion," he said.

"Count me out," I said. "Montez can retain another lawyer."

"Sorry, but you're in for the duration, sis," he said. "See, it's a matter of this for that. The 'this' is that the murder book isn't closed on Pacho's death, in which you remain a prime suspect according to Brian DiMaglio. He thinks you got a great ass, but he'd love to knock you on it."

"Scary," I said lightly, but it was. "What's the 'that?'"

"Work with me and DiMaglio closes the book on Pacho."

"You told me it was already closed."

"Yeah, well, I fibbed."

"The offer is above your pay grade, not to mention illegal," I said. "I was worried you were taping me, but you should be worried I'm taping you."

"I'm too old to worry."

"Where's Laura?"

"In mourning," he said. "Her mother died. Vizcaino found another way to force her to lead him to Montez's treasures—the plate and *dinero*—his war chest for taking over Santa Fe. He snatched her niece, Pacho's daughter, Cleo. He wants to trade cards for the girl."

"Cards? More than one?"

"Seems like," he said.

"He'll hurt Laura," I said.

"Maybe she'll have friends."

"I'm one of them," I said.

Kesey handed me two envelopes as he turned to leave.

"It's almost showtime," he said.

CHAPTER 53

I opened Kesey's envelopes in my office.
In one was a ticket on tonight's Avianca red-eye to Cali, a puzzlement, for Cali was far south of Bogota. Jeepers, I was hitting the road again.

The second envelope contained a note with jagged edges as if ripped from a memo pad. In bold block-lettering written with a Sharpie it said: "Into the valley of $$$," followed by a stick figure wearing a scarf. It was signed "K."

K was Kesey. The $$$ signs were Santa Fe's money. The scarf was a reference to my still being a suspect in Pacho's murder. "Into the valley" was lifted from Tennyson's poem about doomed calvary riding into the valley of death.

Pure Kesey weirdness.

I looked for a deeper meaning but found only one simple reason: Kesey was afflicted by the Lonely Guy syndrome. Live your life of solitude but occasionally enjoy a cryptic exchange with a like-minded loner.

Like me, I lamented.

Quandary: I wanted to bring my modest arsenal to Colombia. But how?

My profiled frequent flying there often set off JFK security alarm bells, and I was a prime target for not-so-random searches for drugs or money. Same deal upon arrival at Bogota's El Dorado, whose computer highlighted me as "known to associate with criminals." These minor indignities come with my territory, so I typically just go with the flow. But it limited certain necessities I could bring aboard a plane.

I rummaged through my office and found an impressive velvet box with a prestigious label that had been evidence in a jewelry robbery case. I blew dust off it, polished my brass knuckles, and put them inside the box. To underline it being a gifted piece of lowbrow jewelry, like diamond-studded teeth grilles, I even wrote a note: "Yo, bro, Happy B-day."

The little Beretta was more problematic. I disassembled its frame and undid its works until it was a harmless little pile of nuts and bolts and springs. I removed the bullets from the clips and added them to the pile.

Then I dug in Mama's closet and unearthed one of her prized shoulder bags, an over-the-top creation of a much-hyped '70s designer whose ascent to stardom ended when he O.D.'d in a mixed-sex restroom in Studio 54. Guy was the fashion equivalent of a penniless Basquiat whose originals now fetched big bucks. Mama could've solved our money problems but refused to sell the bag. She never included it in her daily dress-ups either, which got me to thinking it invoked a sad memory of my father. It was special.

The bag's interior was lined with gold the designer had ingeniously melted and painted on. I put the bits and pieces and bullets beneath the gold lining. Of course, X-rays would detect gold—which was in plain view, clearly flaunted, not surreptitiously attempted to be concealed—and would merge the little bits of metal haphazardly behind it to a wavy, indistinguishable image.

It would do.

But the Beretta's barrel was a too-large giveaway. How to conceal three inches of steel cylinder? Easily. Because I'm a lawyer people think I write a lot. Actually, I mainly doodle, but I get gifted with expensive pens. I selected a Cartier special edition gold widebody ballpoint, unscrewed its top and removed its ink cartridge, slid the Beretta's barrel in, then screwed the top back on. I'd clip the pen in my pocket for all the world to see and the security X-ray wouldn't flag it as suspicious. I hoped.

I needn't have been concerned.

Kesey was waiting for me at the check-in counter. "Where you go, I go," he said.

"Seems to me I'm the one following," I said.

He flashed his badge and led me around the security checkpoint to our gate.

"Why Cali?" I asked. "Why not Bogota?"

"Let me count the whys, starting with *Los CTIs*," he said. The CTI, or *Cuerpo Tecnico de Investigations,* was a supposedly elite division of the Colombian National Police widely known to be riddled with crooked cops.

"Before Vizcaino became a para and a drugster, he was CTI," Kesey said. "Keeps up with his old CTI buddies. Ten seconds after your passport is scanned in Bogota immigration, he'll get a call from them. We don't want that to happen."

Montez had assured me Vizcaino was under control. I wondered if Kesey knew that, or whether there was another reason for going to Cali.

"Trust me, sis," he said.

"I don't, bro."

"You're going in-country through Cali to stay beneath the radar and maintain the element of surprise."

"Same problem entering Cali as Bogota, no?" I asked.

"Nah. Since the original cartels went down, Cali and Medellin are hick towns, cartel-wise. The big action's in Bogota now. Better catch some *Zs* during the flight. May not have time to sleep the next couple of days."

I looked at my watch. "Too early for my body clock to stop."

"Hold out your hand," he said. He took out a phial, and from it tapped a pill into my palm. "My little friend will sweeten your dreams."

"Possessing controlled substances is a side benefit of being DEA, huh?"

A wide grin split his round face like it was carved into a pumpkin. "Narcs are like doctors," he said. "Closet addicts."

Before we took off, I saw him dry-swallow two of the pills. I'm not big on downers, but I took mine. By the time we were airborne, I was starting to nod off. Kesey was already snoring softly. In repose, his blunt features seemed childlike. As I faded to black, my last thought was whether this unwell rogue DEA agent was friend or foe.

Something moved—I opened my eyes and saw red.

I blinked and the red cape of the Avianca stewardess swam into focus. "*Lo siento, señora,*" she said. "*No puede reclinarse,* we are landing."

"Smooth flight," I said, although I didn't remember a moment of it. "*Mis cumplidos al piloto.*"

"*Gracias,*" she said, putting my breakfast tray down. "*Buen provecho.*"

I wolfed my food down and enjoyed the rush of Colombian coffee. Kesey appeared from the restroom. He sat alongside and handed me my gold pen. It felt light so I uncapped it. The Beretta barrel was gone. I looked at him.

He grinned and handed me my reassembled pistol. "You would've gotten by the security people, but no one gets one over on me. Nice bag, by the way. Hey, we're almost there."

I looked below. The Andes begin at the southern tip of South America and extend like a spine through the continent to Colombia, where they split into three ranges. On a topographical map, they resemble a trident.

The plane was banking, and beyond the window, two snow-capped mountain ranges flanked a flat valley checkered with fields. Ahead a white city sprawled across the shoulders of foothills: Cali.

"Your knucks are in your backpack," Kesey said.

CHAPTER 54

When we disembarked, a jeep was waiting on the tarmac.
The driver wore camo. No insignia but obviously a *gringo*. He drove us past multi-colored commercial jetliners snuggled against the terminal to a far corner of the tarmac where a half-dozen unmarked aircraft were parked: a pair of four-engine cargo carriers, a scatter of prop-driven spotter planes, and two helicopters, one of them a plexi-bubbled cockpit four-seater and the other an honest-to-God gunship bristling with missiles. Plan Colombia was, in G parlance, robust.

As we boarded the four-seater, Kesey grunted replies into his phone. As the rotors began to thrum, I heard him talking: "Copy that," he said. "No ma deuce. Need a Barrett fifty. Red Team is going kinetic. K, out."

I'm not fluent in military jargon but I understood enough. A ma deuce was old infantry slang for a heavy machine gun. But Kesey hadn't wanted a ma deuce—too cumbersome, whatever. He'd asked for a Barrett fifty, a big, armor-piercing, long-distance sniper rifle. Kinetic, I deciphered as energy in the form of explosives. Red Team was a strike force. His?

"You going to start a war?" I asked.

"End one that began a long time ago."

The chopper followed a road that meandered between small towns.

It flew so low—literally beneath the radar—that I could read road signs. A mile past one that said YUMBO, we set down by a tall cane field that shimmered in the heat. When the rotors stopped, I heard insects chirping.

A man wearing a black cargo jumper stood on the edge of

the field. He was a lean guy with a black, peaked cap shadowing his face. I felt as if I'd seen him before but couldn't pin when or where. He and Kesey barely nodded, but I sensed they knew each other well. Then the guy removed his cap to wipe his face and I recognized him as Indio, the man who'd escorted her to Pacho's funeral and later killed his ambusher outside my apartment.

I'd been right. He was a DEA undercover. His presence here suggested that Laura was also in Colombia.

He led us along a path that wound through the cane. The tall stalks closed behind us, disorienting my sense of direction.

Eventually, the cane field opened to a clearing occupied by a ramshackle building. Above its entrance a faded sign said CLUB SAHARA.

"Back when Cali was *the* Cartel, its top guys used to confab out here," Kesey said. "Belt *aguardiente,* discuss the latest in the powder trade. Boss man was a guy named Herrera who dug old war movies. Named this place after one of his favorites."

"*Sahara,*" I said. "Bogart. Great film. One of my favorites too."

"Birds of a feather," he said. "Criminal lawyers and criminals."

"You said Cali was just our back door into Colombia," I noted. "Seems like it's more."

"Yeah, well, it is more," he said.

Actually, it was much more.

From outside, Club Sahara seemed a small building hard against the dense cane. But within, it extended well into the field. Its entry foyer was sort of a hatcheck room, but instead of hangers there were numbered pegs. A dusty, time-faded empty holster hung from one.

"Cartel boss protocol," Kesey said. "No personal weapons allowed inside."

A steel bunker-like door was ajar. We followed Indio through to a carpeted room where armchairs were set around low tables. The withered remains of a half-smoked Cohiba lay in a mother-of-pearl ashtray. A half-opened door led to another space.

"Once upon a time, Club Sahara was the Montecristo Cigar

Bar for the Cali cartel," Kesey said. "Back then, their message to the world was, 'Look at us and despair at our might.' Now the only kingpin here is the ghost of Ozymandias."

So Kesey read Shelley too. What a strange bird.

"Time to clue you to the agenda, sis," he said. "Wilkinson doesn't know about our little side excursion because it was privately greenlit by my old buds in DEA Special Ops. Guys whose golden rule is to protect and preserve one another. That extends to our confidential sources. This mission has two objectives. The first is to even the score for a brother we lost. The second is to make sure we don't lose a source. You following me?"

"No. Why bother clueing me?"

"You're our source, sis."

"Stop the sis thing, okay?"

"No problem, Electra."

No one called me Electra except Gino. Kesey's intimacy was irritating. "You've been snooping me," I said.

"Yeah, I have been," he said. "Give me the card."

The card was my leverage. "What card?" I said.

He smiled. "Sure. Later, when you're ready."

From the other room, I heard voices and metallic sounds. When we entered it, I smelled gun oil and perspiration from a half-dozen men cleaning weapons. Like Indio, they wore black jumpsuits with no insignia.

"*¿Todo bien?*" Indio asked.

"*Si, señor*," one replied.

By the tone of the exchange, Indio was in charge. I looked closer at the planes of his copper face, his high cheeks and full lips and tilted eyes. Unusual, I thought. Colombia's indigenous people rarely interact with white Colombians. Much less with American cops.

"These guys are a handpicked crew," Kesey said. "Honest cops and military. We work with them on no-accountability black ops."

"This is a black op?" I asked.

"Pitch black," Kesey said.

"Shine a light, please."

"The action's at another old Cali cartel hangout," he said.

"Now temporarily occupied by a Santa Fe guy who wants to take Montez's place."

"Vizcaino," I said.

"Word is that he's holding a woman there," he said. "He wants to exchange her for the cards. Like the one you're dummied up about."

Laura's niece, Cleo, I thought. An offer I couldn't refuse.

"This is personal for you," I said.

"That makes two of us," he said.

CHAPTER 55

"This is the set," Kesey said.

We were all gathered around a map Indio had drawn with charcoal on dried bark. Hard to make out at first, but then forms assumed themselves: Fields were defined between lines. An irregular shape spilled across a few. A lake, I supposed. Between it and the fields, a single road wound from a small building—a guardhouse?—on the perimeter to a cluster of buildings in the center.

"Thirty years ago, this was Herrera's favorite Cali cartel hideout," Kesey said. "Guy had dozens of *fincas* and used to sleep in a different one every night. Smart boy. He knew extradition was going to be legalized by Colombia and surrendered publicly. Pled guilty here, which immunized him from extradition. Bribed and cooperated an eight-year sentence. Good behavior meant four years in a jail he built himself. Forget conjugal visits, he was allowed conjugal *departures*.

"Herrera was on the jail pitch playing soccer when a guy, whose nephew he had killed, emptied a nine into his head. Voila: The new boss became Montez. He inherited this place. Toylandia."

"Sounds like some kind of cartel Disneyworld."

"It was, back in the nineties," he said. "But Montez isn't into horses and cattle or getting his hands dirty with his private army. He moved his operation to Bogota. Set things up so other people deal with the product; he just oversees the income it generates. Surrounds himself with a few good bad men his Mexican partners provided—the *X*s—and works remotely from wherever the girls are."

Indio pointed at what seemed like a gatehouse. "*Aquí es muy peligroso,*" he said.

"Heavily guarded," Kesey said. "No one gets in without Vizcaino's okay."

"They bring in *putas* every night," Indio said. "The bad boys tell the girls things. Vizcaino was with some last night."

"You got it down, sis?" Kesey asked me. "Make sure, because you're point. Be easy. Flash your smile and you'll walk right in."

"I ain't playing *puta,*" I told him. I meant it to sound lighthearted, but it didn't raise a smile.

"You're not playing, you're lawyering," Kesey said. "Negotiations are your thing, right? Well, you got something to negotiate with. Tell Vizcaino you're ready to deal. You and Laura give him what he wants, and he'll give you Laura's niece."

"Besides a card I don't have, what does Laura have?" I asked.

"Same as you. Paired queens. He'll take the meet."

"Okay," I said. "And then what?"

"The cavalry arrives. Me."

Pequeños amarillos, the little yellows, are the mini-taxis that are ubiquitous everywhere in Colombia.

One was waiting for me on the road outside the cane field. Ten miles later I got out and it buzzed away. I looked around.

No one in sight. Tall cane towered above an empty roadway. Just ahead was a driveway, gated and flanked by a guardhouse. Past it, a road wound between manicured lawns. I walked up it.

Brutal as cartel *jefes* are, they have a strangely childlike side. Could be because their own childhoods were ruthlessly violent and otherwise lacking, so when they became wealthy adults, they indulged their long-repressed fantasies. Pablo Escobar had his very own zoo. Herrera turned a finca into a private park. During the taxi drive, I'd Googled the place. Toylandia had soccer fields, stables and tracks, a lake to powerboat on, a grass strip long enough for ultra-lights, a helipad, a cinema, a disco, and a free bordello.

I reached the gatehouse. Its windows were one-way black. I expected to be challenged but nothing happened. I rapped on the glass. Still nothing,

Cali was five thousand feet above sea level but only two hundred miles north of the equator. The sun beat down. *Muy caliente.* My undies were damp with perspiration. My bra chafed. Insects whined in my ears—

My phone buzzed. "Texted you a number," Kesey said. "Call it."

When I did my screen lit up. A face time image of Vizcaino's mug.

"Ah, the good *Doctora*," he said. "How did you get my number?"

"Laura gave it to me," I said, hoping to elicit her circumstances.

"She's with you?"

"Nearby," I said.

"Where are you?"

"We're in Bogota," I said. "Wanting to do business. Where are you?'

"First, show me what you have."

I took out my device and pulled up a photograph of my card.

"That's one," he said. "Where's the other one?"

"Laura has it," I said. "Where should we bring them?"

"Wait for my call." The screen went dark.

Kesey called again. "Go in," he said.

"Alone? I thought you'd be—"

"No problem. You're covered."

I entered Toylandia, passing a stable. Empty stalls; rotted hay; the skeletal remains of a horse, its empty harness small, befitting a dish-faced Arabian. Long gone now. Like Ozymandias. Like Kesey himself soon would be. A hard man, hell-bent toward eternity but reveling in his last mission and its rewards. But money was useless if you were dead, so perhaps he derived pleasure simply from pursuing it. At least it would spare him a hole in a Potter's Field.

Half-sunken speedboats were moored in mud by the lake. Man-made, it was shrinking, reverting to nature. Its surface was no longer smooth but dotted with vegetation where its bottom had resurfaced. I thought of an overgrown cemetery whose grounds were unkempt. Where there had been roses were thornbushes. Litter everywhere: stubbed cigarettes, beer bottles, used condoms.

Ahead, a *hacienda*. Vizcaino's hideaway, I thought. Mission accomplished, but where's my cavalry? I trusted Kesey, but I took out my little Beretta as I entered the hacienda.

A once-grand entrance hall was in shambles. Mud-caked footsteps on its marble floors. Beer cans in an empty fountain crowned by an angel that looked as if it had escaped Rome, B.C.E. Outside, the sun was a furnace, but inside, the shaded stones were cool. But that was not why a shiver ran down my spine. I was alone in a graveyard, haunted by the ghosts of dead cartel bosses and the bad vibes of their descendants.

At the far side of the space a door was open; beyond it, shaded greenery. I went outside. Beyond the house's shaded eaves was an overgrown garden. A path led through it to a bungalow. Beretta pressed against my side, I went up steps that led to a small portico fronting a bungalow. Its door was closed. On either side were windows, slatted shutters open—

A hand clamped my mouth. It was Indio.

"Shhh," he whispered. "Stay here."

Silently he entered the bungalow.

I knew the scenario was fraught with danger, but a lifetime of resentments welled up in me. Why can guys do things women can't? They hunt but we can't? No way. Anything any man can do I can do better. I'm the huntress from hell and wanted to sate my anger.

Crouched in a shooter's stance, I went into the bungalow.

Two people were there. Indio held a dagger to the throat of a man who looked like one of the *X* brothers. "Where's Victor?" Indio asked.

"He and my brothers went to the kiln."

"If you lie, you'll die," Indio said.

"The kiln, it's the truth, I swear."

"Here's your truth, *demonio*."

Indio slashed the *X*'s throat.

I watched him sag and bleed out and felt not a twinge of

pity, but marveled at how my perceptions had changed. Some people needed killing. Doing so was a good thing.

I wasn't aware of Kesey behind me until he spoke. His eyes were wild. "There's bodies buried under this playground because Herrera liked knowing where his enemies were. Didn't matter; for every contender put down, another sprang up. The one who murdered my bud is still alive. Won't be much longer now. It all ends at the kiln."

CHAPTER 56

An inch on a Colombian map can be a long day's journey, and although our destination was barely one hundred-fifty miles from Bogota, it was at the end of a road that meandered along treacherous high-country hillsides below the base of the *Cordillera Centrale*. It was late afternoon when the jeep carrying Kesey and I pulled over at a bend in the road. Unmarked jeeps were parked there, and Indio's men were waiting. He wasn't among them.

A mile below and away, cooking fires flickered in a small town called La Calera—the name's literal translation was "the limestone kiln." I didn't know why and didn't ask.

Kesey thumbed toward it. "Montez and Vizcaino's paramilitaries operated out of there. Figured he'd head for familiar territory."

"Right," I said. "So?"

"Same deal as we planned for Toylandia. Let Vizcaino know you're ready to deal. Prisoner exchange. Cleo and the plate for your card. Do your thing, sis."

"What about Laura?" I asked.

"Worry about yourself."

I called Vizcaino. His face was shadowed, dimness behind it. "I told you to wait for my call," he said angrily.

"I'm not waiting for you," I said. "I want the girl now."

He hesitated, then, "Where are you?"

"Close to the kiln," I said.

"How did you know—"

"Laura knew," I said.

"Alright. Come now."

The road was in the shadow of a rock-walled cleft so steeply angled downward that I had to lean backward to maintain my balance. From my tilted viewpoint, the sun between the high peaks was a blinding slash of brilliance. I looked away from the light to darkness far below where the cleft narrowed to an unseeable joinder.

The dissonance provoked thoughts.

All my life I'd been alone—yet had never felt lonely. Now I wasn't sure what I felt. I'd come in search of... what? My own salvation? Yes. And also, someone to watch over, or pardon the airhead vernacular, a BFF. Whichever, I was out in the boonies putting my butt on the line for my peace of mind and a person I knew little of and perhaps would never know more. Lord help me, it felt good.

"Every step you take I'm watching you, counselor." Through earbuds, Kesey's voice was otherworldly, but I knew he was close by. I felt his lens on me, an itch I couldn't scratch.

"Look down at the road," he said.

It was ridged by tread marks.

"Vizcaino's armored truck," he said. "Pointing your way. The situation changes, react and adapt. That ledge on your right? Leave your phone there. Don't want Vizcaino thinking you're my GPS puppet. Want him to see you as a lawyer. A negotiator. Leave the gun, and your knucks too."

I left the phone, the gun, and the knucks on a rock ledge and continued down the road. It was beginning to level. Ahead, I saw a massive heap of garbage, heard the caws of birds wheeling above it, as the ramshackle outskirts of a village came into view beyond and below.

La Calera.

The road was the village's main street. On its margins, tin-roofed shacks clung to hillsides. No people in sight, but smoke rose from chimney pipes, and the hearty smell of *sancocho* wafted from behind shuttered windows.

The street was bordered by only a few buildings. A neon Aguila Cerveza sign glowed red in a shop window. There was a bodega whose second-floor sign said HOTEL, a shuttered cinder block church topped by a cement cross, an abandoned

Estación de Policía with a bullet-pocked façade. Not a soul in sight.

But I felt eyes on me.

La Calera was an indigenous town whose populace contained caution in their DNA. They'd withstood Spaniard conquistadors, government death squads, the depredations of drug lords, and attacks by anti-government guerrillas whose wet dreams were of Che. Bad times that worsened when the paramilitary mercenaries of the rich and infamous took over. Lock the door and hide your daughter from the paras, especially *Commandante* Montez and *Teniente* Vizcaino.

The tread marks led past La Calera to where the road dog-legged along the seam in the mountains that ended at another valley. It brought to mind Kesey's bizarro-at-the-time reference to the opening line of Tennyson's *Charge of the Light Brigade*—"into the valley of death"—because on the valley's far end was an enormous stone building, its windowless façade suggesting things best left unseen within.

There was a mobile-home-style trailer ahead. Old, perched on blocks. A big SUV with monster wheels was parked alongside.

"*¡Muévese y muere señora!*" a man said, startling me. He held an automatic rifle leveled at my midsection. "*¿Que quiere?*"

"To talk *con su jefe*," I said. "*El me conoce.*"

"*Túmbese, señora,*" he said.

I lay on the muddy ground. Heard them rummage through my bag. Watched an ant pass my nose. Felt a gun muzzle press against the back of my neck. Then—

"*Bueno. Ve con el.*"

I was lifted to my feet. Vizcaino faced me. He had discarded his lawyer's suit and square-toed shoes for camo tucked into field boots. An automatic pistol was strapped to his thigh.

He had reverted to his paramilitary origins. La Calera was his command post, the trailer his war room.

"Your *carta*," he said. I want it. *Now.*"

"I don't have it. It's nearby."

"And the other? Laura's?"

"She as well. Very near."

"Where? My men will go to her."

"Before anything, I want to see the girl."

"We exchange *simultánaneamente*. Clean yourself before. Such a pretty woman you are—no wonder Martin chose you. When I am in charge, I would like to continue working with you. It would be a good thing. There may be a time when I am in need of a lawyer."

"When do we do the exchange?" I asked.

"Tonight," he said. "Here."

CHAPTER 57

It was still hours before dark, but the sun had passed behind the mountains and the road was purpling toward twilight.

My things remained where I'd left them.

I pocketed the Beretta, phone, and knucks, then called Kesey. When I told him about my meeting Vizcaino, he snorted disbelief.

"Either he's a fucking moron or he thinks you are," he said. "*He* wants to set up the exchange? Counselor, his deck is stacked. Deal his way and you'll get nothing but dead."

"Gimme a break, big guy," I said. "As you pointed out, negotiation's what I do. Conjure me a new script to follow."

"It's already written. Tell me about the set."

"Vizcaino operates out of an old trailer."

"Trash that he is," he interrupted.

"The trailer's on the edge of town," I said. "Far enough so his half-dozen guys with burp guns can see anyone coming from a quarter mile away."

"Fuck meeting in the trailer," he said. "We're going to La Siberia."

"What, like ... Russia?"

"Worse. You'll see."

It was nearly dark in the seam now. I thought Vizcaino's goons might be following me. Or stalking me with drones.

As if sensing my concern, Kesey said, "No one watching you but me and my man."

"What man?" I asked.

"*Hola*," a man said.

I turned and saw a man on the roadway. He lit his phone

and held it to his face, highlighting the porcine features of *abogado* Adolfo Arias. A lightbulb clicked on in my mind as I suddenly understood his role. He was Kesey's informant, confirming that Kesey knew from the start that Laura had skin in the game, and explaining how Kesey knew the obscure objects of everyone's desire were the white plastic cards.

"Please come along, *Doctora,*" he said.

A footpath ran uphill from the roadway. I followed him along it. He seemed loquacious, but I chalked it up to nervousness. Little wonder, considering his actions shouted as loud as his words.

"It is good that Vizcaino goes down," he said. "Santa Fe will be run by new people. Fresh blood, as they say."

His flipping from Santa Fe to DEA didn't surprise me; it was akin to a rat leaving a sinking ship. The Colombian narcos and their enablers changed allegiances as easily as they replaced putas. Gino was right: Trust no one.

"The new bosses will be hungry and make mistakes," he said. "Their workers will be arrested for extradition. They will come to me, and I shall refer them to my American lawyer. You, *Doctora.* Business will be good for us."

Just when you think things can't get weirder, they do. Here I was in a bleak nowhere, actively participating in the rises and falls and fates of ultra-violent cartel wannabes, and now a square-toed Colombian drug lawyer was planning our joint future pumping money from next-gen cartels.

I sighed ... the business I'm in.

The path steepened and grew narrower. I fell in behind Arias. Here, the foliage was sparse but spiny, tearing at my mud-spattered cargo camos. As we ascended, a half-moon appeared in the space between the peaks, affording a view of Arias's wide backside. His aftershave wafted behind him.

"How much longer?" I asked.

"We're here," he wheezed.

Nearly obscured between a rock outcropping and the bushes was a shack. A candle flickered in the space where there once had been a window. In its dim light, I discerned a shadowed figure within.

"I shall wait outside," Arias said.

Holding the Beretta in my extended arms as if it were a divining rod, I followed it to my future. The shack door was ajar. Would it lead to the beauty or a beast? I pushed it open and entered.

A man stood inside. He wore a work shirt and an old cap whose peak bore the faded logo of a wheelbarrow, and the embroidered words CEMENTO GRAJALES. He took the cap off and revealed himself as Indio.

I lowered the Beretta. He raised a quieting palm and cocked his head as if listening. A long minute passed. Then, from outside, came a bird-like call:

Coo-coo-coo ... coo-coo-coo.

"*Bueno*," Indio said. "Arias has departed. No doubt he's telling Vizcaino where Laura is staying at this very moment."

Arias was also helping Vizcaino? The duplicity in the drug trade never ceased to amaze me.

"Where is she?" I asked.

"Arias thinks with you, here. She is nearby, but Vizcaino won't dare search further."

"Why not?"

"The townspeople are in La Calera, where Vizcaino's men can keep an eye on them. But at night we control the hills. It is our land, and trespassers are severely punished. Come."

There was no path now, just rocks and shrubs.

The moon had been obscured by clouds and the hillside was pitch black. As we climbed higher, I could not see anything, but Indio told me to put my hand on his shoulder. Beneath my fingers, his tough muscles told me the story of his life: a worker who'd once lugged cement for an outfit named *Grajales*, the same last name as Laura—not a coincidence, I thought—and had since become an undercover working for DEA.

"La Siberia," Indio said. "It is fitting that we will meet Laura there. This is where it all began, and this is where she wants it to come to an end. To save her niece, Cleo, and punish those who punished her family."

I looked at him blankly. Indigenous Colombians are insular outcasts, discriminated against by others and not prone to conversing with whites. Yet, I sensed he felt a need to enlighten me, perhaps to fortify my resolve for what lay ahead.

"Her father, *don* Ernesto Grajales, was a good man. Sensitive to my people. Cemento Grajales was a prosperous company, and he shared its income with the people of La Calera who worked there. A *comuna,* he called it. I had the honor of being his *organizador*. When the guerrillas were here, they allowed this. Their *comisar* said it was politically *correcto*. Truth? They were so busy with the *coca* trade and their war with the paras they let us alone. But then the bad time began."

"The paras came," I said.

"Yes," he said. "Then."

We reached the crest of the hill. The clouds that had obscured the moon had passed and I saw the crest ran along a ridgeline atop the hilltops encircling the valley. Below, only a few desultory cooking fires defined La Calera, but across the valley, lights shone from atop the massive building I'd seen earlier.

He glanced at his watch, then looked at the ridge behind us. I heard a vehicle in the distance but couldn't tell whether it was from the road below or the ridgeline.

"They told *don* Ernesto that *La Siberia* was to be run for their benefit," he said. "When he refused, Montez instructed Vizcaino to execute him. Publicly. Laura was forced to watch. Afterward, Montez put her brother Pacho to work for him. Pacho was an intelligent boy. He had gone to university, he spoke *Ingles*. To ensure Pacho's loyalty when he worked in America, Vizcaino kept Laura in Colombia. He fancied her."

I felt a pang in my heart. *Fancied was a fancy word for rape.*

"She escaped and joined Pacho in Los Estados," he said. "Now, La Siberia is a ruin, a monument to the past, like the pyramids ... full of tombs."

CHAPTER 58

A Jeep appeared on the ridge behind us.
Kesey drove, smoke trailing from his cigar. "Everything copacetic?" he asked.
"*Si.*" Indio pointed down the hillside where vehicle headlamps were convoying along the road from La Calera. "Vizcaino thinks you are below with *doña* Laura," he said. "He and his best men are on their way to take you both. This is his *importancia*. The two halves, together."
Two halves? Of what? I wondered.
"La Siberia?" Kesey asked him.
"Lightly guarded."
"Your people?"
"Three below."
"Jesus, man, Vizcaino's got a fucking platoon," Kesey said. "Three men? He'll crush 'em and come up here. So much for the best laid plans of mice and rats."
"There you go again," Indio said. "So many expressions you use I do not know whether they are true or things you have read and repeat. One I remember. Thermopylae."
The name rang a distant bell from my school days. A battle in which three hundred Spartans and their allies sacrificed themselves while holding off over a hundred thousand Persians. Indio's two men might be sacrificed, but they would hold off Vizcaino's men.
"When Vizcaino appears, they'll fire from three positions then move and repeat," Indio said. 'Vizcaino will think he's up against many and dig in for a fight."
"My man, Indio," Kesey said. "How you doing, sis?"

From below, gunshots.

"Time," Indio said.

La Calera was deserted.

"The people are at La Siberia," Indio said.

"In," I corrected. "They're armed?"

"With belief."

Kesey downshifted as the road rose. Ahead, a glow illuminated the sky.

Indio extended an arm as the jeep came through a turn and the slope leading to La Siberia appeared. On it, the people of La Calera sat, holding candles whose collective glow illuminated their bronze faces.

On the roof of La Siberia, the few defenders Vizcaino had left behind were shouting obscenities. A beer bottle glittered in the light and shattered on the steps. The snout of a rifle appeared on the rampart.

My God, these people will be slaughtered, I thought.

The steps were suddenly lit by flashes—grenades, I thought—but the flashes were floodlights set on tripods around the area in front of La Siberia. Beside each tripod stood an armed man wearing a jacket brightly lettered "CNP"—Colombian National Police—the force created to combat renegade paramilitaries. But these men were all part of Indio's crew. Some held video cameras pointed at the scene. One raised a loudspeaker.

"*Policía*," he boomed. "*No te resistas.*"

The men on the roof retreated from sight. The townspeople surged up the slope to La Siberia's massive door.

"¡*Viva la raza!*" Indio shouted, raising a fist.

Long live the race. God willing, I thought.

Indio took my hand and quickly led me past the joyous mob. "The guards are confused," he said. "Some will give up. Others will fight. Or use the captives to escape. Hurry."

We hurried around to La Siberia's rear. Empty and dim there. Nothing but a sagging loading platform. Chutes led from it to small openings in the wall. They were boarded shut.

Indio easily pried a board loose and motioned to me, and I sat on the edge of the chute and slid into blackness. The chute was steep but short, and a moment later, I emerged on my feet and looked around.

Dust and cement. Heaps and bags of cement powder. Piles of sand and crushed rock waiting to become cement. All long-dormant and covered by dust, a concrete jungle frozen in time.

Indio appeared alongside me. I followed him down a corridor and into another. And stopped. A harried-looking guard stood there, looking at us uncertainly. He raised his weapon.

"*Tranquilo, hermano,*" Indio said, pointing at the logo on his shirt. "I am *an hombre de mantenimiento*. Here, I show you my identification."

As he reached into his pocket his free hand yanked the guard's gun barrel, and as the man stumbled forward, Indio's hand produced a blade that slashed the hapless guard's throat in a single motion. Then he grabbed my hand—his, slick with blood—and pulled me with him.

We entered a cavernous, vaulted space that, for a moment, reminded me of Rome's Pantheon, for the only light was a shaft of moonlight through a cathedral-like oculus. Cement dust danced in the beam and rendered the rest of the space near-dark. But as my eyes accustomed to the dimness, I saw the floor was pocked with large pits, and I smelled the stink of shit and decay. It was not a cathedral but the oven room of an extermination camp.

I realized I'd been here before—no, seen it before—in the video where Vizcaino had murdered a boy.

Turned out the pits were kilns where cement was once hardened and shaped. But they were cold now, and from the depths of one, a charred skull grinned up at me. From another, a ladder jutted, as if recently used by its captives.

By the ladder, figures took shape in the dimness. A woman and her children. The family of Don J, I knew, for one boy was a younger version of the kid Vizcaino had killed.

Indio pointed at the corridor from which we'd entered. "Run," he told them, and they did.

Two other people emerged from the shadows.

CHAPTER 59

Laura had her arm around Cleo.

The girl's clothing was filthy and hair matted, her gaze unfocused by the sudden shock of release. Laura, overwhelmed by relief, was weeping.

I wanted to comfort her, but words failed me. For want of something else to do, I dug into my cargo pockets and took out the tissue-wrapped earrings I'd bought Laura for Christmas that I'd been carrying ever since in the hope of giving it to her.

I offered them to her, but she did not acknowledge me.

I handed them to Indio. "Hold it for her."

The staccatos of automatic weapons grew nearby. A door splintered open and fleeing guards rushed toward us, shooting wildly. Stunned, I stared as bullets stitched the floor toward me.

Laura tackled me. The bullets struck inches from where I'd been. She lay atop me face-to-face and for a moment our gazes touched. She whispered gently:

"*Esto no se ha terminado. ¿Entiendes?*" Do I understand it's not over?

I understood the words but not their meaning. Was she referring to the local uprising or her own vengeful agenda ... or our continuing relationship?

Then her voice became stern, "*Todos pagan por sus pecados, nena*," she said. "Everyone pays for their sins."

I took that as a stinging reminder, or perhaps a severe rebuke, of what I'd forced from my mind: that Laura had witnessed my killing Pacho.

Before I could reply, she rolled off me and embraced Cleo, protecting her from the maelstrom above. From three directions, bursts of automatic weapon fire ricocheted off the stone floor and buzzed overhead. When the shooters paused to reload, pistol shots replied from just behind us. The automatic fire lessened after each pistol shot. Three, two, one, and then there were none.

Indio stood, smoke curling from the barrel of his lowered Glock.

Three auto-gunners writhed on the floor, gut shot, bleeding out.

Indio offered the Glock to Laura. She didn't take it. She gathered Cleo in her arms and put her hand to my cheek, but her eyes cut to the wounded men.

"My mother died," she said. "She thought that killing was a mortal sin. I am not so sure about that, but I must honor her beliefs. A daughter's duty, you understand."

"You kill the killers, El," she said.

I used my Beretta to kill them. It was easy. One behind the ear thrice and done. I didn't question myself. It was a thing that needed doing by my own hands.

Kesey joined us. "You should have saved one for me," he said.

"You should have been here," I said. "Backing Indio up."

"That boy don't need help from an old fart like me," he said. "Besides, I only got one more fight left in me. Gotta save my strength."

"Vizcaino will be back any minute," I said.

"Nah, he's pinned down on the road," he said. "His armored truck got stuck in a pothole. He called Arias and asked what was going on. Arias says he told him all was cool, come back to La Siberia. Don't know if I believe Arias said that, or if he warned Vizcaino to get out of Dodge. Don't matter. Just a question of time."

Until I met Laura again? Until Vizcaino was dead?

"Tell me what's going on," I said.

"Simple," he said. "Without the hostages, Vizcaino and Montez can't use you and Laura to lead them to the money and the printing plate. You knew Montez was scheming."

I knew, but admitting it was a ticket into a world of trouble. "I don't take jailhouse fantasies seriously," I said.

"Not to worry," Kesey said. "I'll keep your secret, because down the line, you'll keep mine."

"Laura's cooperating with you," I said. "She's going to testify against Montez."

He shrugged. "Indigenous don't rat."

"Laura's not indigenous."

Kesey patted his heart.

"What's that mean?"

"Think about it."

CHAPTER 60

Laura's departing words again raised a question that haunted me.

"Kill the killers."

She'd said it in a tone that reminded me of the black rose she had left on Pacho's coffin. As if she already knew I had it in me to kill. Had I murdered Pacho? I needed to know.

Only Laura could tell me.

What if I had? What then?

Esto no se ha terminado.

It's not finished.

When I returned to New York I had a CorrLinks message from Montez: He wanted me to visit. He said it was important.

I bet it was. By now he must know that the hostages were free and both his get-out-of-jail-free cards had been trumped, so he was going to Plan B: cooperate, cooperate, cooperate, with me continuing to represent him. Some team. A mutual abomination society. But we needed one another.

I had a card that was the key—or half the key, whatever that meant—to finding the money and the plate. Leeds had already made the plate into the major attraction, and he'd further underlined its importance by crediting Montez with saving western civilization or some such nonsense.

I needed to stay in the case because if I didn't represent Montez, there was no justifying my continued presence helping him cooperate, during which I was determined to draw the truth from Laura.

I wasn't pleased by having to visit Montez. Before I did,

AUSA Jenna Wilkinson called. "Your client called me regarding the *Blue Atlantic* matter. In the future, please have him convey such information through you."

"Your guys made the seizure?" I asked.

"El, you know I'm not at ..."

"Liberty to say, right. But since the investigation's ongoing, I'm gonna assume you did. Ten thousand kilos. Big one."

"I'm not confirming anything. Read the press releases."

I went into the SDNY U.S. Attorney's website and there it was: A massive shipment of cocaine intended to be exported to the SDNY had been seized in Cartagena. AUSA Wilkinson was prosecuting the case.

I sighed at my history repeating itself: ethically helping achieve justice for the unjust despite my self-disgust at doing so.

Torn, betwixt and between.

"Cut the crap," Gino said. "The only thing you're torn about is why you keep persevering over a woman who doesn't seem to care about you. To learn if you're a murderer? Hell, don't you know by now?"

"She saved my life."

"Cue the violins," he said. "Accept the fact that you feel the way you feel, then do what you gotta do."

"You have no idea what I feel," I said.

My old mentor was way off, but I didn't correct him. I *did* need to know if I'd killed Pacho, and my feelings about Laura were strong, but limited to sisterly. Motherly, really.

Gino riffled though the letter I'd given him. Montez had mailed it to me, noting that it was the same communication he'd sent Wilkinson. It was a drawing not unlike my Venn diagrams. The boxed entity in the middle was labeled B.A.—the *Blue Atlantic*, no doubt—and the lines from it led to surrounding boxes containing what seemed corporate LLCs and account numbers.

"Looks like your guy's got the skinny on a lot of people," Gino said.

"Kesey called me," I said. "'First Toylandia, then La Siberia, third time's the charm," he said.

"Three, two ... what's one?"
"Akron," I said.

CHAPTER 61

The flight left at dawn and raced the rising sun westward.

It was a small, unmarked jet. Approximating our speed at 450 mph, by my watch, I figured we were over western Pennsylvania. Below, the checkerboard of rural America appeared: ruler-straight county roads running between fields connecting small towns where the sun reflected off early bird traffic.

I sensed the plane dip from its apogee. We'd be landing soon. A short flight, but if we were going where I thought we were, that wasn't surprising.

Behind me, Brian DiMaglio snored softly. A veteran cop, he grabbed shut-eye whenever he could. Asleep, he appeared younger, innocent, even likeable. I understood his antipathy toward me and regretted it. His service parka was draped over his shoulders and he'd removed his boots, but still wore his tactical belt, his holstered sidearm jutting from his hip.

In front of me, Kesey lit a cigar. We hadn't spoken beyond a grunted hello, but I knew he'd been awake throughout. He stared below, his profile silhouetted against the slanted sunlight. His features seemed hollowed, his blunt nose more prominent, the rear twin tendons of his neck visible. *His elevens are up*, I thought. He's dying.

A woman wearing camo emerged from the pilot's cabin. She politely told Kesey he couldn't smoke.

"Piss off," he said.

Flustered, she left.

Another passenger with black wraparound shades sat alone in the front row. A black watch cap pulled low, black cargos and top, and a satellite phone in hand. During the flight, the phone screen had lit up several times, followed by brief, murmured conversations.

A body of water appeared ahead. On its shore the towers of a city. I pulled up my mental map.

Lake Erie. Cleveland.

The plane taxied to a far end of the tarmac.

The person with the satellite phone went into the restroom. Outside my window a pair of unmarked cars were parked. Standing by them were four strapping men wearing peaked DEA caps.

When we disembarked, Kesey asked who was in charge.

"Me," a bearded Black guy said. "I'm Jackson."

Kesey thumbed at DiMaglio. "Brian's my number two. I go down he steps up."

"Cool the bad vibes, chief," DiMaglio said. "You ain't going down."

Kesey looked at me. "Eyes on her at all times, Jackson. Nobody gets close to mussing her hair, got it?"

"Got it," Jackson said deferentially.

The satellite phone guy emerged from the plane. Strands of a green Mylar wig hung from her backpack.

"Hello, Laura," I said.

She nodded wordlessly, and to my dismay, offered her hand. I'd expected a more up-close-and-personal greeting. But when we touched, her grip was tight and she held it for a long, meaningful moment that assuaged my disappointment; she was all business outwardly, but she sent an unmistakably warm message. Sisters in crime. Made sense. We were carrying out a governmental mission that was unsanctioned and illegal.

"These two are riding with me and Brian," Kesey told Jackson. Your team's in the lead car. Let's move out."

Laura and I sat in the rear seat.

She was again on the sat phone. Mostly listening, an occasional acknowledgment, her face expressionless.

"Good?" Kesey asked over his shoulder.

"*Si*," she said and went on listening.

Jackson's vehicle, bubble lights flashing, sped in and out

of traffic. Grinning, DiMaglio followed close behind. A man who loves his action, I thought.

The outside world whizzed by. Kesey stared out at it, brooding, as he had on the plane. I knew what he was thinking: Kesey's Last Tape was about to unspool.

When Laura got off the phone, I put my mouth to her ear and whispered, "We're going to find Vizcaino now?"

"Find isn't the right word," she said.

Up front, Kesey chuckled wetly. "I was thinking of Leeds," he said. "Guy's got pull in D.C. Wasn't for him, we wouldn't have gotten Akron green-lighted so fast."

We passed a Welcome-to-Akron sign.

Jackson cut his flashers and slowed. Now we were just two generic vehicles, driving. Insurance against being spotted by Vizcaino's people?

"Relax, sis," Kesey said. "Victor ain't around."

CHAPTER 62

Akron seemed a nice town—for a day trip.

Kesey thought so too. "Nothing to do in this burg. Take a stroll, whatever. Early bedtime. First thing tomorrow we're out of here."

To where? I wondered, but didn't ask, knowing that he wouldn't answer. Man played his cards close to his oversized vest. So Laura and I strolled along a street where every other shop was a national brand franchisee. Middle America, all right.

"That shop over there looks kind of interesting," she said.

Its sign said FINE AND RARE ENGRAVING. *Very interesting*, I thought, realizing that Laura had not-so discreetly guided us there.

The place was a tidy little emporium. Custom cabinetry, gleaming counters, framed old fonts on the walls. Against one wall sat a massive safe. In front of it was a small antique desk whose polished top was empty except for an old-fashioned pen and pencil holder and a brass sign engraved with a name. Behind the nameplate sat a short man who belted his pants at his chest. Rimless glasses magnified his eyes. He lowered the document he was reading and smiled pleasantly.

I glanced at the nameplate. "Albert Erich Raeder, I presume," I said.

"Folks call me Erich," he said. "May I be of service?"

Good question. I'd broken the ice but had no idea what lay beneath it, so I left the field to Laura. To my surprise she spoke in Spanish, although I thought it far-fetched that Raeder was conversant.

"Your shop is *preciosa*," she said. "May we look around?"

"By all means, *señora*," Raeder replied in fluent Spanish.

Another revelation: Laura knew Raeder was bilingual.

"I welcome an opportunity to converse in your lovely language," he said. "Sometimes it's a necessity, as occasionally I have Spanish-speaking clients."

He looked at me. "If I might ask, what do you do?"

"I am an attorney at law," I said.

"So are my Latin clients," he said.

Laura caught my eye. Your turn now.

I got the message: Get Raeder to talk by listening intently, showing approval, expressing agreement. Be Dr. Simpatico Feelgood to the point where he's so addicted to ego-stroking that he talks too loosely.

I pointed to a wall hanging. A glassed-over, age-yellowed document written in a Teutonic script. "Wow," I said.

"Very rare, indeed," Raeder said.

"I can see that," I said.

"Hand-blocked print."

"It's pure ... art."

"That's how I view it."

We moved on to another hanging. He said something about an early Gutenberg Bible. I said it was amazing how he understood the way an engraver was an artist interpretating God.

He beamed at that. "Indeed."

"Say," I said. "I know quite a few Spanish lawyers who do business hereabouts. What're your clients' names?"

"Hmmm ... I believe one's name starts with a *Vee*," he said. "Victor? The other I'm not sure."

"Don't believe I know him," I said. "Much as I've enjoyed the visit, we didn't just happen to drop in. A Spanish lawyer *I do* know asked me to deliver a message."

"Oh? Really? Er, who is he ... I mean, what is it?"

"To get ready for business," I said. "Whatever that means, I have no idea."

"Nor do I," he said uneasily. "I've no idea whatsoever. None at all."

"*Perdón*," Laura said, tapping her watch.

"Oops," I said. "Lost track of time. We've a flight to catch. Thank you so much, Erich."

"The pleasure was mine," he said, uncertainly.

Outside, Laura moved aside and cupped her phone. She spoke briefly, too softly to overhear, then turned to me.

"You did well," she said. "So did I. While you were doing brain surgery on the engraver, I photographed what he was reading when we entered."

A document brightened her screen. She enlarged it and I saw it was an invoice. The seller was an LLC, offshore and untraceable, muting identity but shouting dirty money.

The original purchase of unnamed merchandise was of guaranteed AAA-quality manufactured by Gwongzhou Industries, Shanghai. Hmmm. China was also the source of fentanyl precursors. Kesey hadn't exaggerated. Paz's cooperation could be a major weapon in the war against that poison.

The sold merchandise was five thousand sheafs of 25 percent linen/75 percent cotton. Rag paper. I'd done counterfeit cases before and knew a bit about the scam. This rag paper was good enough to pass for U.S. money, like the bogus mil Laura had brought me.

The place of delivery was Raeder's shop.

The delivery date was yesterday.

"Raeder doesn't know if we're law or for real," I said. "If we're law, he won't want to explain rag paper in his custom shop. If we're from his old pals in Colombia, he'll want to get ready to set up his presses."

Laura smiled. "Beautiful and smart."

"You don't need to stroke my ego," I said.

Hurt in her eyes. "I meant it, El."

"Sorry, I'm ... I dunno," I said. "Raeder will want to get the paper to the presses as soon as possible. Call whoever it is you talk to—Kesey?—and tell him to put a tail on Raeder. Darn—he might have already left."

"Jackson's people are already on him. He went to Youngstown."

"Why Youngstown?" I asked.

"Where I got your money. And where the plate is."

"So why are we in Akron?"

"Because when I picked up your fee in Youngstown, I saw Raeder and followed him to Akron. He'll lead us to the plate. I have a good idea of the general location, but Raeder will show us exactly where. You wouldn't believe how freaky the neighborhood is."

"Vizcaino is in Youngstown?" I asked.

She nodded. "He came a long way to find the money and plate Pacho took. Bad move," she said. "It'll be his last."

We rejoined Kesey and DiMaglio for dinner.

It was in a dim old tavern nearly obscured between a bright Golden Arch and a neon Whopper, but its burgers were prime beef and the bun fresh-baked. Kesey washed three of them down with draft beers. His cheeks were flushed, his mood optimistic but pensive.

"Like Ike said, we are about to embark on the Great Crusade toward which we have striven these many months—make that years," Kesey said.

"Hear, hear," DiMaglio asked. "Who's Ike?"

"Have another draft," Kesey told him.

"Getting late, K," DiMaglio said.

Kesey's smile faded. He nodded.

We spent the night in a motel outside of Akron. DiMaglio was a stickler for security, so to avoid scrutiny, he signed us in as two pairs of husbands and wives, but when we reached the rooms Laura and I bunked together.

It had been a long day and was going to be an early rise, so after showering we hit the sack. We didn't speak for a while, but the silence was comfortable. After lights-out, I remained awake and sensed that Laura was too.

"Wondering," she said. "You involved? Married?"

"Married to my job, I suppose," I said.

"Never get lonely?" she asked. "For the sound of another voice, I mean."

"I whistle while I work."

"You're a jewel, El. One of these days the right man will find you."

"That so? You don't always get what you don't want."

She laughed. "Then you do want someone."

"In my dreams, I guess," I said.

"Have a sweet one. G'night El."
"Sleep tight, kiddo."

CHAPTER 63

Laura was right; the neighborhood was too freaky to believe.

In the pre-dawn darkness, Youngstown's Mahoning Valley was a poster child for post-industrial middle-America. Abandoned factories dominated the desolate landscape, their blue-collar workers gone in search of greener pastures, leaving the tired, hungry, and poor behind.

Kesey coughed from deep within, lowered his window, and spat. "Stinks out there," he said. "Fucking rustbelt is polluted. Desolation row. Reminds me of how what's-his-name saw it, the guy who wrote *The Road*."

"Cormac McCarthy," I said.

"Him. That dude knew."

"Can't deal with another dye job," Laura said, and put on her green wig. On her it seemed a feathered headdress fit for a princess.

There was an oil drum fire ahead. The fire reflected off discarded needles and phials and a medley of lost Gen Xs and haggard Millennials and wild-child Gen Zs with tattooed faces and fluorescent hair. A robed, bearded man stood among them, his mouth twisted in speech, gesturing as if preaching. From a phial he tapped pills into his palm and held it out. A dozen faces leaned forward, but he closed his fist and arched a questioning brow. When the faces emitted a susurrus of amens, he placed a pill on each tongue.

"Gimme some old-time religion," Kesey said hoarsely.

He's running out of gas, I thought.

"You religious, counselor?" he asked.

"Depends," I said defensively. In truth, I'm not religious,

but I've pretended to be when pitching would-be clients. I've professed belief in Judeo-Christianity, Buddhism, Islam ... once in a mushroom-eating cult run by an organic greenhouse owner. Changeable me. Kesey and I were alike, in that regard. More alike than I'd ever admit to him.

Kesey's phone crackled. Its speaker was on.

"Ah, here," DEA Agent Jackson said.

"Copy," Kesey said. "Sitrep?"

"Two miles ahead on your left is a gated area. Watchman at the entrance. Subject rode around it a couple times, squaring blocks looking for a tail. Didn't see us because we're well back, with a drone on him. He went to the gate. Must be known there because the guard let him in."

"Opposition?" Kesey said.

"Six men patrolling their perimeter. We got drones on 'em too. Say when and we'll take them out."

"When," Kesey said. "Be sure to jam their phones."

"We don't forget things, boss," Jackson said.

"Me either," Kesey murmured as he hung up.

The street was dark but for the glow of Kesey's cigar. He was perched, head atop bent arm, on the fender of our jeep. The Thinker. This was his last round-up, his long-sought closure. But for what?

"Place reminds me of La Siberia," Laura said. "Old ruins in need of restoration."

Kesey's phone squawked: "Jackson here. Got a call from a Secret Service Agent name of Leeds. Wanted to know where you are and what you're up to."

"Tell him we're in the field looking for his thing," Kesey said. "Say we're close. Over."

Seconds later, Leeds called Kesey. "Why didn't you tell me?" he asked him.

"Just found out," Kesey said. "You're gonna need a warrant to get it."

"A warrant?" Leeds asked. "Why?"

"It's in the subject's safe."

I looked at Kesey. A warrant? That would take hours, if not days. Besides, the only safe was in Raeder's shop back in Akron. We were on the move in Youngstown. A warrant wouldn't do jack, but I didn't think Kesey cared.

Neither did I. We were outside the law, now.

We left the car and were walking past and around the shuttered factories. Laura was in the lead, phone in hand. In the darkness, two dots of light shone on its screen. The larger one was stationary. The smaller one slowly moved toward it—indicating us, I figured. I wondered what the other dot was.

Kesey coughed violently and we stopped. He bent with hands on knees and I heard his phlegm splat on the street.

I didn't know where we were, but I didn't feel lost. The opposite. I felt as if I'd found my way to ... what? My true self? It was an out-of-body sensation that made me wonder who or what was guiding us. A greater power? Destiny?

Turned out otherwise.

The dots on Laura's screen were close together—then, from the shadows, someone hissed, and I saw our pathfinder was Indio. He pointed ahead, and then with his left thumb formed an L, meaning to the right, I thought.

Laura said something to him in a language I didn't immediately recognize. An indigenous language? *Quechuan*? She must have learned it when living in La Caldera. He responded in kind. I had no idea what they were saying, but their body language suggested familiarity. Figured. The boss's beautiful daughter and his young *organizador* had a history.

Laura held up a palm, signaling me to stay, and crooked a finger for Kesey and Indio to follow her. They went to the corner and peered around it, speaking quietly.

Then Laura turned the corner and was gone from view.

Half a minute later, Indio left too.

"C'mere," Kesey called to me.

"Hold this for me," he said when I joined him, and put a small leather wallet in my hand. "Jesus, your hands feel hot," he said.

His fingers felt like icicles. In the dim light seeping from around the corner, his face was skeletal and ghostly pale. I pocketed the wallet.

"Ready?"

I nodded.

"You into football?" he asked. Strange topic, considering the moment. Was he killing time or was his life flashing before his eyes? They seemed distant.

"Say again," I said.

"My vocational high school had a team," he said. "Being big, they made me an offensive tackle. I was good at beating on people. College scouts began romancing me. Visions of cheerleaders danced in my head. But then I blew my knee out and the music stopped. So I did the next best thing and became a cop. I was good at that too. Still am...."

He paused and peered around the corner.

"Don't much follow football anymore," he said, his back to me. "Just check the Monday news to see how my teams do. I'm into Detroit, Buffalo, Cleveland, Baltimore—the old cities. Don't give a rat about the players but I like seeing working-class fans happy. Fuck the five-hundred-dollar seats in Dallas, Tampa, La-la Land. Let 'em go play golf. Where'd you grow up?"

"New York," I said. "You?"

"Brooklyn, when it was Brooklyn," he said. "Before high school we played tackle football on the sidewalk. Rough game, lotta hurt. Same deal now." He looked me in the eye. "Listen to me, Electra. For now, you're on the bench. If someone goes down you sub. You good with that?"

"I'm good," I said, but he'd already turned the corner.

I leaned around it and saw the light came from a guard shack at the entrance to the gated area Jackson had mentioned. Two people stood at the gate. A man and a woman. Beneath the light her hair was neon green. Laura.

Indio and Kesey were nowhere in sight. I took that to mean they were off the field: time to send in a sub while the guard was distracted.

I stepped onto the gridiron, but no one cheered.

CHAPTER 64

"You don't want to fuck? I give good head."

I heard Laura talking to the guard from where I crouched behind a burned-out car, fifty feet from the shack and the gate.

The guard wore a machine pistol strapped to his leg. "*Puta* junkie," he said. "Beat it."

Laura unzipped her parka and shrugged it down her shoulders, revealing a skin-tight body suit. She ran her hand down it. "Worth twenty-five, *si?*"

The guard goggled. "Fifteen," he said.

"Twenty," Laura said. "Come, *mi amor.*"

The guard unlocked the gate and went to her. He unbuckled his pants and his holstered weapon dropped to his ankles.

Laura pointed to his shorts. "*Tus calzoncillos.*"

He lowered his shorts and shuffled toward her.

Indio emerged from the area behind the gate and put his arm around the guard's throat. Kesey emerged from behind him and caved the guard's temple with the butt of his pistol.

Breathing heavily, Kesey stood and looked at Indio. "How the fuck did you get inside?"

"He's indigenous," Laura said, as if that explained it.

Indio looked at the inert guard. "He finished?"

"He's had his last woody," Kesey said. "Geez, skid marks on his skivvies."

Kesey followed Laura through the opened gate into the fenced area. I went with them while Indio remained at the gate.

"He's our watchman now," Kesey explained.

"Didn't Jackson clear the area?" I asked.

"Yeah, well, just in case," he said.

"Do not mislead her," Laura said. "The area is cleared. Only the vermin inside remain. Exterminating them is not a thing for Indio to do. It is only for the three of us. A woman they tormented with guilt. A little girl they soiled. A man who lost a friend. *¿Entiendes?*"

I understood. Montez owed Laura and Kesey a debt—payback could only come from us—but as to who Kesey's lost friend was, I drew a blank.

Kesey's phone crackled. "Clear," Jackson said.

"Now's our time," Laura said.

We went through the gate.

CHAPTER 65

Kesey was circling the drain.
Wheezing. Spewing effluvium. Walking unsteadily. He stumbled and I grabbed his arm, but he yanked it free.
"Don't need no help," he said angrily.
Man should be in the hospital, I thought, not in this wretched place chasing his demons. But I understood his choice: forsake being intubated and subjected to the false cheeriness of doctors prolonging the inevitable. His best and only medicine was to take his enemies with him.
"Rest a minute," Laura said to him.
"No need, little girl—we're here."
I saw it too. Down the street, a sliver of light shone from between the slatted blinds of a small concrete building. Steel door, high windows, probably once a paymaster's office, now Vizcaino's hideout.
Kesey handed me a phone. I looked at it, unsure.
"Call him," Laura snapped.
Again, I was bemused by Laura's sudden shift of personalities. She had more facets than a cut diamond. A moment ago, she'd been Kesey's little girl; suddenly, she'd morphed to my senior commander.
"Give me your card," she said to me.
So she *had* seen me take it after Pacho's arrest. I leaned against a wall with one leg crossed over the other, foot up. I reached to my boot and turned its heel hard sideways, and the white card appeared atop the sole where I'd hidden it.
She laid it flat on the ground. Then she took out a white

plastic card identical to mine. She laid them alongside one another and, using Kesey's phone, photographed them.

Understanding dawned. The cards were the two halves.

That was why Montez and Vizcaino believed both Laura and I possessed keys that fit the lockbox of their agenda, why they needed both of us to open it. It was double-locked.

"Tell Vizcaino we'll deliver the real thing in two hours," Kesey said quietly to Laura. I had the impression he was saving his strength for one last effort.

Laura texted a message and the photograph.

"These boys operate on CST: Criminal Standard Time," Kesey said. "To them, two hours means four or six," Kesey said. "While they're anxiously counting down and wondering how come communication with their outside guys is down, we'll hit 'em—in *half* an hour."

Laura sat on her haunches and looked at the building. She'd waited for this moment for years; another half hour was mere seconds to her.

But it was an eternity to me. I'd hyped myself for this gambit and was anxious to finish it. I went for a short walkaround. Nothing worth seeing—anything to kill time.

Across the street, detritus lay scattered about the loading dock of a dark building. Rusting metal pieces whose shapes reminded me of slices of an orange. I looked hard at them and thought, not an orange, not slices....

"The petals of a sphere," Laura said to me.

I hadn't even heard her come alongside.

She pointed at the loading dock.

Behind it a door was ajar.

In Laura's phone light, the space seemed enormous as a 747 hangar.

It was rank with rusted metal and the fluids that once had oiled and greased them.

She moved her phone, its light illuminating an area filled with vehicles damaged beyond repair. Some still wore licenses: the plates of middle-American states.

"The end-product of consumerism," she said. Her light

moved on to an enormous steel vise. "Where the cars are crushed."

Her light fell across a large machine that looked like a giant mold: a pair of opposing cup-shaped steel rims, and the gears and levers controlling them. When the cups met, whatever was inside the mold would compress.

"The sphere-maker," she said quietly.

Obviously, she was aware of the process, but by her reaction, doubtful she'd ever seen it. Her light probed the rest of the space. Nothing there but more dead cars awaiting reincarnation in another form.

Gino's speculation was confirmed. This was where the spheres—ostensibly compacted cars intended for sifting and recycling in Colombian sweatshop yards—were assembled, their cores hollowed to hold drug money being repatriated from the States.

A sphere was half-completed. It looked like an installation from some Madison Avenue art dealer whose clients were billionaires. But this gallery was Santa Fe-owned, its earnings the millions bled from addicted Americans in blighted red and benighted blue states alike.

It was all coming together now. The ship that had been lost at sea was a cover to hide its cargo of hollow spheres....

Another thought flashed in my mind.

On the night Pacho was killed, he'd been accused of deliberately sinking a ship suspected of carrying money in order to cover his theft. Pacho must have known there would be fatalities. I'd figured the man wrong. Behind his jocular innocence lay a murderer.

Laura read me.

"The ship was scuttled off the Guajira peninsula," she said. "As Pacho planned, it went down slowly in calm and shallow water. My brother thought the crew would survive. He was saddened that one man was lost. I wasn't. That man was Xander Monsalve. I remembered him and his *hermanos* from La Calera."

I realized that Laura herself had participated in the sinking and the thefts that preceded it. If so, she also knew where the plate and the money were.

"You've been here before, haven't you?" I asked.

"To pick up the money I brought you, but they blindfolded me until we were in this building," she said. "But not in this part. It was in a garage of cars—nicer than these."

It figured that the plate and the money would also be somewhere close by. Close enough for the money to be put in the spheres by one trusted person. Martin Montez, before his arrest? Afterward, by Pacho? Then by Erich Raeder? Or ... Laura?

She turned from me and scanned the walls with her phone light. They were blank. No doors to other rooms. Nothing.

I turned my light on. Kesey had joined us; leaning against a wall, he checked his watch.

"Twenty minutes to go," Kesey wheezed.

"To go for what?" I asked.

"Clock's ticking," he said.

I ran my phone light across the floor. Dull gray concrete, smooth—too new-looking for the old, weathered building. I saw what appeared to be a seam. Looking closer, I rapped my knuckles. It seemed solid. Kesey unholstered his gun, tapping its butt on the seam. There was a faint hollow sound from below.

We inspected the floor inch by inch. My fingers felt a fractional aperture—a credit card-sized slot.

Laura inserted one of the white cards into the slot. Nothing happened. Undeterred, she inserted the other card. The floor slowly moved—an emptiness beneath—and the cards slid back out of the slot.

"Smart," Kesey said. "Youngstown, the tire capital of the world, knocking out millions of rubber wheels manufactured with dangerous, flammable chemicals stored in blast-proof underground spaces long forgotten in a nearby radius. The chemicals are gone but not the danger. Keep an eye out for booby traps."

I expected the trapdoor to be old and heavy, but apparently Montez had modernized it for easy access, for it was light and so well-balanced an entire section of floor rose, revealing a tilted ramp below.

Guided by our phone lights, Laura and I walked down it.

Kesey followed, grunting with each step. There must have been a photovoltaic switch, for as we left the ramp, an overhead flood light came on.

"This is where I was," Laura said.

A dozen vehicles were parked: SUVs, vans, full-sized sedans. They wore Ohio license plates.

Kesey coughed and wiped a sleeve across his mouth. "Fifteen minutes," he said.

Laura went to a van, the white one that had been outside the house where the bogus money had been hidden. She groped inside the rear tire well and took out a remote; when she pressed it, the sedan's trunk lock popped open.

In it were taped cartons. She reached into her parka and took out a folding knife whose blade she used to open a carton.

It was filled with banded bills. Franklins.

Two million? Three? More in the other cartons? More in the other cars? If so, at least a hundred million, or more. A monthly total of Santa Fe's sales? Or bogus money Raeder had created?

I picked up a packet and riffled through it.

The serial numbers were all unique.

It was Montez's stolen fortune.

The garage walls were unpainted cinder block, their mortar unevenly spaced. But there was another neat slot. Laura slid the cards into it, and a cinder block slid aside, revealing a flat object wrapped in clear plastic. An image was engraved on it—the familiar face of Benjamin Franklin.

It was the printing plate.

Kesey took the plate and put it beneath his parka. His color had returned as if he'd taken a swig of whisky.

"Gonna make it in time," he said.

CHAPTER 66

We circled around Vizcaino's lair to its rear.
　It had a single closed door. Something bright was looped around the door handle. It was a beaded bracelet, and I remembered Laura's response when Kesey had asked how Indio had gotten inside the compound: "He's indigenous," she had replied.
　I understood that she believed Indio was possessed of ancient, avatar-like means of transcending modern problems. Perhaps he was, for somehow he had accessed the compound, scoped it out, and left us a blessing—the bracelet—but not his presence. He understood that this part was for us alone: My absolution, Laura's indemnity, Kesey's closure.
　In the pale moonlight, her face was serene as she removed the bracelet from the knob and slipped it around her wrist. Then she handed the cards to me.
　"Do your thing, counselor," Kesey rasped.
　Sure, I thought. *Just walk in and say let's do business and ... play it from there.* Fine. I gripped the doorknob—it resisted being turned as if it hadn't moved for a long time—then it gave way and the door opened.
　I stopped, looked, listened.
　The space was dark. I turned on my light and entered. Nothing but brooms and mops and another door, light seeping from below it ... and men's voices from past it: Vizcaino, Raeder's proper English, and another man's obscenity-laced comments I recognized as the *lingua franca* of the X-men who, on the night that had forever changed my life, had facilitated Pacho's execution.

Despite the chill, Kesey was sweating. In my light, Laura's eyes shone like a beast's, reflecting the glow of a campfire. I gripped the inner door's knob, beginning to turn it, very, very slowly....

During countless witness examinations I'd learned of people's altered phenomenology during extreme stimuli, their stream of consciousness filtered by a perception of time elongating. It was happening to me now; my world was immersed in the atmospheric syrup of the moment before violence goes hypersonic.

Click!

The door burst open. Inside, a glimpse of three men at a table: Vizcaino, Raeder, and an *X* looking up as Kesey tossed something into the room.

Flash! *Bang!*

A rifle—Kesey's?—spat fire into the fogged room. From it, a desultory spark of return fire. I emptied the Beretta at the unseen shooter.

Then, suddenly as it had begun, it was over. Silence, as the fog of war slowly lifted … revealing a naked bulb swinging above two dead men.

I rushed inside. Raeder, vacant-eyed, mouth open in a silent scream, lay alongside *X* whose body was riddled with red florets.

Vizcaino was gone. So was Laura. The exterior door was open.

I rushed through it and went outside.

The area was empty. There was a bright object on the ground. It was Indio's beaded bracelet, laid as if pointing the way to a dark building lined with a loading dock.

I slipped my brass knuckles on and stepped up onto the dock.

Vizcaino was hunched in a corner with Laura clamped between his bent knees, one arm wrapped around her throat, the other holding a pistol to her temple.

"Give me the cards and I'll let her go," he said, his eyes, bloodshot from the flash-bang, focused on me.

"I will put them down," I said. "Let her go and I'll leave them for you."

I dug in a cargo pocket and took out my wallet. With my left hand, I took out my American Express and New York State Bar cards. In the dimness, all that showed were their shapes.

"Put them closer to me," he said.

"I'll hand them to you. Here."

I tossed the cards to his feet.

As Vizcaino reached for them, his gun moved from Laura's temple. I balled a fist beneath my knuckles and coiled to strike him—

Laura sunk a knife in his eye. He screamed and fell to his knees as she twisted the blade deeper. He shuddered and lay still. She pulled the knife from his socket and tossed it to my feet. I'd seen it before. It was the folding blade that had been my father's, the one she had used on the night she'd prepared our dinner.

She saw me looking at it. "I've sinned twice," she said. "I should have asked before taking it, but I needed a weapon. Then I broke my oath to my mother never to kill."

"I forgive you," I said. "I believe your mother would too."

She smiled. "Yes, I think she would. Alright, my part of this is done—the rest is up to you."

"What do you mean?"

She didn't reply.

Kesey was slumped.

His breathing was labored, face gray. He motioned me closer, and I bent to him.

"You did good, Electra," he whispered. "Promise me that you'll...."

His voice trailed off and his eyes glazed; his last word left unsaid, but I knew it was the same thing Laura had said—that the rest was up to me.

"I promise," I whispered, although I didn't know what.

Indio drove me to the Akron-Canton airport.

We didn't speak. Kesey's death had silenced us.

Laura had disappeared. Jackson's DEA team had arrived as we were leaving, and Kesey's promise and Laura's wish were becoming clear to me—my mission had been to destroy *el Jugador,* but I'd failed. Leeds would have his plate and Montez's cooperation agreement would ensure that his sentence would be minimal.

But I'd find a way. I'd promised.

CHAPTER 67

I received a call from Judge Graff's clerk.
"Status conference on the Montez case tomorrow at ten," Brunhilda said. "Be on time, the old man's pissed."

"I'm no longer Montez's attorney," I said.

"Tell it to the judge," she said.

I braced myself for the worst.

My reckoning had come. Jackson's team must have filed dozens of DEA-6 Reports of Investigations about my unauthorized participation in a clandestine government op, and all the unlawful things that led to its bloody end.

Filled with dread, I went to court.

At the government table, Wilkinson was seated with Brian DiMaglio and Leeds. I wasn't surprised. With Kesey gone, DiMaglio was now the senior case agent. As for Leeds, I supposed that recovering the plate had put him back in good graces, and he still wanted to keep his imprimatur on the case.

Montez was seated alongside me at the defense table. He'd take credit for recovering the plate, and I wasn't about to turn on a client and argue otherwise. The plate had redeemed Leeds, but not Montez, who wore a SHU orange jumpsuit.

"Why am I still in the SHU?" he asked me.

I didn't ask Wilkinson. I was off the case.

Judge Graff took the bench. "I've received several submissions," he said. "I shall discuss them in order so there are no misunderstandings by any of the parties. That clear, people?"

"Abundantly, your Honor," Wilkinson said.

"Clear," I said, although it wasn't.

"The government's moved that attorney Smukler be

relieved as Mr. Montez's co-counsel," Graff said. "That motion is granted."

Amen, I thought. Smukler's shilling for Paz had bridged to criminality, and he was likely facing an indictment and disbarment. Only a matter of time until he flipped on Paz. Might have already.

"Next, Mr. Montez has filed a motion *pro se*," Graff said, "requesting that he be allowed to represent himself. There is case law allowing this, but in this weighty matter, I find that Mr. Montez is not qualified to do so. Mr. Montez, find another attorney."

Montez looked at me. "I already have an attorney," he said.

"Your Honor," I said, "I am no longer counsel."

Graff smiled. "That so? I haven't seen your application requesting to be relieved. Have you, Ms. Torres?"

"No, sir," Brunhilda replied.

"We'll revisit that issue in a moment," Graff said. "In his *pro se* motion, Mr. Montez also requested that the Court cease tolling speedy trial time, as he wishes to exercise his right to be tried forthwith."

Stupefying. Montez was getting a cooperation agreement and could be out in five years—less. But now that Don J would testify, Montez had no chance at trial, and was looking at life. What was up with that?

Sotto voce, I spoke to Wilkinson. "What about the cooperation?"

"We're not offering him an agreement," she said quietly.

"I'll hear from the government," Judge Graff said.

"The government is ready for trial," Wilkinson said.

"But you have the plate," I whispered to her.

She did not reply.

"Revisiting Mr. Montez's request," Graff said. "He has a right to defend himself. Nevertheless, his unfamiliarity with the law likely will create appellate issues. As I made clear at the outset of this matter, I will not allow this case to linger unnecessarily. Therefore, in the interest of judicial economy, since current counsel has failed to request being relieved, she shall act as Mr. Montez's *co*-counsel to advise him."

Huh?

Had the DEA kept me out of their reports? Kesey had instructed Jackson to keep me out of things, and obviously both Jackson and DiMaglio had complied.

"Any comment, counselor?" Graff asked.

"No sir," I replied. "I shall comply."

"Discovery complete?" Graff asked.

"It is now," Wilkinson said. "Let the record reflect that I am now providing counsel with a list of the witnesses the government intends to call."

"So noted," Graff said. "How long does the government anticipate for their case?"

"Four or five days," Wilkinson said.

"Trial date?" Graff asked Brunhilda.

"Monday, June 8th," she said.

I looked at the witness list. There were only three names on it: Joachim Paz, Brian DiMaglio, and Jorge Jaramillo, aka Don J.

Montez read the list over my shoulder. I would've thought that the specter of Don J testifying would have dismayed him, but he was smiling confidently as the court marshals appeared to take him away.

"Tell Laura I'm looking forward to seeing her when this foolishness is over," he said as he stood. "The three of us, we'll have a drink."

DiMaglio had heard him. "No such person as Laura now," DiMaglio told me.

I understood. My ex-cop P.I., the same who had given me DiMaglio's address, had once said that the worst thing that could happen to an agent was to lose a brother agent, and the second worst was to lose an informant they were sworn to protect. So Laura was now beneath the G's protective umbrella, either as an unwilling prisoner or as a willing partner in crime-busting—I did not know which. What I did know was that she would remain anonymous: renamed, relocated, and perhaps rewarded.

"Your client has until June 7th to produce the plate," Leeds said to me.

What? I was stunned. Had Kesey *not* turned the plate in?

Had he disposed of it to ensure Montez would not be able to cooperate? Or was it Laura who'd done so for the same reason?

"See you June 8th, counselor," DiMaglio said.

I looked at him. "What happened to 'Dirtbag?'"

"Kesey told me to lay off," he said. "Dunno why, but he had a soft spot for you. Anyway, me and you, we're good."

"I miss him," I said.

He nodded. "Me too."

CHAPTER 68

On the morning of June 8th, Judge Graff was in a foul mood.

"Bruni, tell the court officers to warn the spectators that any display of reaction will result in their expulsion from the courtroom," he said.

I wished he'd issue me the same warning. Not that I'd normally react—my courtroom demeanor was strictly poker-faced—but I'd have made a mighty public ruckus if I thought it would get me booted from the case without compromising myself. Good Lord, I, a AAA-litigator, had been reduced to a petulant cartel boss's co-counsel.

As Brunhilda left Graff's chambers, I heard the anticipatory buzz from the courtroom. The Southern District of New York is a multiplex of living theater whose stages are the dozens of courtrooms at 500 Pearl Street, where dramas large and small play out. Half an hour before jury selection was to begin, every seat was filled. Word was out that a cartel kingpin was representing himself. Secrets would be revealed from the defendant's mouth to media ears ranging from the *Times* to the tabloids. What was left of my reputation was about to suffer the stings and missiles of insinuation.

"Mr. Montez," Graff said. "Regarding your decision to represent yourself, I take it that includes cross-examination of witnesses. So let me warn you in advance that if your questions are stated as conclusions or concern matters irrelevant to the charges, or are otherwise inappropriate, I will not hesitate to shut you down. Do you understand, sir?"

"I do," Montez said. "My cross-examinations shall be brief and require either denial or agreement."

Montez had prepared for his role. Not only did he sound like a lawyer, in his dark suit and muted tie, he looked like one.

"I won't inquire whether you intend to testify," Graff said. "In the event you do choose to testify, there are two alternative methods. Either by your narrative, or by questions and answers asked and answered by yourself. In the event you do testify, which alternative will you avail yourself of?"

"A narrative, your Honor."

"So you say," Graff said. "Nevertheless, you are not a lawyer and might inadvertently state things the government objects to as inadmissible. I do not want your testimony repeatedly interrupted by sidebars between counsel to argue. Therefore, if you intend to testify, prior to taking the stand, give the government a list of your statements so any objections can be dealt with beforehand."

"It shall be done as you say," Montez said.

"Understand, no deviations allowed, sir."

"There will be none, your Honor."

Good grief. A lawyer's best friend is the element of surprise. Following a long string of yes-or-no questions with a concluding yes-or-no response inapposite to the previous answers is the key to successful cross-examination. But Montez could not deflect because he'd just agreed to reveal his case beforehand. As a self-serving narrative, no less. I started to protest, but Graff cut me off with a frown.

"You have something to say?" he asked me. I knew the old fox had deliberately neutered Montez's testimony, thinking that I'd intervene and demand that Montez's ineptitude was cause to rescind the co-counsel agreement, and thereby I'd become lead lawyer. No loose ends, no endless appeals, end of case.

"I do not," I said.

"Government?"

"No," Wilkinson said.

CHAPTER 69

I'd erected a mental block between me and the spectator section behind the well.

Doing so shrank the field of combat to a smaller arena. One side was Judge Graff's high bench. On the side facing it were the government and defense tables. To the left was the jury box. To the right was the door to the pens. Justice in a quadrangle.

Judge Graff interpreted the Federal Rules of Criminal Procedure's jury selection dictates to the letter. He alone interviewed prospective jurors. People clearly conflicted—loved ones in law enforcement, those who thought an accusation equated to guilt, those who expressed malice toward Latinos—were excused. So much for dismissals for cause.

Peremptory challenges to disqualify—strikes, based on lawyers' gut intuition—were limited: the G had six, Montez had ten.

Jury selection began.

Some strikes Wilkinson used surprised me because I thought the jurors she struck were pro-G types. Could be she was nervous, this being her first major trial. Could be she was getting bad advice from Brian DiMaglio, seated alongside. I didn't really care what the reason was, I just wanted this exercise in futility over.

In federal courts, only five percent of indicted persons go to trial, and of those that do, maybe one wins. Do the math: one in a hundred defendants win at trial. Make it one in a thousand if the defendant's an extradited Colombian drug kingpin representing himself.

There were a few prospective jurors I was certain should be struck for cause, but Montez made it clear he wasn't interested in my opinion. Like Wilkinson, Montez committed what I thought were egregious mistakes. Although I was his attorney in name only, I felt legitimately embarrassed by his choices. I suppose I wore my feelings on my sleeve, for across the well, I saw DiMaglio smiling at me as if he found my discomfort humorous.

It took three hours for twelve jurors and four alternates to be selected. It wasn't until they rose to be sworn in that I realized I'd seen the trees, not the forest.

Against all odds, fourteen of the sixteen jurors were women. Adding to my amazement, both Wilkinson and Montez had selected them for some beyond-coincidental yet clearly gender-biased reason, or for some other criteria I could not ascertain. I got it that Montez thought he might charm the women jurors; conversely, I would've thought that would prompt Wilkinson to select men, yet she hadn't. Was there a method to her madness?

Graff swore in the jury. Then he banged his gavel. "Court is adjourned. At two o'clock, trial will commence."

My longtime habit before the first day of trial was to skip food and fuel with black coffee in keeping with a lean and hungry mindset. But having no intention of going hungry on Montez's behalf, I lunched in my usual place in nearby Chinatown, hoping Shanghai spaghetti would fill my belly and sharpen my own noodle.

Before court, I went to the restroom.

Jenna Wilkinson was on her knees in a stall, puking into the toilet. I thought she was ill and went to assist her.

She waved me off. "Thank you, but I'm okay. I'm just a little...."

Stage fright, I thought.

"It's okay," I said. "My first big trial my knees were wobbling. Don't worry. Soon as things begin, you'll settle down."

"Thank you," she said. "Hard picturing you nervous. I mean, they say you're an ice queen."

Among other things they say, I thought.

Wilkinson's opening statement furthered my bewilderment.

Opening statements are like first impressions: at best they can set a favorable tone, at worst they might instill lingering doubts. My style is to state them as a short story with key points in plain English. In my closing statement, I would refer to them in the context of "as I told you so at the outset."

Other lawyers prefer to ignore the specifics and concentrate on emotional aspects that are the foundation of sympathy or empathy.

Still other lawyers mix and match these, or express societal injustices, or whatever they think might work, but all know that whatever the chosen format, openings are the bedrock of the case to come.

Whether due to inexperience or ineptitude, Wilkinson's opening statement was weak. Oh, she touched on the important points. The trial would reveal beyond a reasonable doubt that Montez had broken a host of United States' laws, that he ran an organization that contributed to the drug crisis, that he employed thugs to maintain control. But her delivery was dry and passionless, and, astonishingly, took a mere ten minutes.

Another thing puzzled me: she seemed to deliberately mete mere lip service to the two male jurors, yet spoke eye-to-eye with the female jurors. I wrote that off as a younger woman's shy unwillingness to confront the so-called stronger sex, yet as she returned to the G table, she seemed satisfied and confident.

Still, although she might have double-dribbled her opening, her case against Montez was, to use the time-honored phrase, a slam dunk.

"Defense?" Judge Graff asked.

Montez did not immediately respond, instead, he remained seated with his head bowed in thought. I wondered if he was having second thoughts about representing himself, which meant I'd have to pinch hit without warming up. Not a welcoming thought.

"Defense?" Graff repeated.

Montez raised his head. He had donned framed glasses that gave him a somewhat sincere aura.

"Yes, your Honor," he said, gathering yellow legal pads,

although I hadn't noticed him writing word one. He started toward the jury box, paused and shook his head as if reconsidering, then returned to our table, and set the pads down. Finally, smiling apologetically as if for having delayed the process, he went to the podium.

"Good afternoon, ladies and gentlemen," he said, then turned to face Judge Graff. "Forgive me, I'm new at this, but I believe 'Good afternoon your Honor' is the proper way to begin, so may I start over?"

Graff, who never smiled, did. "You may, sir."

"Thank you. So. Good afternoon, your Honor."

Like a wave moving through a sports crowd, amused expressions spread across the jurors, and one woman chuckled aloud. Another of my habits is to nickname jurors according to how I evaluate them: the Thinker, whose opinion frequently changed; the Tailor, who'd already made a decision before trial; the Soldier, who resolutely abided by the law; and, if luck's in my corner, the Spy, my secret sympathizer. The woman who had laughed was near the wrong side of middle age but attractive, and I dubbed her the Cougar, possibly a.k.a. the Spy.

"So, once again, good afternoon members of the jury," Montez said disarmingly. "Oh, nearly forgot, good afternoon to representatives of the government as well."

Leeds, DiMaglio, and Wilkinson remained stone-faced, but the jurors' smiles widened. Even Graff was still smiling. I was too surprised to smile.

Montez had gotten to the jurors and Graff at hello!

I'd thought his demeanor would be a defiant rebuttal, but I was wrong. The Player might not know the rules, but his instinctive genius was manipulating the final score. I hated to admit it, but no denying his bumbling self-effacement had been a dazzling ploy, and he too deserved a courtroom nickname: the Natural.

Wilkinson had addressed the jury from a podium, but Montez slowly walked back and forth. Wilkinson had lectured the jury as to what the evidence would prove, but Montez suggested he had no idea of what the evidence was at all.

"I, um, tried writing down what I thought I should say,"

he said. "But then I thought why bother, I know exactly what I need to say, so from my lips to your ears, here goes."

From behind my mental block, I sensed the spectators were rapt, as were the jury and Graff. And I.

"I've been around a while and have the gray hair to prove it," Montez said. "I'm the first to admit I've made mistakes in my life. I mean no offense when I say you jurors may have as well. It is, as they say, the human condition. I'm sure you're wondering what mistakes I have made. I can't deny that I've befriended people I shouldn't have. People who, well, let's just call them bad company. People who might have—no, to be honest—probably committed the crimes Ms. Wilkins—sorry, Wilkinson—accused me of."

Good start, I thought. Despite my extreme antipathy toward Montez, the defense lawyer in me couldn't help but admire him.

Now he paused at the podium, removed his glasses, and slowly ran his gaze across each of the jurors.

"Please forgive me if I'm making you uncomfortable," he said. "I'm rather blind without my glasses, but I don't want to hide behind them. I hope you'll just look at me, unencumbered by goggles and allegations."

The Cougar sure was looking at him, along with a few other female jurors. *I'm watching a star being born*, I thought, *you insufferably brilliant turd.*

"The man you're looking at is not the man Ms. Wilkinson described," he said. "I committed none of the crimes she accused me of. I didn't even know of them until I was arrested. I will not be able to speak to you until after the evidence—or lack of evidence—is presented, or not. At this moment I stand before you as an innocent man. When I stand before you again, I'm confident you will still see me as innocent. I believe in justice. I know you do too. Thank you for your time and consideration."

Montez put his glasses back on and sat at our table.

For a long moment the courtroom was dead silent.

"Call the first witness," Judge Graff said.

CHAPTER 70

Joachim Paz was dirty, but AUSA Wilkinson cleaned him up.

She began direct examination by defanging him, as it's called in the parlance. She'd have him admit his transgressions to blunt the defense's doing so on cross-examination.

"Tell us about a false threat you created," she said.

Paz's career had been spent advising clients how to evade law enforcement, but now that he'd flipped, he went all-in on enabling it.

He said he knew of inmates who were told to lie about a threat he had devised, a scheme in which the inmates stated that they heard Mr. Montez planning to kill a government prosecutor. He did this by referring these inmates' cases to a lawyer named Morton Smukler, who then relayed their false accusations to the authorities.

"You knew this was a crime?" Wilkinson asked.

Paz said he knew. Wilkinson asked whether Smukler could corroborate this. Paz said he was certain Smukler could have, but soon after his arrest, he had passed. Heart attack. Stress.

"You've been visiting Mr. Montez, correct?" Wilkinson asked.

"Yes."

"You represent another person in this indictment known as Don J, who allegedly was a partner of Mr. Montez, correct?"

"Yes."

"Both Don J and Mr. Montez confided to you that they were partners in an organization that transported illegal drugs to the United States, correct?"

"Yes."

"You told Mr. Montez that Don J was about to export cocaine aboard a vessel called the *Blue Atlantic*, correct?"

"Yes."

"You did so knowing that Mr. Montez would convey that information to the government, correct?"

"Yes."

Whoa. Montez's attempts to cooperate the *Blue Atlantic* being obtained via Paz's perfidy didn't surprise me. But I was doubly bewildered hearing the details: First and worst, Wilkinson had elicited that Montez had cooperated, or tried to. Second, and nearly as unbelievable, she was casting shadow over the credibility of her soon-to-be prime witness, Don J.

Yet when I glanced at DiMaglio—who surely was wise to what was happening—he seemed perfectly at ease with it.

"You first represented Mr. Montez when he commanded a paramilitary organization, correct?" Wilkinson asked.

Object, Martin, I thought. The trial was about the Santa Fe conspiracy, not about long-ago unrelated evidence of other crimes.

"Correct," Paz said.

"In that capacity you represented him in an investigation of atrocities committed by that organization, including rapes, tortures, and murders, correct?"

Object, you egotistical know-nothing, I thought. But Montez, unperturbed, was making notes. Over his shoulder I saw doodles. Three-dimensional geometrics.

"Were these acts related to drug trafficking?" Wilkinson asked.

"Yes, ma'am," Paz said.

Kesey, you devil, I thought. Now I understood why he was adamant about going after Paz. It was to use him to open the door to introducing testimony that would otherwise not be admissible—testimony of prior bad acts that had not resulted in convictions and were otherwise unprovable. But linking drug trafficking continuing from the past to the present was related, therefore admissible.

"Did you know these allegations to be true?"

Paz said he personally did not know whether the allegations were true but had discussed them with both American and Colombian authorities. They had showed him video evidence confirming that Montez had ordered and participated in trafficking, although he had succeeded in convincing both governments that prosecutions were unwarranted.

"How did you convince them?"

"Mr. Montez bribed them."

"You didn't represent him in this case but advised him regarding the drug and money-laundering charges he faces in it, correct?"

"That is correct," Paz said.

I stood. "If your Honor please, a sidebar?"

Graff nodded and Wilkinson, myself, and Montez went to the side of the bench. Graff leaned over and spoke quietly to me. "I'm aware there is a taped recording in which Mr. Paz admitted advising Mr. Montez," he said. "Now you're anticipating the government will introduce that tape, and for a variety of reasons, you object to that."

"Judge, I am on that tape," I said. "If I'm revealed as a participant in the case I'm clearly conflicted from representation."

"Which would mean a mistrial and a new lawyer would take months to get up to speed," he said. "Which I will not allow. Nor do I think it necessary to consider. The government submitted an *ex parte* letter in which they stated they do not intend to use the recording because Mr. Paz will acknowledge its contents, but not your presence. Do not request a sidebar again. Continue."

"No more questions," Wilkinson said to Graff.

"Defense?" Graff said.

Montez stood. His glasses were back on.

"Mr. Paz," he said evenly. "You mentioned a paramilitary organization I allegedly belonged to. Isn't it a fact that organization was an agency of the Colombian government created to counter communist guerrillas?"

"That was my understanding," Paz said.

"The crimes you mentioned were disseminated by the media. Do you believe the media?"

"Irrelevant," Graff said. "Next question."

Irrelevant but nicely done, I thought. No better punching bag than the media.

"Your fees were substantial amounts paid in cash," Montez said. "Did you report them to the tax authorities?"

"Some," Paz said. "Not all."

"Next question," Graff said.

"Are you aware that your false threat resulted in my being confined in a solitary cell whose lights were on all day and night, and that for months, my only human contact was when I saw a guard's hand when my one daily meal was slid through an opening in a door?"

"Objection," Wilkinson said. "Inadmissible, bolstering, and—"

"Question withdrawn," Montez said. "I'm done, your Honor."

I felt a twinge of awe. Montez had naturally accomplished two things that take most lawyers years to learn: don't ask questions you don't know the answer to, and the question is more important than the answer.

Montez sat. "How did I do?" he asked me.

"You were excellent, professionally," I said. "Personally, you're a turd who needs flushing."

CHAPTER 71

Case agents are the indispensable ingredient to prove a drug conspiracy.

Bricks of cocaine and pebble-sized pills and drums of powder are meaningless without the mortar that binds them to the accused, that being the case agent. Sometimes they're the first G witness, setting the stage as a preview of what will come. Other times they're the last G witness, drawing verbal road maps of how seemingly discrete evidence actually fits together perfectly.

But Wilkinson put her case agent on the stand right in the middle of her case. Another tactical blunder, I thought, to no strategic end.

"Agent DiMaglio, you are a DEA investigator assigned to the Santa Fe joint task force in which you partnered with DEA Special Agent Kesey until his recent death, correct?"

"Correct," Brian DiMaglio said.

He looked good in a suit. Lawyerly. Made sense because I knew he'd been a pre-law student before dropping out of school and joining DEA. I also knew he was a Dead Head, had a Semper Fi tat on his right bicep, and a putting green in his backyard, courtesy of my peeking into his daughter's social media, all of which I'd erased from my computer, knowing he'd rip my head off if he discovered I'd been intruding on his family again.

"My understanding is that you and DEA Agent Kesey have been investigating the Santa Fe organization for several years, during which you became familiar with its means and methods and members, am I correct?"

"Yes."

"Tell us what you learned," Wilkinson said.

"Santa Fe is involved with all aspects of the cocaine trade. Cultivation of *coca,* laboratory refinement to cocaine, transportation and sale to and in the United States, and shipping proceeds back to Colombia. Additionally, they produce and sell large amounts of a controlled substance known as fentanyl."

"How do they ship the proceeds to Colombia?" Wilkinson asked.

DiMaglio detailed the junk metal operation that produced seemingly solid spheres that were hollowed, during which Wilkinson interrupted to put corroborating photographs into evidence. I wondering how DiMaglio knew about the spheres. Had to have been through Laura, because Kesey hadn't known about them until just before he died, and since we'd been together in his final moments, I knew he hadn't told anyone else.

The jurors were enthralled by DiMaglio's reality show. Montez sat quietly, brow raised as if it was news to him. Like, really?

"Agent, did you create a profile of Santa Fe?" Wilkinson asked.

DiMaglio had. The lights dimmed and an ELMO projector lit the far wall with a pyramid of mug and telephoto shots. Montez was at the top, Lucho and Don J labeled just below, beneath them a tier labeled *Los Xs.*

"Can you identify the man on top?" Wilkinson asked.

DiMaglio pointed at Montez. "That's him there."

"Identifying Martin Montez," Wilkinson said. "Who do Lucho and Don J and *Los Xs* refer to?"

"Lucho and Don J were Montez's lieutenants. *Los Xs* are *sicarios,*" DiMaglio said. "They kill for Santa Fe."

"Thank you," Wilkinson said. "No more questions."

Montez stood. He was in his Clark Kent mode again, peering over his thick-framed glasses, now halfway down his nose.

"You identified a photograph as me," he said to DiMaglio. "Prior to my arrest, did you ever see me in person?" He took his glasses off.

"No."

"You mentioned spheres and drugs and money," Montez said. "Your information is limited to what others told you, correct?"

"Correct."

"You referred to a group of killers," Montez said. "You have no direct evidence linking me to them, correct?"

DiMaglio hesitated a moment, then nodded. "Correct."

I wondered why he'd paused. Something there?

"Then why—I should ask how—do you connect me to...?" Montez's voice trailed off and he shook his head as if perplexed.

The Cougar and the other jurors seemed puzzled as well. So was I. DiMaglio hadn't cemented the case together, he hadn't even scotch-taped it. Secondhand hearsay testimony was essentially worthless. All bun, no beef.

"No more questions," Montez said.

"Court's recessed until tomorrow morning," Graff said. "I want counsel in my chambers now."

I figured Wilkinson was about to be reamed out for allowing DiMaglio to do nothing but opinionate. I'd figured wrong.

"I assume the defense has read the government's latest submission," Graff said.

Montez had no access to ECF bounces, and I hadn't yet bothered to read them. "I haven't had an opportunity," I said.

"Allow me to educate you, counselor," Graff said. "The government has one more witness before they rest their case."

Don J, I assumed.

Maybe there was a method to Wilkinson's madness after all. Paz's testimony that he'd tipped Montez to the *Blue Atlantic* had been tailored to imply Montez's involvement in trafficking. Have DiMaglio talk theory, then have Don J inject reality. Putting the pudding before the proof, so to speak. Well done, Jenna.

"The problem is that the witness was not on their witness list," Graff said.

Huh? Don J had been front and center on the witness list.

"The government states that is because they just learned of the new witness's availability," Graff said. "I'm not pleased it took them this long, but I'm bound to allow it. Which in turn creates problems I find deeply troubling."

I was deeply troubled as well. The defense was entitled to review whatever new discovery came along with the witness, perhaps in the form of physical evidence. At the least, the defense would have the right to review DEA-6 Reports of Investigations summarizing what the witness had told the government. Meaning the trial would be delayed, and I'd continue playing court jester.

I'd promised myself to keep my trap shut, but the prospect of an extended trial loosened my tongue.

"Your Honor," I said. "I don't understand why the witness is deemed new. Don J, as he is known, was on the witness list."

"Don J will not be testifying," Wilkinson said.

Wha...? I was stunned. "Why not?"

"He violated his cooperation agreement."

I flashed back to Montez's second communication about the *Blue Atlantic,* detailing offshore LLCs connected to the ship. The bright boys at IRS, probably with a little help from their Interpol friends, must have traced the entities to Don J, who, by continuing to traffic, violated his cooperation agreement, thereby negating him as a useful witness. Montez had known this, which explained his confidence.

"I'll be damned if this case will be prolonged," Graff said. "I've communicated with the MCC. This evening, for however long it takes, Mr. Montez and co-counsel will be allowed to review the new witness's discovery material."

"When did the government first learn of the new witness?" I asked. "Who is it?"

"Review the discovery, counselor," Graff said.

CHAPTER 72

It wasn't until seven that Montez and I were locked in an MCC room. A monitor was set up, next to it a file labeled with Montez's case index number. Inside the file was the *ex parte* letter from Wilkinson to Graff, a clip of DEA-6s, and a flash drive.

Montez was chipper. He had good reason to be upbeat. Thus far, Wilkinson had not made a case and, unless the new witness was substantial, there was no case at all. I figured the new witness was a previous FNU LNU the G had previously deemed unnecessary but, given Don J's absence, was better than nothing. Like throwing feces against a wall and hoping some might stick. Incredible as it had first seemed, Montez's scheme might actually come to fruition.

Montez paged through the sixes and laughed. "These policemen write as if they're a subspecies. Gorillas in uniform."

I glanced at Wilkinson's letter. I suppose I should have read it earlier but thought it would just be obfuscations of how and why the still-nameless new witness had just now appeared. Didn't really matter—Graff would green-light the witness.

There were several attachments. One was a voice-print analysis. Aha, the flash drive contained a conversation, but I'd save that for later. I needed to see the video first. It would tell the tale. Or not.

Montez held the sixes. "What are these black lines?"

"Blacked-out redactions of the witness' name thought too sensitive to be distributed," I said. "Should have been removed by now, but you'll find out who it is tomorrow. Good luck, Chuck."

"You despise me, don't you?" he said.
"I won't cry when you go down."
"You'll cry after I walk."
"That a threat?"
"No. A fact."

I inserted the flash, hoping its contents would wipe Montez's smile off his supercilious puss. The screen flickered and a video came on.

It was shot from above. Two men were in a room below. They wore rubber gloves, their enlarged hands making them look like characters in a comic strip. But nothing comical about them, for I recognized the two *Los Xs* who had been in Pacho's house on the fateful night he'd been murdered.

"Meaningless," Montez muttered. "What's the significance?"

I was wondering the same thing. Apparently, the government had a camera in Pacho's home, one the *Xs* hadn't disabled. But no, I would've received its video in the discovery. So the video was not taken by a G camera—

Oh my God. Had it been rolling when I appeared?

Couldn't have been, I decided. My presence at the murder scene would've disqualified my being Montez's co-counsel. Or worse....

Onscreen, Pacho appeared, ushering a fourth person into the living room. The person's face was visually redacted to a blur, but I couldn't hide from myself.

The video jittered and moved to a new vantage point.

It had been taken by a phone. Laura's? From the start, I'd suspected she was present when Pacho was murdered. But I had dismissed the possibility, thinking that she would have told me.

But she hadn't, and there was no denying the supporting circumstances: Laura's Porsche was there before and gone after, the way she'd avoided talking about Pacho's murder, the manner in which she vacillated—close to me one moment, distant the next.

As if caring for me, yet unforgiving as well.

I paused the video and read Wilkinson's cover letter. Its

first paragraph stated that the new witness had unexpectedly come forward.

Was it Laura?

Yet she had been known to the government well beforehand. She'd refused to testify when Cleo was a hostage, but now that Cleo was free that no longer mattered. Yet, she had still refused to testify. Kesey's voice whispered from the grave: "Indigenous don't rat."

But they do make deals, I thought. Twenty-four bucks for Manhattan. Immunity from prosecution in exchange for testimony.

The second paragraph of Wilkinson's letter acknowledged that the contents of the video might be grounds for a mistrial because of the presence of the defendant's co-counsel at the scene of what it deemed to be most damning evidence in the case.

The third paragraph was a proposal that my presence be blurred so the jurors would not recognize me.

Ridiculous, I thought. The jurors would need to be instructed to ignore the blurred woman. But how could they? She could not be explained as a confidential source or a cooperating individual, for the jury would wonder why one in such a role was not a witness. The truth was that the video would trigger a mistrial.

Three proposed exhibits were attached to Wilkinson's letter. One was an affidavit from a forensic voice analyst who concluded with 100 percent certainty that the two voices he'd analyzed were one and the same speaker.

The second was a response to a government subpoena verifying that at the time in question, a call had been placed from one designated phone number to another.

"What does it say?" Montez asked.

I ignored him. One of the few still-missing pieces of my memory reemerged.

While zoned on *burundanga,* I'd overheard a call over a speakerphone.

I restarted the video and watched the scene unspool: Cocaine on a coffee table. Pacho, urged to indulge. Him reluctantly doing so. An *X* putting a gun on the table and telling me to do the same with mine. When I did so, the other *X* brandished a gun. I was told to snort cocaine to prove I was not a federal agent.

A phone chirped.

An *X* answered over speakerphone and a recorded voice asked if he would accept a call from a federal prison. The *X* grunted acceptance. Relays clicked and whirred. The recorded voice said the call could proceed.

"Xavier?" the caller said. "Where are you?"

I recognized Montez's voice. That explained the voice-print analysis. Federal inmate calls are recorded, but rarely monitored. Still, given the givens, this one had been.

"At Pacho's," Xavier said. "He is here, listening."

"Pacho, you stole my money," Montez said. "I am a pragmatic man. Return my money and you're forgiven."

"I don't have it," Pacho said.

"*¿Dónde está Laurita?*" Montez asked.

"I don't know," Pacho replied.

"Ximeno, do it," Montez said.

Xavier nodded and Ximeno picked up my Sig and put it in my left hand. Then he lifted my arm and covered my hand with his and pointed the Sig at Pacho's head.

"*Doctora*, kill the thief," Ximeno said to me.

"I can't," I said. "I won't.

Ximeno pulled the trigger; Pacho fell lifelessly atop the couch. Ximeno whipped the Sig across my forehead where the mysterious bruise had lingered.

The video faded to black.

CHAPTER 73

I stared at the dark monitor screen.
I'd been true to myself. I was innocent.
"Here's what you need to do," Montez said.
"Shut up," I said. "I know what to do."
My presence in the video created unsurmountable problems. Even if my presence was blurred, I'd have a right to inquire as to who the person was—a sure ticket to my being removed from the case. Graff would be furious but would blame the government. As for the video itself, I'd clearly been a victim, not a perpetrator. I had my ticket out.
"Tell the judge you object to the video because of your presence," Montez whispered urgently. "Tell him you are resigning from the case. He will have no choice but to declare a mistrial or ban the video being shown."
"If I resign, it would only delay the inevitable until next spring while another attorney gets up to speed, during which you will languish in the SHU. If that's what you want, it would be my pleasure." And, I thought, a wintry season of my discontent.
"I'm not a fool," he said. "I was careful to phrase my words. What does it matter if I called a friend? Or inquired about his sister? That I told a man he stole my money? That I asked my friend to collect it? The manner in which he did so was not at my bidding nor knowledge."
"The judge won't ban the video," I said. "Because the government won't use it."
"Why not?" he asked.
I pointed at Wilkinson's letter. "Says so here. They don't

need the video because the new witness will testify as to your crimes."

"Nonsense," he said. "Other than Lucho and Don J, I have always done business through intermediaries. The new witness is some peasant who knows nothing but rumors."

"She's many things, but no peasant," I said.

"She? *Laura*? She wouldn't do this to me."

"She will, *con gusto*," I said. "For her family."

"She doesn't know what happened at Pacho's. She can't testify as to the video."

"She took the video, fool," I said. "Now she'll take your future. You robbed her innocence."

"I did nothing but teach her to be a woman," he said. "Which she enjoyed."

I dress sedately when I go to court—maybe one of Mama's low-key Valentino suits, vintage croc Lanvin low-heels, whatever—but being a fixture at this trial felt constricting, so I'd jazzed up to a colorful Yamamoto dress paired with bright Jimmy Choo stilettos, one of which I brought down on his thin jail slippers with a vengeance, literally nailing him to the floor.

He let out a yowl.

"Laura's been cooperating all along," I told him. "She'll talk about everything. This is a Manhattan jury. Smart people. Women with strong feelings. They'll fall in love with Laura when she tells them you raped her and all the rest. 'Me Too,' they'll think."

I stuffed the discovery in my bag and stood to leave.

"Wait," he said. "Let's see what she testifies. Knowing her, she may not respond as the government believes."

"She will," I said. "And you'll lose the trial, and your prior history as a para will inspire Graff to sentence you to life. You can be sure Wilkinson will recommend the Bureau of Prisons designate you to a supermax where the underground solitary cells make the SHU look like the Four Seasons. Hey, did you hear about Tony Handsome?"

"What?"

"Sawed his wrist with a plastic knife," I said. "Wrote a message in blood—something about not being able to take it anymore—before he bled out."

His face paled. "If I plead, how much time?"

"I might be able to convince Wilkinson not to make an adverse institutional recommendation in her sentencing memorandum," I said. "Then it's up to Graff. For starters, you're looking at ten to life. You're loaded with negative enhancements that won't help. Bosses tend to be sentenced at the high end. Think thirty years ... or more."

Eyes squeezed shut, he shook his head.

"On the other hand, there's positives working for you," I said. "If I demand the video be played, I'll be off the case and your new counsel will take months to get up to speed. There's a ton of appellate issues but Graff wants this case off his docket now. If you plead guilty, he may reward you, maybe take into account your cooperation in taking down the counterfeit presses. You can be sure Leeds will inflate it."

"How much time, do you think?" he asked.

I shrugged. "Maybe, ten, fifteen...?"

"Ten," he said thoughtfully. "Less for good behavior is eight and a half. Less for time served here and in Colombia is six. Less for credit from work and study programs, say five. A motion for early compassionate release ... speak to the prosecutor and let me think about it."

CHAPTER 74

Downtown Manhattan at three a.m.

The Shark cruised through deserted streets. My bag lay on the seat. The DEA sixes in it would include Laura's statements. I wanted to read them but drove aimlessly because I dreaded what I might learn. Wilkinson might cut corners, but no way would she allow Laura to testify unless she first proffered truthfully about everything. I'd crossed lines at La Siberia, but Kesey and company had conveniently forgotten them. Jenna Wilkinson wouldn't share their forgiveness; she was a straight arrow, and I was sure she'd see to it that Laura's testimony would include my behavior.

I'd known about Montez's scheme but had gone along with it. In La Siberia and in Youngstown, I'd aided and abetted killings. I was guilty by both dissociation and association.

Reading DEA sixes was like watching the old cop show *Dragnet*. Detective Joe Friday, limiting answers to "Just the facts, ma'am," just as Laura's inquisitor had done. It was DiMaglio who had proffered her.

Laura's sixes were still redacted. She was ID'd as CS-1. The details were bare-bones minimal: CS-1 had firsthand knowledge that Montez had trafficked in cocaine and fentanyl, laundered the proceeds, and murdered while doing so.

No surprises there.

What was surprising was that there was no mention of Pacho's murder or Laura's participation in Montez's crimes. I thought about this and smiled appreciatively. If Laura had inculpated herself, she would have been charged and signed a plea agreement admitting it, which would have been in the discovery provided to me.

But she had not.

Clever Laura. She had negotiated an extraordinary—perhaps even extra-legal—deal in which her own guilt was carved out. And, by extension, mine as well, for our joint participation at La Siberia was unauthorized, and therefore illegal.

DiMaglio had gone along with her concealments, probably out of some sort of post-mortem loyalty to Kesey, whose own behavior had been beyond egregious. Or because he, too, was incriminated by his knowledge of the black op in La Siberia.

If Graff were apprised of these off-the-record ventures, he'd severely sanction the G. But I knew that would not happen. During the direct examination of Laura, AUSA Wilkinson would not open that door because DiMaglio had locked it.

Trial was to resume at ten.

I knew Wilkinson would be at work early, polishing her examination Qs and her to-do lists like the striver she was. At nine I went to her office.

"My guy wants to plead," I said. "What's the deal?"

"None," she said. "He pleads to the indictment."

"No credit for the counterfeit ops he gave?"

"When he chose trial, he blew cooperating."

"How about letting Graff know about them?"

"Your client, your choice."

"Jenna, give him something."

"How about my regards?"

"Lawyer to lawyer," I said. "I have reason to believe you cut a deal with your new witness that Graff will not like."

"Are you threatening me, Counselor?"

Go figure. Mild-mannered Ms. Goody Two-shoes crosses lines, then dares me to call her on it. Well, if Wilkinson wanted to play hard ball, that was fine with me. I threw her a slider.

"I also have reason to believe your witness didn't suddenly appear but has been here, talking to your agents."

"Untrue," she said, but her expression said otherwise.

"Tell it to the judge," I said. "All I'm asking is your

sentencing memorandum request that Graff reward Montez for his counterfeiting cooperation."

"It won't fly. Against SDNY policy."

"I'll include it in my sentencing memo," I said. "Just don't respond negatively."

"All right. I'll leave it up to Graff."

"Another thing. No supermax."

"That's up to BOP," she said.

"If you recommend it, they won't."

"My agents will go ballistic," she said. "They've been after Montez for years and know what he perpetrated. They want him to pay for his sins in a supermax."

"They'll back off," I said.

"Kesey spent his career chasing Montez," she said. "I, we, owe him gratification."

"Kesey was good people," I said. "I knew he had a vendetta for Montez. Thing is, both he and DiMaglio cut a lot of corners nailing him and the rest of Santa Fe. Be a real shame if I'm forced to stain their records by revealing them."

"Do that and you'll go down with them," she said.

"So will you, for playing along. You knew about Kesey and DiMaglio's black op in Colombia and the assassinations in Youngstown. Your ass will be on the line too."

"You'd do that to us for dirt like Montez?"

"I'd do that because it's my duty," I said.

"What they say about you is right," she said. "You're a conniver."

"You're not bad at conniving yourself, Jenna," I said.

To my surprise, she smiled. "You're my heroine. When I grow up, I want to be like you."

"Then we have a deal?" I asked.

"Of course, we do ... you bitch."

CHAPTER 75

The SDNY courthouse is a billion dollars' worth of marble and mahogany, a high-rise testament to the never-ending War on Drugs.

Judge Graff's court was on high, the uppermost twenty-seventh floor, befitting his tenure as a prominent jurist. Between the corridor and the court was an anteroom where witnesses awaited their turn in the box.

When I entered the courtroom, DiMaglio was planted outside the anteroom. Its door was closed, but I knew Laura was inside. If the plea deal foundered, she'd be testifying. I hardly hesitated, but I supposed my expression was a giveaway.

"Keep walking, El," DiMaglio said quietly.

I spoke to Montez in the court pens. Overnight he had shrunken to a shell of himself. Gone was the dashing charmer, replaced by a dejected loser.

"Please," he said. "Tell me no supermax. I can't bear the thought."

I let him suffer a few seconds.

"No supermax," I said.

"All rise!"

Graff took the bench. He ran through the boilerplate that was the necessary foundation for a plea.

Did Montez understand? Was he pleading because he was guilty? Would he now verbalize what he was guilty of?

Montez's eyes were wet. His voice thin. He said he had trafficked in drugs and laundered money in the SDNY and elsewhere.

Graff asked Wilkinson if the government thought that was enough. She said the government was satisfied.

"Plea accepted," Graff said.

He set a sentencing date in November. I hurried from the courtroom, but the witness room was empty. I looked down the corridor and saw Laura at the elevator bank. There was a bong and an elevator door slid open. She entered and it began to close. I stuck my foot in the door and entered the elevator.

"I want to talk," she said. "But not here, not now."

I pressed every floor button. "I understand that you couldn't tell me you've been cooperating all along," I said. "What I don't understand is why you were hiding at Pacho's, taping what happened."

The elevator stopped. A lawyer got on.

"I've got the new virus," I told him, and he quickly stepped off. The elevator resumed its descent.

"Why hide and tape?" I repeated.

"Martin sent *Los Xs* because he knew Pacho was stealing," she said. "I didn't think he'd let them harm Pacho because only he knew where the money and plate were hidden. They were there to kill you, if *necessario*."

"Why?" I asked. "Why would Montez sacrifice his attorney?"

"*Abogados* are disposable," she said. "Shooting you would scare Pacho into giving up the money and the plate."

"You *knew* this?" I asked. "Why didn't you warn me?"

"I thought you were another of his crooked lawyers," she admitted. "If I warned you, Montez would know Pacho had confided in me. For that alone he would have killed my brother."

"He did. To your point: why kill Pacho if only he knew?"

"Martin thought I, too, knew." She smiled. "I did."

"Why didn't you tell me I didn't kill Pacho?"

She shrugged. "I assumed you knew."

Gad. I'd been torturing myself for nothing while Laura apparently had no idea that I needed her absolution. "Pacho should've warned me not to come," I said.

"He didn't know the *Xs* would be there."

She stopped talking as the elevator door slid open. A

woman got on. I did my COVID routine, but the woman ignored me. I sensed Laura's impatience at having to wait to continue. The elevator stopped and the woman got off.

"My brother was not a thief," Laura said vehemently. "He didn't take Montez's money for himself. He had a vision."

"Sure," I said. "Protecting his sister and making her Montez's whore as a prelude to his taking over Santa Fe."

She slapped me, hard.

"Fool," she said. "Pacho could've given up what he stole from them. He didn't because he thought they'd kill you if he did."

"Nice of him," I said. "They just set me up to do twenty-five to life for a murder I didn't commit."

"I would have come forward with the video if it came to that," she said. "Pacho died so you, an innocent, might live."

"And you?" I asked, "Will Montez let you live?"

"Martin would never harm me," she said.

I looked at her, waiting for more.

"Because he...." Her voice broke.

"Loves you," I said.

She began to weep. Montez was a monster who'd destroyed her family, but by nature she was a kind soul, and his love, as poisonous as it had been, tempered her hatred of him. I again saw her as the naïve girl who'd been at Pacho's daughter's *quinceañera*. In her way she had actually forgiven Montez. I used my trademark blue Hermès scarf to wipe her cheek.

The door opened to the lobby floor. Many people were there, hustling and bustling. We left the building and walked across Police Plaza, and I wondered: *what now?*

Wind gusted across the open space. She stopped in the lee of a so-called artwork: five large, conjoined steel circles representing the five boroughs of the city.

She put her hand on my cheek. "We truly are sisters, and I will always love you. Goodbye, Electra."

"Where are you going?" I asked her.

"I've things to do," she said.

CHAPTER 76

I had nothing to do.

There were no live case files on my desk. Just the paper proof of my looming bankruptcy: bills and delinquent tax notices I couldn't pay and letters and lawsuits demanding refunds to the clients I'd abandoned.

I'd earned fortunes but spent them as if there were no tomorrows. Now my tomorrows were today. I was broke, busted, and self-disgusted. Just when I thought things couldn't get worse, they did.

Gino called and said Pops had passed.

It hit me like a punch to my gut. Dear old Pops was the last tenuous link to my past. "Gino? You knew Pops?"

"He was the cop-doc, remember?"

"You're not a cop," I said.

"I was," he said. "Once."

I drove Gino to the cemetery. His wheelchair was folded in the Shark's big trunk, just as it used to be when he was teaching me how to lawyer.

"How did you know I knew Pops?" I asked.

His eyes refocused as if seeing another time.

"When 'Nam ended, the G found another war to distract the public from the real haps," he said. "Hello, 'War on Drugs.' Fancy Nancy telling people to just say no while Ronnie's CIA was deploying DEA Johnnies to the new 'Over There.' The Spanish Main. It was perfect. In our own backyard. The Monroe Doctrine and Remember the Maine to rah-rah public support."

And create the industry in which I labored, I reflected.

"I was one of DEA Southern Command's foot soldiers," Gino said. "Our true agenda was left unspoken. Go along to get along with the Colombian government, which was owned lock, stock, and gun barrels by the cartels. Herrera, the guy who built Toylandia? He put his own man in the presidency. Crook name of Samper."

"The G went along with that?" I asked, incredulous.

"Deal was to allow the cartels to work so long as they occasionally gave up a guy who had fucked the wrong someone's wife or was too ambitious. We were consorting with the enemy. Our job was assassinating rival guerilla and paramilitary bosses. Same numbers game as 'Nam. The bad-guy body count makes the front pages. Count goes up, we're winning, everyone's happy."

The rain increased and I sped up the wiper blades. Gino stared at the smeared glass.

"Night mission," Gino said. "I'm one of a three-man team code-named 'The Triplets' deployed in the Magdalena basin. We're crawling through mud toward the houseboat where our target, a para commander, is holed up. My boot snags a tripwire, and a mine explodes. Blows our cover, and with it, my legs. Me and one of my bros are captured. The para boss decides to make us an example of what happens to bothersome *gringos.* They sit what's left of me against a tree to watch them work my bro over. Oh, geez."

He wiped a sleeve across his eyes.

"Sorry," he said. "Worst day of my life. I worshipped my bro. We called him the old man because he was one of the first agents when DEA was created in '73. Badge number fifty-four. Five-Four was his call sign. Best man I ever knew."

He drew a steadying breath.

"The para was a sophisticated guy," he said. "Fuck *aguardiente,* he drinks wine. Uncorks a white chilling in a silver bucket and does the aroma inhale tip-of-the tongue taste test. Pours himself a glass and sits back and watches his number two work on Five-Four. *Agh,* this is bad shit you don't want to know."

Gino knows I want to know and that he will tell me, but I get it's his way of apologizing for a coming ugliness.

"The number two uses his boss's wine corkscrew to drill holes in Five-Four. My bro Five-Four doesn't react. The para's number two ups the pain. Sticks hot chilis into the holes. Asks him how that feels. 'Hot,' Five-Four says. 'Bring me a *cerveza*, waiter,' he says.

"The number two freaks and puts one in Five-Four's head."

Gino winced at the memory. Drew a reinforcing breath.

"A moment later, a flash-bang explodes and Kesey comes in blasting. The para and his number two escape but Kesey doesn't go after them. He tourniquets my legs and calls in for a medevac. Which is how I'm still around. Part of me, at least."

The rain sounded like a drummer boy on the Shark's soft roof.

"Thirty-five years since Kesey swore to find the para and his number two," Gino said. "The obsession ruined his marriage and his health. Operated on cigars and booze and shit food. Spent his days taking bad guys down. First thing he'd ask them was if they know the bastards who killed Five-Four."

"Montez and Vizcaino," I said.

"One down, one to go," he said.

"They're both down, Gino."

"Vizcaino's dead." He barked a harsh laugh. "But thanks to you, my law student and adopted niece, Montez will still have a life. Don't let that happen, Electra. Put him in a box forever."

"Too late," I said. "The deal's done. What can I do?"

"Never too late," he said. "Find a way. You can."

The rain had diminished to a drizzle, and I turned the wipers down a notch. Ahead I saw the turnoff to the cemetery.

"My stumps ache when it rains," Gino said.

I looked at him. He had never spoken about his disability before. His expression was distant, seeing an old memory.

"I was in rehab when Kesey showed up at the V.A. Hospital," he said. "He grabs a wheelchair, tells everybody to fuck off, and wheels me out. 'Where we going?' I ask him. 'To a christening,' he says. 'What christening?' I ask. 'You'll see,' he says."

"What year was this?" I asked.

"Eighty-eight ... Memorial Day."

I did the math. It added up. I turned into the cemetery and left the blacktop for dirt lanes between rows of graves. Gino looked at them as he continued.

"So I get to see a new mommy holding a beautiful baby girl while a priest is waiting for her to name the baby so he can do his thing," he said. "Maybe the new mommy's still a bit sedated or maybe it's that postpartum thing, whatever, but she can't make up her mind, which makes her sad. Funny thing, she's crying, but the baby is laughing. Kesey to the rescue."

"What do you mean?" I asked.

"His literary allusions," he said. "He picks up the laughing baby and says, 'Mourning becomes Electra.' The priest says that's a strange name. Kesey tells him in mythology, Electra was the heroic daughter of a powerful king. The priest looks at the new mommy, and when she says she likes the king tie-in, the priest goes on with the show."

"And here I am," I said.

CHAPTER 77

There were a dozen-odd cars parked by the gravesite. A mix of police cruisers and unmarked prowlers. Their occupants, along with Gino and I, stood graveside as Pops's coffin was lowered. Someone turned on a phone and played "Taps" while the cops stood in a line and took out their service sidearms and fired a single salvo.

"Wasn't exactly a twenty-one-gun salute, but Pops wasn't one for ceremony," Gino said. "Kesey neither. Knew he was dying so he made a will. Just two requests. One, that he be cremated and his ashes dumped in the Gowanus Canal. Man loved Brooklyn."

"What was his other request?" I asked.

"All those years he was hunting Montez and Vizcaino he was carrying Five-Four's badge with him. He wanted you to have it."

I was wearing the parka I'd worn in La Siberia. I unzipped a pocket and took out the leather wallet Kesey had given me in Youngstown. Somehow, I'd forgotten all about it, or maybe some greater power had bidden me to wait. It was a buzzer case. I flipped it open and saw a DEA badge numbered fifty-four.

"Why was Kesey so hard on me?" I asked.

"Tough love," he said. "Teaching you."

"Kesey was my father," I said.

"No, Electra. Five-four was."

My apartment overlooks Central Park. Beyond its flat expanse there's a digital clock atop a midtown skyscraper. I watched it blink to 12:01. December had begun, and with it came my usual melancholy in the season of togetherness. I shuddered and pulled my Mama's fur wrap tighter around my bare skin.

After leaving Gino, I'd gone straight home. Flushed my valiums and poured away my vodka. I wanted clarity, not self-absolution. I wanted to strip my veneer. Literally.

I was on my terrace, butt naked beneath Mama's mink.

I laughed, sending frozen breath into the stillness.

My deepest wonderings had been answered. At long last I knew who my father was and what had become of him decades ago. But I was not ready to mourn him. Gino had been right.

I had something to do.

CHAPTER 78

I needed to submit a sentencing memorandum asking Graff to consider Montez's initial counterfeiting cooperation.

I hated the thought of helping Montez but hated violating my ethical responsibility as a defense lawyer even more. Sometimes I hate myself for being so straight by the book, but then I think how much worse it would be if I were bent.

I received an ECF bounce on the case. I thought it might be a notice that Montez's sentencing was delayed. But when I read it, my apprehension flared to anger. Montez, still representing himself *pro se,* had submitted his own sentencing memo.

"Think positively," Gino said.

"Nothing positive about it," I said. "Montez's sentencing memo claims I convinced him to go to trial by saying I had a close relationship with the only witness who could implicate him, that I assured him she was so unstable and bipolar she couldn't testify. He says I lied about her so I could take him to trial and keep collecting fees."

Gino shrugged. "Devilish fellow."

"You bet," I said. "A … a … scumbag."

"Tut-tut. Such language from you?"

"He claims he always wanted to cooperate," I said. "That he had told me where the plate was, but I didn't give it to the G."

"He claims," Gino said.

"You don't get it," I said. "How can I reply? I can't deny what happened in Ohio and I won't drag Laura into it."

"It's you who doesn't get it," Gino said. "Stop thinking about how to reply. Just don't. Montez is his own lead counsel. If he submitted a sentencing memorandum, you don't have to."

"At sentencing, Graff will ask me about what I told Montez about Laura being nuts."

"And you'll answer truthfully that you never told Montez that," he said.

"Graff wants to keep the record clean. No controversies. He'll order a hearing. What if Montez subpoenas Laura to testify?"

"He'll have to serve her," he said. "You don't know where she is. What makes you think he does?"

"Even if he can't serve her, she'll be exposed as a confidential source. This case is big news in Colombia. Montez has friends who'll kill her."

"Good bad point," Gino said. "Montez knows you won't let that happen, right?"

I nodded.

"Therefore, you won't deny."

"What?"

"You'll admit you discussed it with Montez."

"I do that and Graff, being the contrary sonofabitch he is, might cut Montez a break. Adding Leeds's praiseworthy letter to that, he might backtrack and give Montez credit for the counterfeit cooperation scam. Montez could be out in less than five years. Not to mention that Graff will see to it that the G crucifies me for lying to my client. Gino, they'll take my ticket to practice."

"Up to you," he said. "Deny, maybe you destroy Laura. Admit, maybe you destroy yourself. Your call."

Gino was right. It was my call … to action.

I needed retribution to satisfy myself and as a tribute to Agent Five-Four, my father. Only then would I be free from the baggage I'd carried my past life. Free at last.

Almost.

CHAPTER 79

I did not see Montez until sentencing day.
When he emerged from the pen into the courtroom, he'd regained a modicum of his former imperious self. When he reached the bench and stood alongside me, he whispered softly.

"Tell me," he said. "How is our lady?"

"You'll never see her again."

"Never say never, *amiga*."

"I've received sentencing memorandums and the defendant's motion," Graff said. "Does the government have any additional comments?"

DiMaglio sat at the government table. He was looking at me expectantly, and I realized he knew my quandary and was curious as to how I would deal with it.

Wilkinson had kept her word. Her sentencing memo had not responded to Montez's request for cooperation credit and stated that the government took no position as to an appropriate sentence.

"No, your Honor," she said.

Graff looked at me. "Which brings us to the defense submission," he said. "Mr. Montez has made some serious allegations about co-counsel. I'd thought they would've elicited a response from co-counsel, but nothing has been submitted. Does co-counsel now wish to respond?"

I drew a steadying breath. I felt the same anticipatory rush I'd get when about to cross a witness with a sudden question that thrust to the heart of all he'd lied about.

"I do," I said. "Mr. Montez's statement is factually correct.

He told me he went to trial because he believed the only witness with personal knowledge of his crimes would not testify."

As if smelling blood in the water, Graff leaned forward eagerly. "Did you tell him the witness would not testify because she was mentally unstable?"

"We discussed that," I said.

"But in fact, the witness was willing to testify," Graff said. "That right, Ms. Wilkinson?"

"Not at first," Wilkinson said. "The witness changed her mind."

Kesey had said Indigenous don't rat but I figured someone—DiMaglio via Indio?—had told Laura that without Don J's testimony all the G had going was DiMaglio's hearsay and Paz's self-serving testimony. Without her, there was no case, and she'd agreed.

"Did you find the witness unstable? Bipolar?" Graff asked Wilkinson.

"The government had no basis for that belief," Wilkinson said.

Graff looked at me. "But you told Mr. Montez that, counselor."

I glanced at Montez. Still with the phony smile as when we'd first met. The consummate Player, already figuring the next moves. I was, too, and didn't like what I figured: that Graff would reward Montez's quirky but dignified manner—he had actually made him smile—then the grump would turn his ire on me and reward Montez with a generous sentence reduction because, as Leeds had overstated in the presentence report, "Montez had saved the United States from a catastrophic economic calamity."

The dirty dog could be out in five years. Still in his prime, still rich and powerful, still finding and taking whatever he wanted—including his *Laurita*.

"Mr. Montez and I discussed the witness's mental state, your Honor," I said.

"My question was whether you told Mr. Montez that the witness would not testify because she was mentally unstable and bipolar? Yes or no?"

I drew a breath. This was my moment. I shook my head.

"No," I said. "It was Mr. Montez who told me that."

For a long moment the courtroom was dead quiet until Montez's chair struck the floor as he sprang to his feet.

"Your Honor," Montez said. "I never said that."

"The Court might find these helpful," I said, and handed Brunhilda documents she passed to Graff. "The first is a printout sent to me by Mr. Montez via CorrLinks. Attached is a Bureau of Prisons certification of that message."

Graff's brows knitted as he read it, "Mr. Montez refers to a psychiatric evaluation of the witness," he said. "Might it not be a response to your telling him that she was unstable?"

"I contacted the doctor who prepared the evaluation," I said. "When I explained the situation, he replied. That's in the next documents, if your Honor pleases."

Graff looked at the next documents. "It is a notarized affidavit from the referred-to psychiatrist concluding that the witness suffers from extreme bipolar disorder that often causes mood swings and changes to recollections," he said. "Regardless, the Federal Rules of Criminal procedure clearly state a document is inadmissible in place of live testimony. Is the psychiatrist present?"

"No, sir," I said. "Nor is he necessary because, as your Honor is aware, an exception to the rules is sworn documents from a foreign country. As you can see from his affidavit, the examining doctor practices in Colombia and did swear to the affidavit in support of his conclusions. However, if your Honor prefers, we can adjourn the sentencing until the psychiatrist appears."

"No adjournments," Graff said. "I want this case over now. Show the letter to Mr. Montez."

"I paid the doctor to write it," Montez said. "It was a joke."

"You paid a doctor for a joke?" Graff asked. "Did you inform co-counsel it was a joke?"

"I'm sure she knew I was joking," Montez said.

Graff looked at me. "Did you, counselor?"

My final twist of the blade: "No, sir."

Graff's mustache downturned. "Bruni, show the alleged joke to Ms. Wilkinson, who will then inform us if the government was aware of this evaluation."

As Wilkinson read it, I thought she smiled. "No sir," she said. "Had we been aware, we never would have allowed the witness to testify."

"I should think not," Graff said. "In any event, the witness did not testify, so the matter is moot. All right folks, the sideshow is over. I find that Mr. Montez's allegations about co-counsel are unsubstantiated. I further find that when Mr. Montez went to trial, the government was no longer bound to honor a cooperation agreement. The presentence report, having applied the sentencing guidelines, recommends a thirty-year sentence. It appears there may have been some fruitful cooperation regarding the seizure of counterfeit monies, but I find that the defendant's subsequent prevarications cancel them. Taking the defendant's previous bad acts into account, I find that the appropriate sentence is a term of life imprisonment without the possibility of parole. I shall recommend that the Bureau of Prisons confine him in a Level Five facility."

Stunned, Montez asked me, "Level five?"

"Supermax," I said. "Enjoy."

CHAPTER 80

I thought Montez was history. But several months later I received an ECF bounce—notice that he had filed a motion for early compassionate release. His litany of complaints included a diagnosis for a heart condition, and his dental implants were falling out, and proper treatment for his maladies was nil in the level five penitentiary he'd been designated to. Moreover, as an older inmate he was bullied by the hard-case inmates housed there.

Hours later I received another bounce:
Graff had denied Montez's motion.

I received a video message. In it, Laura and Indio stood in sunlight. They wore matching T-shirts with a logo on the breast: around its rim, lettering read *La Communidad Grajales*; within it a clenched bronze power fist.

Much activity behind them. Construction trucks trundling in and out of the entrance to La Siberia. Apparently, the locals had restarted the factory. I wondered how they'd financed themselves, then realized Laura had kept the cards that were the keys to the stolen money—not for herself—but to restart a communal business.

"Thank you," Laura said, her smile white against her tanned face as she touched the earrings I'd bought. They looked as if they'd been made for her, and I thought perhaps they had been for her family's matriarchs. Then she gestured at the factory behind.

"Told you I had some things to do," she said. "*Hasta la vista*, Electra."

Gino invited me to Thanksgiving at his place. Just the two of us, but there were three empty settings at the table.

He proposed a toast: "Absent friends."

"Pops, Kesey, and Five-Four," I said.

"Here, here," he said, and we drank.

"I wish I'd known him … about him."

"Perhaps your mother declined to tell you due to her refusal to accept reality. She chose to live like he was coming back."

"Why she dressed up every day, I guess," I said. "Not just for herself, but so I wouldn't feel lonely. But I did."

"You were never alone," he said. "Kesey and I were watching over you. We both were in love with your mother, but knew she'd never love another. So, we kept an eye on you from afar. When you got into sex, drugs, and rock 'n' roll, we stepped in."

"Say again?"

"It wasn't a coincidence that we met when you were driving a cab. You see, I asked for you specifically."

"Why?"

"Getting there," he said, "You look like your mother but you're more like your father. Pragmatic. Me too. I couldn't work DEA anymore, so I became a lawyer. A damn good one. Figured you'd be successful at it, too. And you are. With a little help from me and Kesey and Pops."

I looked at him blankly.

"No point in lawyering unless you've got clients," he said. "Pops kept your business cards in his waiting room. Kesey pointed people your way."

"Pops, I get," I said. "But a DEA agent recommending a lawyer to criminals?"

"To his sources," he said.

"Pacho?"

He nodded. "Who Kesey knew would lead you to Montez. You were brilliant."

"Only cost me my practice," I said.

"What goes around comes around," he said. "Graff smelled something off. *Ex parte*, he interviewed Laura personally. Yeah, sounds wild, I mean, who does that? But that's Graff. The codger fell in love with Laura. Had her expunged from the Clinton List and went through his old-boy network to make sure DEA didn't bother her."

"You and Graff are in the same old boys' network," I said.

Gino winked at me, laughed, said, "Auld acquaintances."

I left Gino and walked home along the East River Promenade. There was a chilly wind, but I was not cold. My hand was in my jacket atop my father's badge, whose warmth I felt above my heart. The river was gray as the sky, and its surface was choppy. I thought of my nights listening to a bell buoy's echoed pealing, and of poor lost orphaned Billy, and felt grateful that I no longer thought myself an orphan.

That wasn't all that had changed.

Professionally, I no longer was guided by the system's ethics. Sure, I'd practice law, but according to my new take on justice, which was both lawyering within and without the system. No putting that genie back in its bottle.

Personally, I no longer wanted to be alone. Perhaps it was Laura's newfound happiness, or my own loneliness, but my outlook had changed. I looked below my window at an avenue laced with neon and sidewalks filled with people.

Hmm …

I glossed my lips and applied a tad of mascara. From my mama's closet, I selected a slinky Schiaparelli dress and early '90s satin pumps. Then I put on her mink cape.

I was strolling down Central Park West when I became aware of being watched by a pair of roguish eyes. The fellow introduced himself and asked my name.

"Call me Electra," I said.

FIN

Photo by Austyn Sprouse Visuals

About the Author

Todd Merer, a New York University Law School graduate, boasts a four-decade career in criminal defense law. Throughout his tenure, he specialized in representing individuals facing drug crime allegations, particularly those extradited from Latin America. Notably, his clientele included prominent figures such as leaders of the Cali Cartel, the Pablo Escobar family, the Bogota Cartel boss, and Colombian associates of El Chapo.

Drawing from his wealth of experience, Merer authored *The Extraditionist*, a widely acclaimed novel that achieved best-selling status and earned recognition as an "Amazon book of the month" selection. This literary triumph captured the attention of industry luminaries, leading to its optioning by Alexandra Milchan, co-producer of *The Wolf of Wall Street*, to be directed by Oliver Stone. Additionally, Merer wrote a compelling sequel titled *The White Tigress*, inspired by his advocacy for Asian defendants embroiled in the "China White" heroin trade.

Made in the USA
Las Vegas, NV
09 April 2025